THE
GREATEST KID
IN THE WORLD

ALSO BY JOHN DAVID ANDERSON

JOHN DAVID ANDERSON

WALDEN POND PRESS

An Imprint of HarperCollins*Publishers*

Walden Pond Press is an imprint of HarperCollins Publishers.

The Greatest Kid in the World

Library of Congress Control Number: 2022947988
ISBN 978-0-06-298603-0

Typography by Carla Weise
23 24 25 26 27 LBC 5 4 3 2 1

First Edition

To Isabella and Nick,
who get my admittedly biased vote

"Some are born great, some achieve greatness,
and some have greatness thrust upon 'em."
William Shakespeare, *Twelfth Night*

"When you wake up in the morning, Pooh," said Piglet
at last, "what's the first thing you say to yourself?"
"What's for breakfast?" said Pooh.
"What do you say, Piglet?"
"I say, I wonder what's going to happen
exciting today?" said Piglet.
Pooh nodded thoughtfully.
"It's the same thing," he said.
A. A. Milne, *Winnie-the-Pooh*

A Foiled Plan

Zeke's letter informing him that he might be the greatest kid in the world came while his brother was baking in the driveway.

It was a slow process, even with the yards of aluminum foil Zeke had wrapped around Nate's scrawny frame. He'd emptied the whole box—enough foil to wallpaper the living room, making his little brother look like the world's very first Reynolds Wrap mummy. The sky was spotty with clouds, the sun peeking through and glinting off the metallic statue of Nathan Stahls standing with his arms straight out like a scarecrow.

"Do I have superpowers yet?" Nate murmured from the hole Zeke had poked with a butter knife close to where he assumed his brother's mouth should be.

"Not yet," Zeke said. "Patience. It will happen when it happens."

Or not, Zeke thought, but it had been important to tell Nate *something.* If Zeke had said *I want to wrap you up in aluminum foil and stick you out in the sun and see what happens,* Nate might have balked at the idea. So instead, Zeke put on his straightest face (much practiced, nearly perfected) and said, "I learned in science class that if you can find a way to harness the energy of the sun, it can give you superpowers."

This sounded like a fabulous idea to Nate, who had posters of Spider-Man on his wall, which was really *their* wall given that they shared a room in their rather cramped three-bedroom house. "What kind of powers?"

"Oh, you know. Laser vision. Thermonuclear stomps. Supersonic speed. The classics."

"Frost breath?"

"Pft," Zeke scoffed. "Seriously? How are you going to get frost breath by harnessing the power of the sun?"

Nate shrugged. "Superman has frost breath."

Point made. Then again, Superman had everything. Total overachiever. "Okay. I'm not sure about the frost breath. But I know it will make you awesome."

Nate wanted to be awesome. Zeke long suspected that his little brother thought *he* was awesome, which explained why he was so eager to be Zeke's guinea pig all the time. Nate was always imitating Zeke: copying his walk (chin jutty, slightly strutty, like the world's coolest chicken), echoing his words (even the naughty ones) (especially the naughty ones), snagging Zeke's socks and T-shirts out of his laundry basket to wear (though Zeke drew the line at letting his little brother steal his underwear). It was annoying occasionally, having a pint-size shadow of himself, but mostly it felt good to be looked up to. It made Zeke feel powerful. Important. Like the president. Or Genghis Khan.

"But how *do* I harness the sun?" Nate had wanted to know.

"That's the easy part. We just wrap you up in aluminum foil and stick you in the driveway for a few hours until you absorb an adequate amount of solar radiation."

Nate said he could handle a few hours of radiation easy.

So far it had been three minutes. "*Now* do I have superpowers?" he whined.

Zeke checked his watch—a ten-dollar digital from Walmart with a plastic band that was already breaking—and squinted at his brother. Nate actually looked like a robot from one of those bad black-and-white sci-fi movies, the kind where the rockets are made out of toilet paper tubes and the planets are painted basketballs suspended on strings. Zeke's dad loved those movies, forcing his family to sit and watch them every Friday night— when he was home, that is. He said they were campy. *Campy*, Zeke decided, was just another word for dumb. Still he figured his brother would have looked perfectly at home on the set of *Invasion of the Killer Automatrons from Zelnar Seven*, their father's personal favorite. "We've barely started."

3

"But I have to pee," Nate said, listing back and forth from one foot to the other like an unsteady canoe. He couldn't bend his knees or cross his legs. Five layers of aluminum foil had transformed him into the Tin Man. *If I only had a heart*, Zeke thought, though he knew his brother wasn't lacking in that department.

Zeke reached out and touched Nate's shiny, crinkly forehead—barely warm. Did foil absorb heat or reflect it? He probably should have researched this. He stood close to the ear holes so that his seven-year-old brother could hear. "You ever seen Captain America complain he has to take a leak?" Nate admitted that he hadn't. "Exactly. Superheroes can hold it indefinitely. It's one of their powers. Except Aquaman. He just goes in the ocean." At least that's what Zeke would do, though admittedly he'd never even *seen* the ocean. Not firsthand.

He heard a car approaching and spied the mailman coming up the road. Normally, someone passing by might see a kid wrapped in aluminum foil standing in the driveway and think, *Huh. Why is there a kid all wrapped up in aluminum foil standing in that driveway?* But Frank Rawles had been delivering mail to 4882 Grayfox Lane for fourteen years, which meant he should surely be used to such things by now. Kids hanging from the gutters. Bonfires in the yard. Garter snakes in the mailbox.

Zeke waved amiably.

Frank Rawles shook his head and moved on to the next house.

"How much longer?" Nate pleaded.

4

Zeke didn't even bother to look at his watch again. "At least another twenty minutes. Then we'll take your temperature."

That, Zeke had explained, was how you could tell if the superpowers were budding. In truth, he just wanted to see how long Nate could take it. He'd read somewhere that enough heat can make your brain cook in your skull like pulled pork in a Crock-Pot. Not that he wanted to fry his brother's brains. He didn't even want Nate to pass out or anything terrible like that. But it was summer, Zeke was bored, and a little brain warming in the name of scientific experimentation never hurt anyone. Probably.

"I'm going to get the mail," Zeke said, leaving his brother in the middle of the driveway, reflecting a miniature landscape of the neighborhood in his silver suit.

The mailbox squeaked open. Bill, bill, credit card offer, coupons for takeout, his sister's latest edition of *Elle*—he'd have to think of something clever to do with that—a flyer advertising roof repair, a brochure for the local community college also addressed to his sister, another bill.

And a letter in a plain-looking envelope, addressed to the parents of Ezekiel Stahls.

He frowned.

Zeke had gotten letters like this before, addressed much the same way—*to the parents of,* still including that erroneous plural after more than three years. They were usually from school and they were almost never good news.

Strike that—they were *never* good news.

This is to inform you that your son screwed up yet again—that was usually the gist of it. Zeke tried to intercept them whenever possible, get them from the mailbox before his mother could, though often it just delayed the inevitable: that look on her face and the sigh that could be heard 'round the world. A blindfolded Zeke could still pick his mother out of a crowd by her sigh.

He ripped one end of the envelope with his teeth and pulled the single sheet of paper free. He would read it first and decide if it was something he should flush down the toilet or not. From the driveway he heard his brother squeak, saw him slowly spinning, peeping out through his too-small eyeholes. "Z? You still there?"

"Mm-hmm."

"It's gettin' kinda itchy in here."

"That just means you're going to be impervious to bullets," Zeke called over his shoulder. He unfolded the letter. It wasn't from Stanton Public Schools at least. He'd feared it was notification that he'd finally been kicked out of the district, banned from all forms of education for life. Not that that would be such a tragedy, but Mom would flip. He'd be grounded for centuries.

But this wasn't that kind of letter. This letter was from some group calling themselves the Klein Agency. Zeke had never heard of them. They sounded like lawyers, which wasn't good either. (Not that Zeke had ever done anything he would be taken to court over—not that anyone *knew* about at least.) He read on, ignoring the murmuring behind him.

To Ezekiel Stahls and Parents:

Congratulations! You have been chosen as one of five finalists in the Greatest Kid in the World competition! Based on our analysis, you have been selected to compete for the Grand Prize: a $10,000 cash award; an all-expenses-paid vacation for you and your family to beautiful Honolulu, Hawaii; and the title of World's Greatest Kid.

You will be contacted personally sometime in the next three days regarding your participation in this event, at which point the details of the competition will be revealed. If for some reason this letter has reached you in error, please notify us immediately at the phone number listed below. Otherwise, we will see you soon!

Sincerely,

Gordon Notts, Director of Charitable Programming

The Klein Agency for the Betterment of All Mankind

There was a phone number and an address—somewhere in Texas. Zeke read the letter twice. Then he just stared at that one sentence at the top, repeating it over and over in his head.

World's. Greatest. Kid.

He let it sink in for a moment.

Then he laughed out loud.

Because it was ludicrous. Like *basketball planets dangling from strings* or *flashlights pretending to be laser guns* level of unbelievable. In no dimension was *he* the greatest kid in the world. Obviously, somebody somewhere got their wires crossed. It had to be a mistake. Or a scam. Or a joke.

Zeke crumpled the letter into a walnut-size wad and tossed it in the bush at the end of the driveway.

Ten feet away, Zeke's little brother was trying to reach his face, maybe to pull the foil free and feel some fresh air on his cheeks, but the kid's elbows wouldn't cooperate. He moved like an old Barbie doll, all right angles.

"Be still," Zeke said, taking the thermometer out of his back pocket. The tip of the thermometer disappeared into the foil mask and Zeke watched the numbers marching up, quickly at first, then slowing dramatically. 98.7. 98.8. Finally stopping at 98.9. You couldn't even stay home from school for that.

"I really gotta go," Nate murmured, shifting and crackling in his armor. "Can I just try and get superpowers later?"

Zeke looked up at the sun. It was still early afternoon. Plus they had all summer to do stuff like this. "Yeah, okay," he said. Then he carefully unwrapped his brother's sweaty face.

Nate blinked four times and then stared intently at the driveway for a few seconds before frowning. "No lasers."

"Sorry, man."

"Do you think I can deflect bullets at least?"

"Probably shouldn't test it," Zeke said. "Come on. Popsicle time." Nate smiled at his consolation prize. Didn't take much to make the kid happy.

Zeke headed into the house with rest of the mail in hand, his shiny little brother waddling after him, leaving the one crumpled letter in the bush and wondering how long it would take to even *get* to Hawaii and how much pee was really in the ocean and if that Boy Scout Superman ever got tired of being perfect all the time.

Couldn't be me, he thought, and shut the door.

A Cheesy Prank

Coming in from a humid June afternoon, air-conditioning feels heavenly. A blissful kiss of cool.

If only theirs worked. It had been out for four days now, the condenser kaput, leaving the Stahlses sweating through their shirts.

There were plans to get it fixed, of course. There were plans to fix a lot of things. The dishwasher that made a horrible knocking noise. The baseball-size hole in the living room drywall. The minivan door that wouldn't lock. The outside spigot that leaked. The ceiling fan in Zeke's room (turns out the blades aren't strong enough to support the full revolving weight of a twelve-year-old pretending he's Indiana Jones). The fifth dining room chair with the duct-taped leg that was seldom ever used anymore. Of all of these, the air conditioner was the first priority. After all, nobody was going to steal the decade-old minivan complete with french fries shoved between its seats. And it was kind of funny to watch someone try to sit in the taped-together chair. But central air was kind of a must in the throes of a Midwest summer.

Zeke had to settle for sticking his face in the freezer, feeling his hair stiffen. The chill was delicious. Nate looked around anxiously. Zeke knew what he was looking out for.

"Don't worry. I'm sure she's hiding in her cave." Because of course she was. The boys' big sister hadn't slunk out of her room since lunch. Odds were good that they wouldn't see her again until their mom got home. Not that she would begrudge her brothers a Popsicle, but then they'd have to listen to her lecture them about only eating them in the kitchen and not dripping on the counter. Jackie was in charge during the summer while Mom was at work, and she was paid handsomely for it, Zeke thought; a hundred bucks a week to sit in her room and be on her phone, occasionally venturing out to make a pot of mac and cheese.

Not that he minded her hiding away. In fact, he preferred it. It wasn't that he didn't love her—he wouldn't want to see her thrown into a volcano or mauled to death by a wild grizzly bear, for example. Just that the number of things he had come to dislike about her over the past few years—her ever-rolling eyes, her constantly condescending tone, her dismissive attitude, the way she chewed her gum (all the smacking) or flipped her dirty-blond hair—mostly outweighed the things he liked: namely that she could drive them places and she let them watch whatever they wanted on TV.

They *used* to watch TV together. As a family. Huddled on the couch, fighting over the pillows and stealing the chip bowl from each other. Now the only time they were in the same room was for a half hour at dinner. If it even lasted *that* long.

Zeke handed a cherry Popsicle to his brother, who still had bits of foil stuck to him in places. The rest of it lay in shimmering strips on the kitchen floor. "Thanks," Nate said.

"Don't mention it." Zeke gave his brother a stern look. "Seriously. Don't say anything about the experiment. Not to Mom or to Jackie. They won't understand the complex inter-thermodynamics of sunlight absorption and superpowers."

Nate nodded. Zeke could usually count on the kid to keep a secret . . . or at least to try, though their mother was not to be underestimated; her interrogation techniques rivaled those of the FBI. Zeke took a grape Popsicle for himself, then grabbed a slice of Great Value American cheese from the fridge.

"What's that for?" Nate asked.

"Just a little fun," Zeke said. He opened to the middle of his sister's new magazine and placed the cheese in the center of the page, covering the top half of an ad showing some airbrushed celebrity in a five-hundred-dollar dress. Zeke's entire wardrobe probably didn't cost that much. Nate's cost almost nothing at all—the curse of the younger sibling who only gets hand-me-downs. Zeke carefully closed the magazine again, placing it on the floor next to his brother's feet. "Hulk smash," he said. His brother grinned and stomped. Zeke bent down to inspect the effort. "Now one-hundred-percent cheesier."

Nate snorted. That's how his little brother laughed, in snorts and hiccups, like a drowning pig. He looked at the magazine with the slice of processed cheese smashed inside of it, the pages smeared shut. "Isn't she gonna be mad?"

"She's always mad about something," Zeke said. "At least this way we'll know why."

Nate shrugged. It seemed some days he was the only one who could follow Zeke's logic.

Zeke opened the refrigerator again and grabbed a can of Diet Dr. Fizz. No Dr Pepper in this house. Their pantry housed Fun-Time Chocolate Sandwich Cookies and Tastee-Brand Wheat Squares. It was simple math. One parent with one job plus four mouths to feed equals off-brand soda and a lot of bologna sandwiches. He looked at the rest of the six-pack sitting in the fridge and the engines in the most Zekey part of his brain fired up. He turned to his brother and grinned his bolt-of-inspiration grin—the one his mother called his "supervillain face."

"Have you ever seen a can of pop explode?"

Going Commando

As far as smiles go, Zeke supposed his was a little on the malevolent side. Maybe it was the way his eyebrows arched or his slightly crooked teeth, but there was definitely something maniacal about his grin.

Zeke wasn't actually evil, though. He wasn't even a bad kid. Per se.

That's how his fourth-grade teacher put it. It was actually how she started the parent-teacher conference, her voice hoarse from a day of begging students not to glue things to the desk or use a shirtsleeve as a tissue or, in Zeke's case, to put origami sailboats into the class aquarium with the hopes that the goldfish would re-create a scene from *Jaws*.

"It's not that your son is bad *per se*," Mrs. Riles said to Zeke's mother.

Zeke didn't know what *purr say* meant, but he guessed it meant something like *not quite* or *almost*, as in, your son's not *exactly* terrible. Not *completely* rotten. Not *necessarily* a reincarnation of Attila the Hun. Zeke tried to imagine where he stood on the badness scale in Mrs. Riles's eyes: Worse than Dr. Doofenshmirtz? More sinister than Darth Vader? At least he hadn't Force choked anyone yet—not successfully, anyway; sticking out his hand and saying *you have failed me for the last time, Lunch Lady Marris* ultimately just resulted in a dirty look and an extra spoonful of cooked carrots.

"Zeke is incredibly smart," Mrs. Riles went on to explain. "Very creative. But he has a mischievous mind. He *schemes.*"

Schemes. *That* word he knew, and he took no offense. Being a schemer implied ambition and forethought, which were things to be proud of. Scheming was just another word for dreaming. It was a quality he came by honestly: his father was a dreamer too, always making plans upon plans upon plans. Zeke just happened to be better on the follow-through.

Zeke's *fifth*-grade teacher, Ms. Crawford, the one he'd recently said goodbye to when the summer started, had come to a similar conclusion about him, though hers came saddled with an ultimatum.

"Zeke can be a rascal sometimes," Ms. Crawford told his mother, adopting a stern look despite her big brown eyes and colorful butterfly sweater. It was nearing the end of the school year,

15

and Zeke's mom had been called in, again, for a little roundtable discussion about her son's behavior.

"What was it this time?" Mom asked, already sounding exasperated. *Exasperated* was another word Zeke was readily familiar with because his mother used it constantly. She turned to him. "Please tell me you didn't put vinegar in the hand sanitizer again."

Zeke smiled involuntarily, then flipped it to his rehearsed look of guilt and shame: head down, lip out, hands folded neatly in his lap. The vinegar incident had been the subject of the *April* parent-teacher conference, and he'd already served his time in the Choices and Consequences room for it. In the C&C room you were supposed to think about what you did and what you might have done differently, so Zeke thought about how he should have put vinegar in the soap dispenser as well and doubled his chances of getting a reaction.

"No," Ms. Crawford sighed. "No, today during indoor recess Zeke decided he was going to start a revolution. Didn't you, Zeke?"

Teachers always made it sound worse than it really was. Ms. Crawford said it like he was Katniss Everdeen bringing down the Capitol when that wasn't what he was trying to bring down at all. "It wasn't a revolution—" Zeke started to explain, but Ms. Crawford cut him off.

"He stood on his desk and gave the order to the other fifth-grade boys to 'go commando.' Then he proceeded to *pull his underwear out of his pants* and wave it around like a flag."

Okay, that was pretty accurate.

Zeke watched his mom's face carefully—so many colors. Peach, red, purple. Like a sunset. "Your *underwear?*"

"Not the pair I was *wearing*, obviously," Zeke explained. He couldn't even wrap his head around the logistics of how *that* could work. "It was a spare that I stuffed down my pants beforehand. A prop."

"Yes," Ms. Crawford said, "but the pair Micah Johnson was wearing *was* his only one—and unfortunately it didn't stop him from trying to take them off."

Zeke's mother's mouth opened and shut silently. Another parent might have had a hard time suppressing a giggle at least, but when you're that exasperated, apparently nothing is funny.

His father would have laughed.

"Micah just got caught up in the moment," Zeke explained, remembering how the kid had managed to get his joggers halfway down to his shoes before Ms. Crawford stopped him. Gullible, that one. Even more so than Nate.

Of course, even better than seeing Micah's Incredible Hulk undies was seeing the look on Amanda Troxell's face, sitting right behind Micah, staring at both cheeks, probably worried he was going to topple backward off his desk and plant his jolly green butt right in her lap. Zeke didn't know someone's eyes could get that big.

Zeke's mother put her head in her hands. She clearly didn't appreciate her son's charismatic hold over his classmates.

"Ms. Stahls, we've talked about this before." Ms. Crawford checked her notes. "*Five times* before. Your son is a disruptive presence in the classroom. He pulls these kinds of stunts constantly. Last week he went around informing everyone that his cat had bitten him and now he was slowly turning into a catman."

"Werecat," Zeke corrected. "Big difference."

His mother glared at him. He shut up.

"That wasn't the problem, really," Ms. Crawford continued. "I can appreciate Zeke's imagination. But as the day went on, he started hissing at people. And then he coughed up a hairball in the middle of Language Arts."

Zeke looked down again to hide his smile. The hairball had been pretty fantastic in his estimation. The Stahlses didn't even own a cat—Mom constantly reminded them they couldn't afford one—so the hair Zeke "regurgitated" was collected from Jackie's brush that morning. It looked gross enough when mixed with a little vanilla yogurt, and he felt his hoarking sounds had been spot-on. He couldn't help but think that his dad would have been impressed by the special effects.

No sense trying to explain that to these two, though. They simply wouldn't get it.

"There's a pattern here," Ms. Crawford concluded.

Zeke's mom sat in her chair, silent. She had run out of excuses a long time ago. The only one she had left usually started with the words *His father*, but she didn't even use that one much anymore. She just sat quietly, holding hands with herself, drafting the lecture she would give him in the car. Or maybe she would just do that thing where she stared out the window and said nothing at all the whole ride home. Zeke wasn't sure which was worse.

"Ms. Stahls, let me be honest with you," Ms. Crawford said. "In some ways your son is an exemplary student. He gets all of his work done on time and his test scores are outstanding. Unfortunately, he also makes my job of teaching the *other* twenty-five students in class difficult. He doesn't always stop to consider his actions. He is disruptive on an almost daily basis." She stopped to give her pencil a tap. "I'm sure it hasn't been easy. . . ."

Zeke's teacher trailed off, giving Zeke's mom an opening. She didn't take it.

Ms. Crawford frowned and shook her head. "If Zeke continues to act out like this, I'm afraid I will have no choice but to recommend him to a different school. One that specializes in students with behavioral problems."

"Behavioral problems?" Zeke's mother repeated.

"I don't want to go to a different school," Zeke protested.

"I understand," Ms. Crawford said, looking straight at Zeke now. "But this really has to stop. I can't have you standing on your desk, waving your underwear around. There are only two weeks left in the school year. Let's see if we can just get through them without another incident. Do you think you can do that, Zeke? For me? And for your mom?"

Ms. Crawford stared at him. She looked exhausted—maybe even a touch exasperated too. But his mother looked flat-out

19

desperate, pleading with her eyes. *Please be good*, those sea-greens said.

"Of course," he said. For her.

And he probably would have. If it weren't for the mouse.

The one he cornered in their cluttered garage three days later and managed to smuggle to school in his backpack, the temptation too much to resist. In the chaos of morning arrival, with nobody looking, he dumped it from its box into Amanda's desk. He wanted to see if her eyes could get any bigger.

They definitely could.

Zeke spent most of the last week of school sitting in that all-too-familiar room, thinking about his choices and their consequences.

It was only three weeks after that that a letter arrived in the mail telling him he just might be the greatest kid in the world.

Greetings from Keystone, South Dakota, home to the most famous rock carving of four dead white guys in history. Did you know that originally Mount Rushmore was going to feature heroes like Buffalo Bill Cody and Lewis and Clark? Or that it took fourteen years and four hundred men to carve the darn thing? Miraculously nobody died even though they mostly used dynamite. (Don't get any ideas, kids.)

I hope we all get the chance to come out here together as a family someday. Rushmore is only cool for about five minutes or so, but the Black Hills are absolutely gorgeous—at least what little I got to see of them from out the window. Be so much better to hike through them with you guys.

Miss you all. Hugs all around.

Dad

P.S. Why did they pick Mount Rushmore for the carving? Its beauty was unpresidented.

It's Always Something. And Something.

Zeke was still thinking about the obviously erroneously sent letter when he heard his mother's key jiggling in the door, the signal to turn off the television and grab the book that he'd strategically placed beside him so as to look intellectually stimulated. Nate dropped his own game controller, rolled off the couch onto the floor, and began fiddling with some LEGO. Zeke heard Jackie's feet in the hallway. She had probably seen Mom pull in and was coming to make sure her younger brothers hadn't set fire to anything.

"Nate, why is your chin bright red?" Jackie charged over and began furiously scrubbing at Nate's face with a spit-moistened thumb just as the door swung open, revealing their mother in all her business-suited glory.

"You're home!" Nate dodged around his fussing sister and bolted to the front door for a hug, then quickly stepped back. "God, you *stink*."

Their mother sighed. "Half the store called in sick today, so I had to work fragrances."

Zeke's mom was an assistant manager at the Penney's in the mall, but only an assistant, which meant she went wherever she was needed. Some nights she came home smelling like she'd fallen into a vat of Axe body spray and then rolled around in a bed of potpourri.

"There were these three teenagers," she continued. "I swear they tried everything. You could see the fumes drifting up from their bodies. I have the biggest headache." Ms. Stahls went to the first kitchen cabinet and fished some pills from the top shelf, swallowing them without water. She eyed her sons. "How about you? What did you rascals do all day? Please tell me it wasn't all video games." Clearly the book hadn't fooled her.

"Course not," Zeke said. "We played outside mostly."

Ms. Stahls's eyes narrowed. She wasn't buying that either, which was a shame seeing as how it was mostly true. "And did your sister look after you?" She looked from him to Jackie and back again.

"If by 'look after us' you mean locking herself in her room and texting her friends for seven hours, then yes, there was top-notch after-looking."

Jackie's cloudy blue eyes—their father's eyes—suddenly caught fire, making Zeke thankful *she* didn't have laser vision. "You little twerp! I did too watch you. I made you lunch like always." She pointed to the dirty pot rimmed with orange gunk still sitting on the stove.

Their mother sighed again. "Well, that nixes *my* idea for dinner. Nuggets and tots it is." Mom reached into the freezer and started gathering bags. Frozen chicken was cheaper than fresh and came prebreaded. She opened a drawer and stopped. "Where's all the aluminum foil?"

Standing beside him, Zeke's brother whimpered like a scolded puppy.

"I swear I had a whole new thing of foil. I *just* bought it, and now it's gone."

"Don't look at me," Jackie said. "I was in my room texting all day, remember?"

Zeke's mom skipped clear over him and leveled her eyes at Nate, going straight to the weaker link. Her auburn hair, carefully bunned at the start of the day, was loose and frazzled now. She held a spatula in her hand like a club.

Nate bit his lip; Zeke could sense his brother was already about to break and she hadn't even started with the questions.

"We were playing knights," Zeke said, jumping in with the first feasible lie that came to mind. "In shining armor. We made swords and shields and everything. We used up all the foil." At least it sounded better than *I tried to bake my brother like a potato.*

"You used it all? Do you know how much that stuff costs?" His mom stopped to think about it. "All right—so it doesn't cost *that* much, but that's not the point. The point is we can't go around wasting stuff. I'm not made of money, you know."

He knew. She reminded him constantly. She wasn't made of money. Money didn't grow on trees. Nobody poops nickels—as if *that* was something somebody would even wish for. "Sorry, Ma," he said.

"Sorry, Ma," Nate echoed.

Zeke's mother shook her head, then turned and opened the fridge. "And who drank all the soda?"

Zeke couldn't help but marvel; the woman was like Sherlock Holmes.

She spun back around, hands on hips. "There were six cans in there this morning and now there's only one."

That's because Nate and I shook four of them up and launched them off the roof pretending they were hand grenades, Zeke thought. The fifth one, they split.

He was about to make some excuse but his mother said, "You know what? Just forget it. Go wash your hands. And if your teeth fall out it's your own fault. I'm not buying you new ones."

"Diet soda doesn't rot your teeth," Zeke said. "No sugar."

The hard stare from his mother didn't have a lick of sugar in it either. Zeke shut his mouth and followed his brother to the bathroom. Clearly it had been another long day at work, and he was already testing her patience.

Then again, it was always a long day at work. And she didn't seem to start with much patience anymore.

Twenty minutes later the four of them sat around the dining room table over plates of dinosaur-shaped chicken and tater tots. Dinner at the Stahlses' always had an *and*. Mac *and* cheese. Rice *and* beans. Hamburgers *and* fries. Noodles *and* sauce. Sometimes there were peas *and* carrots to go with it. Sometimes it was canned peaches *and* pears. Most everything came out of a can or a box or a frosty bag. It's not that Zeke's mother couldn't cook from scratch. Once, she used to enjoy it, filling the house with the snap of oil in skillets and the sweet tang of minced garlic or a savory waft of rosemary chicken simmering in a pan. More often than not, Dad would help her, the two of them bumping into each other, sometimes stopping to waltz for a moment to whatever song he was humming, causing Jackie to groan and beg them to stop before she barfed in the salad. Mom was usually the pilot in the kitchen; Dad was her wingman.

Except on Sunday mornings; that's when Zeke's father would fly solo. Most every Sunday his dad would get up with the sun to make his famous Stahls family breakfast feast, waking them all an hour later with the smell of sizzling bacon and homemade buttered biscuits, fresh fruit cups and pancakes loaded with sprinkles or chocolate chips drenched in real, honest-to-goodness maple syrup out of a glass bottle. Zeke and his sister always used to fight over the sprinkled ones.

That was before the house got quiet and the waltzing stopped. Before Mom got the promotion at the store and started begging for overtime, coming home late and filling the kitchen with the sound of the microwave's ding and the smell of Juicy Couture.

26

Serious cooking required time and effort and a constant supply of fresh ingredients, not to mention a head free of aches.

So instead it was nuggets and tots. Zeke sat next to Nate as always, across from their sister. Mom sat at one end, across from the empty chair with the wonky leg that would probably only take fifteen minutes to fix. "Did somebody think to check the mail today?" she asked.

"Jackie got a magazine," Nate said, chuckling into his glass of milk. "Looked kinda cheesy to me." Snort, cough, snort. When you're seven, things stay funny much longer than they should.

Zeke considered saying something about the letter. The one that was balled up somewhere in the bushes. His mother had obviously had a tough day at work. It might give *her* a laugh to know her son might be *the* greatest in the whole entire world. It would certainly give his sister one. Maybe that's why he kept it to himself; Jackie didn't need any more ammunition. "Bills mostly," he said. "I put 'em on the counter."

"Blood from a turnip." Another of his mother's favorite sayings. Zeke always wondered why a turnip; it was just as impossible to squeeze blood from a banana or a head of broccoli. Or, apparently, from his mother's checking account.

"Jackie also got something from some school," he added. "Walton Community College."

"Ugh," Jackie grunted, rolling her eyes. Like every other seventeen-year-old confronting the onset of their senior year, Zeke's sister was deep in the throes of figuring out what she wanted to do with the rest of her life. She had her sights set on college and had accumulated a list of places she planned to apply to. Apparently, Walton Community was not at the top of that list.

"You shouldn't dismiss it," Mom said. "Walton's a nice school. Nice campus."

"Just because it has a Starbucks, doesn't make it nice," Jackie snipped. "Only the tech kids go to WCC. They probably don't even have a music program. Angela's applying to Michigan and Chicago *and* Berkeley, and my grades are just as good as hers."

Another sigh. "I'm not saying you couldn't get in somewhere better. But it's a helluva lot more affordable, and the credits would transfer. Plus it's close, so you could continue to live at home for a couple of years," Zeke's mother countered.

"Terrific," Jackie murmured with less than zero enthusiasm. She picked up one of her nuggets, stared at it for a moment, then tossed it back on her plate. She was clearly finished, with both her dinner and the conversation. "Jasmine invited some girls over to her house tonight. They wanted to know if I could come."

"It's a Thursday."

"It's Friday, actually," Jackie countered. "And it's summer, so what difference does it make?"

"Is it really Friday already?" Mom looked at Zeke, who shrugged. It *was* summer. Who could keep track?

"So can I go?"

Their mother nodded, then raised a finger. "But only if you promise to watch your brothers tomorrow night. Sondra needs me to take her shift and we could use the extra hours. And I mean actually watch them this time, not hole up in your room tweeting your business to the world."

"Twitter is for crusty politicians with nothing better to do than bully each other. And why can't the boys just stay home by themselves? Zeke's twelve. You made *me* start babysitting when *I* was that age."

Stay at home on a Saturday night without the threat of his big sister looming over him? Zeke nodded eagerly.

"True," their mother said, "but . . ." Zeke knew what was behind that "but." *But you know your brother. You know what he's capable of.* Instead, she said, "You're a girl. Girls are just more mature and responsible."

"That's gender bias," Jackie said. "It's illegal."

"I don't think anyone is going to sue me for making my daughter stay home and babysit. Besides, the store closes at ten. I won't be late. And you better not be either tonight, understand? I want you home before midnight."

"Yes, Fairy Godmother," Jackie said, her sarcasm dialed to ten. "Should I also leave a slipper on the steps of the palace on my way out?"

"If it means you'll find some prince to marry you and come pay off the Visa, be my guest." Zeke's mother stopped and

29

considered what she'd just said. "On second thought—keep your shoes on. I've got enough to worry about."

Zeke wasn't sure his sister was listening, though. She was already up out of her chair, her tongue set to rapid-fire. "Jaz said to come at seven and I have to stop and pick up Angela on the way also can I take the van 'cause I'm almost out of gas promise not to wreck it thanks you're a saint and you smell really good love you bye."

In a whirlwind, Zeke's sister managed to kiss their mother on the cheek and fish the keys out of her purse. She was halfway to the door before Ms. Stahls knew what was happening.

"No texting and driving!"

"Texting, bad. Total obedience to overbearing mother, good," Jackie called back in a flurry, followed by the sound of the front door slamming shut.

Zeke's mom rubbed her temples and sighed. It seemed like dinners usually ended this way. With Jackie finding some excuse to leave the table first. Though that was better than the ones that dragged on in silence, where you could hear the clink of everyone's forks against their plates, his mother staring across the table at the empty chair.

Zeke finished his tots quickly and Nate followed suit. Mom left most of her dinner uneaten. "You and your brother clear the table. I'll get the dishes later," she said, her voice soft.

Normally Zeke would protest. It was technically Jackie's turn to get the table. It was *his* week to take out the trash—though he hadn't actually done that yet either, which could explain why it was overflowing, with two hundred square feet of aluminum foil shoved down somewhere toward the middle. But it seemed best to just follow orders tonight. He stood up and grabbed his plate when he heard a knock on the door.

It obviously wasn't Jackie coming back for forgotten Chap-Stick or a hoodie. Could be the neighbor, Mrs. Gwon, who sometimes stopped to pawn off her leftovers or to comment on something she'd learned from the neighborhood crime watch. *Now they are just breaking windows and tearing up the car looking for money to buy drugs. I swear, this neighborhood is going to h-e-l-l.* Mrs. Gwon liked to spell out her curses, thinking that Nate wasn't old enough to figure them out. Zeke looked to the door and then to his mom.

"I'll get it," she said. "You just do what I asked you to, please."

Just do what she asked.

She made it sound so easy.

KABAM and Kerpow

Zeke stood in the kitchen, peeking around the corner with a ketchup-smeared plate in each hand as his mother opened the front door.

On the other side was a tall, lean man with gaunt cheeks and tanned skin, his hands cupped prayerlike before him. He wore an all-white suit with a peacock-blue shirt and a yellow bow tie. His hair was a bush of golden, looping curls—a cherub's 'do. His broad, toothful smile was capped by deep dimples. He looked kind of like a little kid dressed up for an imaginary tea party. He pressed his finger to the bridge of his wire-frame glasses, giving them a boost, Clark Kent style.

Zeke had never seen him before. He surely would have remembered.

"Ms. Charlotte Stahls?"

Zeke's mother nodded.

"Good evening. My name is Gordon Notts. Is your son Eze-kiel home by chance?"

Gordon Notts. Where had Zeke heard that name before?

"You're not with the police, are you?" his mom asked.

"Oh, most definitely not. I'm with the Klein Agency for the Betterment of All Mankind. KABAM for short."

Right! The letter! Zeke nearly dropped both plates he was holding.

There was a pause, then his mother said, *"Kabam?"*

"Kerpow!" the man shouted, making an explosion with his hands, causing Zeke's mom to take a cautious step backward. "Sorry. Just can't help myself sometimes. So, *is* your son here?"

"Well . . . yes, but—"

"Excellent," Gordon Notts said, suddenly stepping right inside the front hallway without permission. Zeke moved a little farther back into the kitchen, keeping one eye peeping around the corner. He felt a tug on his T-shirt.

"Who's that?" his little brother whispered.

"Gordon Notts," Zeke whispered back. "From KABAM."

"What's Kabam?"

"I'm not sure," Zeke said, then pushed Nate back, completely out of sight of his mother and this stranger facing off in the hall-way.

"Sorry to just drop in on you," Mr. Notts continued cheerily, "but we find it works better when there's an element of surprise. We prefer to capture you in the moment." His voice sounded like something out of a commercial daring you to compare laundry detergents.

"*We?*" his mother said.

"Oh right. Sorry. Come on in, Logan." Notts waved outside and a much larger man entered the house with a video camera perched on his shoulder. Unlike Notts, who looked lithe and slippery, like a well-dressed eel, Logan was bulky, shaped almost like a Mr. Potato Head. He wore flannel and jeans and high-top sneakers. He seemed young, but his beard was already streaked with gray. "This is Logan, one of our cameramen. Logan, this is Ms. Stahls."

Logan reached out with the hand not anchoring the camera. "Pleased to meet you, ma'am," he said. His voice was much deeper than his companion's. And much less grating.

"Is that thing on?" Zeke's mom asked.

Gordon Notts grinned. "Yes, but don't worry—it's not going out live or anything. We're just getting some footage of the initial meeting in case we need it."

"Need it for what? What are you talking about? Who *are* you?"

The man cocked his head to the side, perplexed. "Didn't you get our letter?"

In the kitchen, Zeke bristled, pressed tight behind the doorframe. He watched the cloud of confusion settle over his mother's face, but it was just as quickly replaced with annoyance. "Letter.

No. I didn't get any letter. I don't even know who you are or why you are in my house. I certainly don't know why you are filming this. I suggest you leave this instant."

"I understand, but perhaps you should ask your son if he knows anything about this first," Gordon Notts countered, still sporting his smile as he pointed toward the kitchen. The cameraman shifted, panning the camera's glassy eye in the same direction. Zeke ducked all the way inside, but it was too late.

"Ezekiel Samson Stahls, come here, please. *Now.*"

Zeke knew he couldn't ignore the name trifecta. He took a step out, then realized something was holding him back: Nate still fixed to his shirt. They emerged in tandem, engine and caboose. Zeke kept his eyes on the two strangers—it was better than making eye contact with his mother beside him.

Gordon Notts clapped his hands. "There he is. The man of the hour. Logan, get a shot of him, will you?"

Zeke watched the camera trace him from toe to head and felt himself blush. He wasn't one to get embarrassed easily. After all, he had stood on his desk at school waving a pair of his underwear around. But something about the camera made him instantly uneasy. Or maybe it was something about Gordon Notts, whose hand shot out toward Zeke so fast, he was afraid the man was about to slap him.

"A pleasure to meet you, Ezekiel Stahls, or Zeke, as everyone calls you."

"How do you know what everyone calls me?"

"That's the least of what I know," Notts said with a wink. "And you must be Nathan," he added, reaching around and shaking Nate's hand as well. "I'm guessing you're pretty proud of your big brother, huh?"

Nate nodded even though he had no idea what, exactly, he was meant to be proud of.

"Excuse me, Mr. Notts," Zeke's mother interrupted. "But if you don't want me to call the actual police, I suggest you explain who you are and what you're doing here."

"Of course. My apologies. As the letter indicated"—Notts raised an eyebrow at Zeke, who looked down at the floor—"I work for the Klein Agency for the Betterment of All Mankind. Of course we've been wanting to change that to *"Humankind"* but KABAH doesn't have the same *oomph*." Gordon Notts tugged at his shirt collar, his forehead beading with sweat. "Is it hot in here, or is it just me?"

Zeke's mom ignored the question. "You were saying?"

"Right. Yes. KABAM is a nonprofit with the mission of highlighting the achievements and general goodwill of *human*kind all around the world. Do you watch the news, Ms. Stahls?"

Zeke's mom nodded, then shook her head. "I Yahoo mostly. I used to watch *Ellen*."

Logan the cameraman piped up. "I was a *Judge Judy* man myself." Zeke noticed the camera had gone back to his mother.

Better her than him, he supposed. She wasn't blushing. Not out of embarrassment, at least. The pink in her cheeks was 10 percent no AC and 90 percent irritation.

It didn't stop Notts, though. "You are exposed to the news then. So you must know that it is every day full of atrocities and inequities, social injustices, heinous crimes, and people just plain being nasty to each other." He said all of this while still sporting that cheese-eating smile, accentuated by that bright yellow bow tie. "Frankly, it can be enough to make one lose all hope in humanity."

Zeke's mom nodded as if she finally understood what this was all about. "Ah. Okay. Listen. Whatever you've heard about Zeke, I'm sure it was surprising, but I hardly think it would be enough to make you lose hope in *humanity*."

Gordon Notts laughed. He had a cartoon witch's cackle. *Ree-hee-hee-hee.* "No! No! Of course not. I was speaking about the world at large. You have to admit, humans as a whole do some pretty terrible things to each other. Our mission at KABAM is to go out into that world and recognize the *positive* potential of humanity. To be a beacon of hope, as it were. *We* do good by highlighting the good in others. Share it with the world. Think of us as cheerleaders."

"Cheerleaders," Mom repeated.

"*Goooo* humanity!" Notts said, shaking a pair of imaginary pom-poms. He waited for her to say it.

"Um . . . hooray?"

"That's it!" Notts chirped, putting his pretend pom-poms down. "There is no way to overemphasize the need for positivity in this world of ours. Which is why we do everything in our power to showcase the fantastic, wonderful, amazing things that people are capable of. And it's for that reason that we've recently launched our latest awareness campaign—to find the World's Greatest Kid and reward them for their endeavors."

"The greatest kid in the whole *world*?" Nate whispered in awe. He was still holding on to Zeke's shirt.

"Well, not the *whole* world," Notts amended. "Our funding doesn't allow us to extend internationally yet, and the legal ramifications prohibit us from acquiring the necessary records and such. It's complicated, but let's just say that Greatest Kid in the World looks better on a bumper sticker."

"Okay. And you are here, what? Collecting money? You want to know if we know someone we'd like to recommend?"

"Oh, no, Ms. Stahls. We've already accepted all the recommendations we can handle. In fact, we've already narrowed the field down to five worthy individuals." The man licked his sweaty upper lip, pausing for effect. "No. The reason we are here is to let you know that your son is one of them."

In the silence that followed, Gordan Notts's dimples resurfaced. Logan's camera danced back and forth from Zeke to his mother, no doubt wearing similar dumbfounded expressions. And this wasn't even the first time Zeke had been told this news.

"Hold up a sec," Mom said finally. "You're looking for the world's greatest kid and you think it might be my *son*?"

"Yes."

"*My* son?"

"Yes, ma'am."

"My son *Zeke*?"

"The one and only." Notts shot Zeke with the pointer fingers of both hands, *pow pow*. The camera shifted to focus solely on him again. Zeke wasn't sure what to do, so he just smiled and waved, halfheartedly.

His mother shook her head. "Is this some kind of a joke? Did Zeke put you up to this? Did he blackmail you somehow?" She turned to Zeke. "What do you have on this man?"

Zeke didn't know whether to be proud of or offended by the suggestion.

"I assure you this is no joke," Notts insisted. "It's all in that letter."

"In that case I think there's been a mistake. Don't get the wrong idea, Mr. Notts. I love my son. *Very* much. And I know that deep down—deep, *deep* down—he has a big heart. But I'm not sure he's somebody you would want to put on a T-shirt advertising . . . you know . . . *goodness*."

"Greatness," Notts corrected. "There are millions of *good* kids in the world. Hundreds of millions. We are looking for the greatest. And we have it narrowed down to five."

"Yes. Well. In that case, I think there's been some kind of

error. No offense, sweetie."

Zeke returned his mother's look with a shrug. As much as he would have loved to hear her say otherwise, it was hard to argue. After all, he'd thought the exact same thing, hadn't he, the moment he read the letter?

Gordon Notts was undeterred, however. "You don't have to be modest, Ms. Stahls, though I appreciate your leveled appraisal. Humility is one of the many admirable traits we see parents instill in their exceptional children. But it's all right to be proud of the boy you've raised. Your son is a remarkable individual with a record of inspiring behavior."

She turned and looked at Zeke again. "Is there something you're not telling me?"

Zeke blinked. There were plenty of things he wasn't telling her, starting with that letter and what the aluminum foil was really used for, then stretching back for years, to when he was five and peed in the neighbor kid's lemonade at a birthday party on a dare. But *this*—this Notts and the camera and the contest—it had flustered him, and he couldn't find the words to even get started.

"Ms. Stahls," Gordon Notts said softly, settling a hand on her arm. "I assure you this is no mistake. As an organization partially funded by a grant from the federal government, we are given access to certain records—nothing overly personal, of course. Not medical histories or social security numbers or anything of that nature. But we do have access to grades, test scores—as well as

40

other pertinent information: news reports, local media files, public records detailing each nominee's achievements. It's different for everyone, of course, and some applicants have a richer history than others. . . ."

Zeke knew exactly what his mother was thinking: Zeke had a rich history all right. So did Ivan the Terrible.

"We enter all of this information into our computer program for every kid in America, and based on a highly complex algorithm the details of which I hardly understand myself, it provides a rankable score for each one—between the ages of ten and fourteen, that is."

"Why ten?" Nate asked, peering from behind his brother's back.

"Well, Nathan—"

"It's just Nate," Zeke corrected.

"Right. Well, Nate. After careful consideration, we decided that anyone under the age of ten hasn't had quite enough years to accumulate a life history suitable for ranking, and anyone over the age of fourteen can hardly be considered a kid anymore—at least they certainly don't want to be. But don't worry, my boy. You'll get your chance someday. Provided our funding holds out." Notts laughed again.

Zeke's mom gently massaged her temples. "Hold on. You're saying that your computer got access to Zeke's test scores and school records and whatnot and somehow decided that he was the best kid in the world?"

"Greatest," Notts corrected. "In the United States," he corrected further. "And no. It did not decide that he was the greatest. It decided he was one of the *five* greatest. Which is exactly why I'm here. To help determine if he is, in fact, *the* greatest . . . with a little help from the rest of the country. Well, a lot of help, actually. It's a purely democratic process."

Zeke felt his mother squirming beside him, felt her hand clutch one of his shoulders. It was a familiar feeling. Most of the time she did it as a warning, leading him away from whatever trouble he was about to get into. But this time she gave a much softer squeeze.

Then she let go and reached for the doorknob.

"I'm sorry, Mr. Notts, but this is all too much," she said. "It feels like a scam, honestly. And I think you should go before I report you to the authorities."

Gordon Notts didn't budge, however, even as Zeke's mom opened the door. "I know it sounds crazy. After all, there are hundreds of millions of kids out there. Each of them with so much potential. And yet, what mother doesn't think she has the world's greatest?"

"*I* don't," Mom said sharply, then covered her mouth with her hand as if a bird just flew out of it. She glanced at Zeke and then went back to Notts. "And even if I did, it would be a pretty biased opinion, don't you think? My guess is your computer made some kind of error."

"I highly doubt that," Notts countered. "The computer doesn't make mistakes."

"Then maybe your secretary did. Maybe something got mistyped or misplaced or something, because as much as I love Zeke, as much as I think the world of him, there is simply no way this could be."

She motioned toward the open door. Gordon Notts sighed, crossing his arms. "So then you are saying you do *not* want your son to participate in the contest? This once-in-a-lifetime opportunity?"

"I'm saying my son should not have even *entered* the contest," Zeke's mother said. "I don't even know how it happened."

"So then you are willing to forfeit your chance at the grand prize?"

Zeke's mother dropped the hand that was pointing the way out. In the silence that followed, Zeke swore he could hear her brain working, gears clicking. "Grand prize?" she repeated.

"You didn't tell her about the prize for winning?" Notts asked, looking at Zeke with mock admonishment. "The trip to Hawaii? The ten thousand dollars?"

"Hawaii?" Zeke's mother said. She seemed to almost choke on the word.

"Ten thousand dollars," Nate repeated breathlessly. "That would make us millionaires!"

"Not quite," Zeke informed him. But it would make them

thousandaires at least. And judging by the bills crowding the counter, it might *feel* like a million bucks.

"Mr. Notts—" Zeke's mother began, but the man with the curly hair cut her off with a raised finger.

"You know what? You don't have to make a decision right this minute. The competition doesn't start until Monday. We will need a day to get set up, of course, sign the contract, go over the rules, but that still gives you all day tomorrow to mull it over." He reached into his Colonel Sanders suit and produced a business card shiny as a tinfoil mummy. "Here's my card, since you seem to have misplaced the letter. That's our website right there. I've written Logan's number on the back."

Zeke's mother took the card by the edge, as if one end of it were on fire.

"Just understand that, while we call it a competition, it's really nothing so intense. It simply entails Zeke going about his daily routine, doing all of the things that he normally does, being the spectacular individual he is. We just want to get an honest picture of Zeke in all his glory for the rest of the world to see."

"His greatness you mean?" Mom said.

"Exactly!" Gordon Notts said, shooting his fingers again. "I look forward to your call, Ms. Stahls. And you all have a fantastic evening."

The man from KABAM smiled—his teeth as blazing white as his suit—then reached around Zeke's mom and offered Nate a fist that hung there for three seconds, unbumped. "Until we meet again," he said to Zeke before turning and slinking back through the front door.

"Nice meeting you all," Logan said, bowing ever so slightly. The cameraman followed the director of charitable programming out to the black van parked in the road, leaving the three Stahlses framed in the porchlight.

Zeke's mom didn't close the door right away. She just stood and watched them leave, Nate still pressed to her legs, Zeke beside her with his hands stuffed in his pockets. He expected her to laugh. Maybe whisper "world's greatest kid" like some kind of punch line. If she did, he thought, he would laugh with her—at the absolute absurdity of it all.

But instead of laughing, she looked up at the star-freckled sky and said three words that seemed to have stuck out even more than *world's greatest kid*.

"Ten. Thousand. Dollars."

The Question Mark

They waited until Nate was tucked in to discuss it, filling the rest of the evening with Uno and ice cream sandwiches that Mom had managed to hide in the freezer behind a giant bag of mixed vegetables that nobody dared touch. Finally, with his little brother asleep and Jackie still out with her friends, Zeke and his mother sat side by side on the juice-stained sofa. She gave him a full minute of staring—maybe expecting him to cough up some details voluntarily, but she really should have known better. Zeke Stahls took his right to remain silent seriously.

"Okay," she said at last. "Let's have it. What have you gotten yourself into this time?"

Zeke couldn't even count how often he'd been asked that question. The answer almost always fell under the general category of *trouble*, but underneath that there were numerous subcategories:

trouble at school, trouble at camp, trouble with his sister, trouble with the neighbor's dog, trouble with that old man across the street, trouble with the cranky dude at the library who doesn't appreciate when Zeke puts the tawdry romance novels with their scantily clad steamy-embrace covers in the children's section next to the Elephant and Piggy books.

But this didn't fall under any of those categories. For once, Zeke wasn't even sure what he'd done, which made it easier to actually tell the truth for once.

"Here," Zeke said, producing the crinkled letter that he'd saved from the bushes while his brother was being tucked in. The one that had been addressed to Ezekiel Stahls and Parents, plural. Obviously the computers at KABAM made *some* mistakes. "I threw it away because I thought it was a joke. I never expected anybody to actually show up. I mean . . . who *was* that guy?"

His mother read the letter over quickly. Her face softened. "You're right. It does all seem a little . . ." She paused, searching for the right word. Zeke wondered if he should help her. *Unbelievable? Outlandish? Screwball?* "Suspicious," she concluded. "I mean, KABAM? Really? And Gordon Notts? That *can't* be his real name. And that suit. And that *smile*. Please."

"Has to be fake," Zeke agreed. Except the letterhead looked real enough. And the camera the guy named Logan was carrying seemed expensive and professional. And the van actually had the letters printed on the side: KABAM. It seemed like a lot of effort for a practical joke. "Still . . ." he added, letting the empty sentence loiter between them. He could see it in her face. The doubt. But also the doubting of the doubt.

The possibility.

Zeke's mom pulled the business card out of her shirt pocket, flipping it over and over. It looked legit too. "Can't hurt to look, I guess." She grabbed her phone and typed in the web address. Sure enough, a home page for the Klein Agency for the Betterment of All Mankind popped up. It looked authentic, like the business card—though any ten-year-old with a laptop could make a professional-looking website nowadays.

The agency's logo stretched across the banner, and a handful of news stories ran underneath. They were all stories of people "making a positive difference in the world." A woman helping to vaccinate children in the Congo. A man teaching immigrants how to read English so they could get their GEDs. A band of off-duty firefighters building a new playground. An old lady adopting fourteen stray dogs out on her farm in Iowa. Just like Gordon Notts said, the website celebrated *the fantastic, wonderful, amazing things that people are capable of.* If these were real people, Zeke thought, and not just made-up stories, then they probably earned more brownie points in a day than he'd earned in his whole life.

Zeke's mom swiped around the site until she found what she was looking for—a headline that read *Greatest Kid Competition Underway!* She clicked on the link and suddenly four tween faces stared right back at them.

Four faces and one big question mark.

Four of the Finalists Have Been Determined, the headline beneath the pictures read. *Who Will Be the Fifth?*

Zeke leaned in a little closer and looked at the photos in turn. A white girl with straight blond hair and rainbow braces. Another girl who looked Indian, with smart-looking, thick-framed glasses and a thin-lipped, confident smile. An Asian kid wearing a baseball cap backward and pointing cheesily at the camera. And the smallest of the four, a wiry, brown-skinned boy with a worried smile and eyes that refused to look straight on. Only first names were given, listed beneath each picture. Hailey. Aadya. Kyo. Dom.

According to a computer algorithm, these were four of the five greatest kids in the world. Or at least in the United States.

"Click on one—see what comes up," Zeke said.

His mother clicked on the picture of the first girl. Suddenly the photo became animated, replaced with a video of Hailey speaking in a bubbly, singsong voice. "Hi there. My name is Hailey Richter and I enjoy ice-skating, music, horseback riding, knitting, calligraphy, crossword puzzles, and helping those in need. When I grow up, I want to be secretary general of the United Nations. I think greatness means putting others' needs ahead of your own each and every day."

She finished with a colorful smile. Then the video disappeared, revealing only her photo again.

"Wow," Zeke's mom said.

"Yeah."

"She's a *lot*."

"So much."

"What kid likes crossword puzzles?"

"Click on another one," Zeke prodded.

His mom went down the row.

"My name is Aadya Gupta, which is the name given the original power of the universe. I enjoy bird-watching, stargazing, karate, robotics, cooking for my family, helping the needy, and writing manifestos. When I grow up, I want to be the first woman to land on Mars. I think greatness means always doing your best."

"Bird-watching?"

"She's lying," Zeke replied. "What's there to watch?" Though he made a mental note to start working on his own manifesto as soon as possible. It seemed like something he should have done years ago.

"Hi, everyone. My name is Kyo, but my friends call me Special K. I play soccer and baseball and lacrosse, and I also enjoy rock climbing and deep-sea fishing. I'm not all about sports, though. I like to volunteer at the retirement community and I run my school's annual canned food drive. When I grow up, I want to be a member of the US National Soccer team and maybe run for Congress. I think greatness is making the most of the gifts God gave you."

"Nobody plays soccer *and* lacrosse," Zeke said. "It's redundant."

"Good answer, though."

"I guess."

His mom clicked on the last one.

"My name is Dominic Jones, but everybody calls me Dom. I like reading and running track. But mostly I just like hanging out with my family and friends. When I grow up, I want to be a leader in my community. I think greatness is doing what's right instead of what's easy."

"Now *that* kid I like," Mom said. "Did you hear what he said? He *likes* spending time with his family." She glanced back at the front door that Jackie had escaped through hours ago.

Zeke nodded. At least Dom seemed normal, or if not normal, then at least not superhuman, though they all reminded him of the suck-ups at school. The ones whose names would be called six or seven times at the end-of-year ceremony, taking home fistfuls of certificates with foil stars. He stared at the question mark on the other side of Dom's picture. *Who will be the last contestant?*

Zeke's mom dropped her phone in her lap and took up the business card again. "I still don't buy it. I mean—you can't actually pick the World's Greatest Kid. Not with a computer. It's some kind of publicity stunt. They're going to use this to sell toys or cereal or something. There has to be some kind of gimmick."

"It *looks* pretty real," Zeke admitted.

"I'm sure it's *real*. But it's not . . . what's the word . . ."

"True?"

"Exactly. It's not *true*. Just because they pick one of these kids, it doesn't actually make them the greatest. You know what I mean?"

"Sure," Zeke said, though he only half agreed. They all seemed pretty great to him. In an over-the-top, make-you-want-to-hurl-your-nuggets-and-tots kind of way.

"It's like those World's Greatest Mom coffee mugs. How many of those are there in the world? Like a zillion?"

Actually, there happened to be one sitting in their kitchen cupboard at that very moment. Except it wasn't even a real World's Greatest Mom coffee mug. It was just a plain white Dollar Store mug that Zeke had written over in Sharpie when he realized at the last minute he hadn't gotten her anything for Mother's Day. He'd been careful to make the letters look neat at least. And he'd drawn a smiley face next to it. At the time she'd said she loved it—that it was one-of-a-kind—but that she was afraid to use it in case the marker washed off. Since then, it had just sat in the cupboard.

Maybe she'd forgotten about it. That's what happens to things that get tucked away. At least some things.

"It's actually kind of obnoxious if you think about it," his mother continued. "All the ranking. Those lists you see all the time. Top ten hottest celebrities. *New York Times* bestsellers. *Time*'s Person of the Year. Is that really what makes you great, just somebody saying you are?"

Wouldn't know, Zeke thought. He gave her a shrug.

"It's all about who has the most likes or the most followers or whatnot," his mother continued. "And for what?"

Zeke knew exactly for what. At least in this case. Ten thousand smackaroos and a sweet Hawaiian sunburn. "I mean, it *would* be pretty cool to go on a vacation," he murmured.

His mom frowned, with him not at him for once, then she hooked him with her arm, pulling him close. Normally he would fidget and fuss, try to squirm away, but this time, Zeke felt like letting her hold on, even though the stench of so much perfume stung his eyes. He could feel her chin digging into the back of his head. "Tell me honestly, what really happened to all the soda?" she asked softly, no trace of anger or accusation in her voice this time.

Zeke swallowed. He'd already told the truth about the letter, and she had her arm wrapped around him so there was no chance of running away. She was so much stronger than she looked.

"Me and Nate made grenades out of them," he admitted. "We shook them up and then threw them so they'd explode and spin around. We didn't break anything, though. And nobody got hurt." He considered that last piece of information to be the most crucial.

His mother frowned. "And the aluminum foil?" she pressed.

Now she was pushing it.

"I told you. Swords and shields."

"Right," she said, "my noble knight."

Zeke guessed she was really asking him something else but couldn't come out and say it without hurting his feelings, so he said it for her.

"Assuming it is legit. And there really is this contest. And by some fluke, I really am the last contestant. There's like . . . no way I could possibly win, right?"

His mother took a deep breath. "What do you think?" she asked.

Zeke bit his lip. He had as much chance of winning something like this as Nate did of getting superpowers from the sun. Even on his best behavior—and he couldn't remember exactly what that looked like—he couldn't compete against these four, with their manifestos and their fifty thousand hobbies and their perfect smiles. Of course he couldn't win.

But it would be different if *she* thought he could.

"Ten thousand dollars. You know that's about what I'll make all summer," his mother said.

It'd be enough to get the air conditioner fixed, at least, Zeke thought. Or maybe buy a new one. Maybe fix everything—the van and the wall and the dishwasher too. He had no idea how far ten grand could stretch.

He knew where Hawaii was, though. In the middle of an ocean that he'd only ever seen in movies and on postcards. It would be pretty great to gather shells with his little brother and sprinkle sand in his sister's hair while she slept on the beach. It would be cool to see how far the world stretched.

And there was actually a huge difference between *totally* impossible and *nearly* impossible.

"Then again, if you think about it, I've already gotten this far. Somehow or another, I'm already in the top five."

He told himself not to think about that *somehow* too long. Good fortune. Dumb luck. A glitch in the system. Divine intervention. It didn't matter. It was a chance, however slim. And Zeke knew an opportunity when he saw one. He was a schemer after all.

"We don't even know what all is involved," his mother said, her gears starting to turn the same direction as his. "Who knows what they are going to expect you to do?"

"Be great. Duh."

"Of course," she said. "Silly me." His mother pulled him even closer. He couldn't remember the last time she had hugged him this long. Then again, he couldn't remember the last time he'd let her. "All right," she concluded. "Let's give it a shot."

It was decided.

But she still didn't let go.

Instead of waiting until the morning to call, they sent Mr. Gordon Notts an email letting him know they were interested. They got a response back five minutes later.

Outstanding! So happy that you decided to take part!

It was followed by a brief overview of what was involved and a promise to be back in two days to sign forms and get everything settled.

Zeke crawled into his bed an hour later than usual, tiptoeing past his brother's. Once his mother had hugged him good night and shut the door, Zeke brought his flashlight from his pillowcase and pulled out the letter he'd swiped back from her, looking for some disclaimer, some embedded code, some secret phrase that would solve the riddle of how he had been chosen. He'd submitted plenty of fake applications in his life; just last week he'd applied to work at Target at one of their little kiosks. For name, he'd put Ima Jess Teezen. For past work experience, he'd claimed he was an underwater dolphin wrestler. Under special skills he'd written that he was "fluent in Old Fartish."

He had never applied to be the world's greatest kid, though. He didn't even know there was such a thing until today.

If for some reason this letter has reached you in error, please notify us immediately.

That's what a good kid would have done. Called that number and said, hey, just letting you know you've got the wrong guy. No way am I supposed to be a part of this.

A good kid.

But a *great* one would seize the moment. A great kid would win his mother the money she needed to cool the house. And buy his brother that hundred-dollar dinosaur Lego he'd been pining for since Christmas. And get his sister a ten-dollar Starbucks gift card. No. Make that a *fifteen*-dollar gift card. Because that's what *great* kids do.

Except Zeke had a guess at what really great kids did. They traveled around the world digging wells with their bare hands before donating a kidney, eyeball, and lung to shark attack victims, all the while composing their next symphony and writing the great American novel. Obviously the other four contestants hadn't been chosen by mistake. They probably had handwritten recommendations from the president. Zeke knew there was really no way he could contend with the likes of an Aadya or a Dom.

But then again, he didn't really know the rules yet. Maybe it wasn't all about being a brownnosing, multitalented, overachieving superstar. Maybe there was a loophole. A workaround. Some gimmick he could exploit. Maybe, just maybe, he could find some way to win that didn't involve him being all that great to begin with.

Zeke lay there and listened to his brother's soft snores. The *fwip* of the ceiling fan blades would have drowned those out if Zeke hadn't broken them. He could also just make out the sound of his mother cleaning up the kitchen—just one more thing to be done while she waited up for Jackie—or fell asleep on the couch trying.

She deserved a walk along the beach.

Zeke closed his eyes and pictured himself standing in the sand, water up to his knees, foaming waves crashing against the shoreline, tugging at him, begging him to come out, to see how far he could go and still touch the bottom. The image was drawn from a photo he'd seen at least a dozen times. It made his chest ache just thinking about it.

With his flashlight guiding him, he bent over the side of his bed and reached for the cedar box he'd hidden there, the one he'd stolen from his mother's closet months ago, opening it up to reveal all the memories and broken promises it held. He dumped them out on his bed and began to read.

When he sobbed, he sobbed softly, so as not to wake up Nate.

Greetings from sunny Sacramento, the City of Trees. Also known as The Big Tomato (the apple already being taken). Did you know that the Pony Express started here? Or maybe here was where it ended. All depends on how you look at it, I guess. It took ten days for a letter to get all the way from Missouri to California. Now if you put a letter in the mail . . . well, it seems like it still takes about ten days. Hopefully this postcard will get to you sooner than that. Hopefully I will too.

The California coastline is beautiful. No wonder people sell their firstborn children to come live out here. Ocean on one side, hills on the other, all the rich people in between. A man can always dream.

Tell Zeke to save some fireworks so we can launch them when I get back. And tell Jackie that I'm sorry I won't be able to make it to the orchestra concert, but I'm sure she will be great. The next Yo Mama. :-)

Love, Dad

P.S. What's the fastest way to mail a little horse? I'll give you one guess.

Seeing Red

The decision had been made, the email sent, the meeting arranged, but it wasn't until the next morning that Zeke and his mother told Jackie, who had snuck in at 12:02 in the a.m. with both shoes on and no princes in tow. They were all sitting around the table, eating donut holes straight out of the box, when Mom made the official announcement.

"Your brother has been invited to take part in a contest," she began.

"What kind of contest?" Jackie asked. She was dressed in her flying rhino pajamas. She would probably still be dressed in her flying rhino pajamas six hours from now. It was summer, after all. "Please tell me it's World's Largest Walking Parasite, because I really think he'd have a shot at that."

Zeke stuck out his tongue. Jackie returned the favor.

Their mother cleared her throat. "It's for the World's Greatest Kid, actually," she said.

Jackie looked at Mom. At Zeke. Back at Mom. "Funny," she said, and popped another donut hole, licking the powdered sugar from her fingertips.

"I'm not kidding." Zeke's mom pushed the business card across the table. Zeke stayed quiet and just let her explain, about Gordon Notts, KABAM, the competition, the ten-thousand-dollar prize, Hawaii, all of it. He enjoyed watching his sister's mouth continue to drop like a drawbridge with each new revelation. "Turns out he's one of five finalists," Mom finished. "Can you believe it?"

The answer was obvious. Jackie laughed. At least until she noticed nobody was laughing with her. "Oh my god. You're serious."

"The competition starts Monday. They'll be here tomorrow to go over the details."

Zeke couldn't help it—if ever there was a smirk-worthy moment, it was this one. Jackie took a few more seconds to process before throwing her hands in the air. "Wait . . . hold on. How is this even possible? What kind of butt-backward people would pick *Zeke* as the world's greatest kid?"

"Let's not say *butt* at the table," Mom chided.

"But," Jackie stammered, "but—"

"Butt butt butt butt butt," Nate said, racing his ninth or tenth donut hole around his glass of milk, leaving a powdered sugar trail in its wake.

"But *Zeke?*"

"Buttzeke," Nate said, making his donut hole hop up and down.

"I mean, this has to be some kind of mistake, right? How did you even get nominated? Have they *met* you?"

"Actually, we met with them just last night, and Mr. Notts assured me that it wasn't an error. Your brother really is a finalist. The contest is up on their website and everything."

Jackie's face turned as red as her nail polish. She held up the business card. Zeke could see Logan's name and number scrawled across the back. "You actually *talked* to this guy? He came to our *house?*" She turned to Zeke. "Did you tell him about the time you superglued my dresser drawers closed? Or the time you replaced my hair spray with 7 Up? Or the time you cut all my bras in half and used them as parachutes for your action figures?"

Right. The bra-chutes. That one was admittedly a fail. After only ten minutes on the roof, Zeke learned that women's undergarments just weren't ideal parachute material. There was still a stormtrooper with half a bra strung to his back in one of the gutters somewhere.

"I'm sensing a little jealousy," Zeke said. Honestly, even if he didn't stand a chance in a million of winning, he had to admit it was worth it already, just to see this look on Jackie's face.

"Jealous? Of you? Please. The day I'm ever jealous of you, Ezekiel Stahls, is the day I find a really tall building and jump off of it."

"Jacqueline!"

"You could try the bank building downtown," Zeke suggested. "It's ten stories."

"Zeke!"

Jackie jutted her chin. "Do you hear how he talks to me? It's like this every day. Every. Single. Day. There's no way he could be the greatest kid in the world. He's not even the best kid sitting at this table by *far*."

"Says the girl who got a C on her math final," Zeke countered. He knew his sister was particularly sensitive about her grades. Especially since his were usually a touch higher than hers. And with college looming . . . and scholarships on the line . . .

"It's freaking calculus! And it's freaking hard. I'd like to see you try it, butt munch."

"Butt munch, butt munch, munch-a-bunch-of-butt-lunch," Nate sang.

"Nate, please."

"Well, maybe if you spent more time on your homework and less time on the phone with your friends talking about how 'sexy' Daniel Timmerman looked in his new jeans," Zeke said, giving her a powdered-sugar smile.

"You little twerp!"

"'Soooo tight,'" he added, doing his best to imitate her giggling whisper while making an imaginary mold of Daniel Timmerman's back end with his hands.

"Zeke!"

"You're eavesdropping on my phone conversations now?"

"Only when they're interesting," Zeke admitted. "Which is like, one percent of the time."

"You slimy little puke wad!"

"That means one out of a hundred." He was about to express it as a decimal when a cup slammed down onto the table.

His mother scowled at both of them. "That's enough. Is this how you are going to act when the cameras are here?"

Total silence. Jackie sat up, suddenly alert, like a squirrel homing in on an acorn's drop. "Cameras?"

Mom took a deep breath. "Apparently that's how the process works. They need to film him, just a few hours a day—you know, being good." She flashed him a look.

"Great," he reminded her, giving his sister a wink for added effect.

"Right. They film him being *great*," his mother continued. "That way people can see it and vote for him. You know. Like on that singing show we used to watch."

Jackie's scowl momentarily retreated. "Hold up. So you're say-ing we're going to be on *TV*?"

"I don't know if it will be televised, but it will be on their website at least," their mother said. "That's where all the voting takes place."

Zeke watched his sister process this new information. She was definitely thinking something, but he couldn't pinpoint what.

"But if we want this to happen," Mom continued, "if we are even going to *try* to make it happen, we are going to have to pull together as a family. We have to support Zeke . . . *All* of us."

"Fine," Jackie said. "But if they ask to interview me to tell everybody how 'great' he is, I'm not going to lie."

"Jackie, please."

"Please what, Mother? This is the same kid who played hockey with my pet turtle four years ago. Remember Shelley? Remember coming home to find him hiding behind the fridge, completely traumatized?"

Zeke didn't remember the behind-the-fridge part, though he did remember the turtle skidding pretty well across the linoleum once you flipped him on his back. Zeke honestly felt bad about that one, but he was young and bored and Shelley really did look like he was having fun. His little legs paddled the air as he spun.

"I know how difficult this will be for you. All I'm asking is that you two try to get along. No more name-calling. No more eavesdropping. No more pranks or punishments or flicking each other in the back of the head. Just for me, just this once, give it a rest."

She looked back and forth from Zeke to Jackie. Zeke nodded

first. Jackie cued up the expression that meant *whatever*. He had them all catalogued. He figured one day he'd write a field guide: *Eye Rolls of the North American Teenager.*

"Okay. This is going to be okay," their mother said unconvincingly.

"It's going to be a disaster," Jackie muttered.

"*Sooo* tight," Nate said, and reached for another donut hole, but the box was empty.

The truce—like all of the truces their mother negotiated between her children—was tenuous. In the past, they would last a day, maybe two.

This one lasted three hours.

That's when Jackie came into the family room, dragged a dining chair (not the broken one) over to the window, and perched herself right in front of the only box fan in the house. Mom was busy with laundry, trying to find any two socks of Nate's that matched. Zeke and his brother were working on a comic they'd been making about a kid with chainsaws for hands who causes carnage everywhere he goes.

Aggression was already in the air. Aggression and 90 percent humidity.

Zeke glowered at his sister. "You can't sit there," he said.

"Watch me," she quipped.

"You're stealing all the cool air."

"You can't steal air. It's all around us. Besides, you're young. You'll live." She turned and pressed her face to the fan, letting her hair wisp out behind her like on the cover of one of those tawdry romance novels you might find in the kids' section of the library.

"It's not fair. It's like a hundred degrees in here," he said.

"Stop being so dramatic. You could have sat here if you wanted to." Jackie turned back to face the fan and began to hum contentedly.

Zeke took a deep breath. *What would someone like Kyo or Aadya do in this situation?* he wondered.

Honestly, he hadn't the slightest clue. He knew what *he* was going to do, though. Zeke set down his pencil and casually walked over to the window. Then he plopped straight into his sister's lap.

She immediately stared shoving. "Move, you little fartweed."

"You said I could sit here if I wanted."

"That's not what I said!"

Jackie growled and pushed even harder, but he managed to grab hold of her arm and pull her out of the chair with him, sending them both to the floor, rolling and grappling and hissing at each other. Except Jackie was bigger and stronger and soon had Zeke pinned to the floor with his arms behind his back.

"Not so great now, are you?" she taunted. She pressed his arms even harder against his back. "Is *this* tight enough for you?"

"Avengers assemble!" Zeke grunted.

From out of nowhere, Nate leaped on top of his sister, making a three-scoop Stahls sibling sundae, wrestling, sweating, and screeching. That's when their mother appeared.

"Come on!" she said, her voice ricocheting off the walls. "What did we *just* talk about? Jackie, get off your brother. Nate, get off your sister. Zeke, get off the floor. What's going on here?"

"She's an air hog."

"He's an annoying butt pustule."

"I'm Spider-Man!"

Mom stood with her hands on her hips and considered their respective cases. Then she did something unusual. Something unexpected.

"All right. Everybody get your swimsuits on and get in the car."

Was she actually suggesting that they go somewhere? Together? All four of them?

Zeke didn't question her. The van, at least, had air-conditioning, even if the locks didn't work. And swimsuits could only mean one thing.

Salvation.

Thirty minutes later they stood in a line stretching twenty or thirty long. You could see through the fence that the YMCA aquatic center was swamped, bodies packed in so tight you could barely dog-paddle. But it was a pool, which meant it was wet and cold, and five dollars per person seemed a reasonable price to pay to avoid heatstroke—or in Zeke's mother's case, to keep her children from murdering each other. Zeke knew once they got in, they would milk it for all its worth, staying for hours.

Provided they got in.

Zeke kept his eyes focused on his flip-flops, doing his best to tuck behind his sister when they reached the front of the line. His danger-sense was already tingling.

"One adult, three kids."

Mom held out her twenty to the teenager with the sunscreened nose who reached for it, but then hesitated, head cocked sideways. "Wait. Don't I know you?" he asked, looking directly at Zeke.

"Oh god," Jackie muttered, shielding her face. "Not again."

"I do," the teenager said, pointing. "Your name is Zeke, right?"

Zeke shook his head. Nate nodded emphatically.

"Yeah. I remember. You're that kid who pulled that stunt last summer with the food coloring."

There was no denying it now. He'd been identified. Technically it was fake blood, not food coloring, but the young man was not misremembering. It was one of Zeke's more inspired moments. He'd picked up a giant tube of the stuff for a dollar three days after Halloween and held on to it for the next eight months until he got the perfect opportunity to use it. Hiding the fake blood under his swim shirt, he ventured into the shallow end, looking for the tightest cluster of bodies. He wedged the tube underneath his foot and squeezed as he screamed, "Something *bit* me!"

The effect was just as he imagined. Almost instantly some other kid shouted "Blood!" and then everyone started screaming, rushing for the edges of the pool. The lifeguard jumped in as people were scrambling out, Zeke among them, leaving all the evidence behind. The lifeguards found the empty tube in a matter of seconds and realized it was just a prank. But they still had to completely drain the pool. Everyone was sent home.

Nobody knew who did it. Though one person had her suspicions.

The confession took less than thirty seconds to extract.

The next day she marched Zeke right back to the YMCA to apologize. The manager gave him a lecture on pool safety combined with a follow-up lecture on common decency and then asked the Stahls family not to return.

Zeke thought they just meant for the rest of that summer.

He was wrong.

"Yeah. Sorry. There's no way I can let you guys in."

"What? That was last July!" his mom protested. "He came and apologized. Look. You can check our bags. Check his pockets. No fake blood." She turned to Zeke, suddenly unsure. "You're not hiding any blood or vomit or dog poop anywhere, are you?"

Zeke shook his head, patting his pockets. He was actually out of all three of those, though he knew where he could get one of them; Mrs. Gwon rarely cleaned up after her Pomeranian.

"I'm sorry, ma'am. We have a list of people who are banned from the pool for life. Your son is on that list. You can try the community pool on Forty-Sixth Street, though they probably know about you guys too. You're kind of famous, kid," the gatekeeper said.

Zeke wasn't quite sure how to feel about this. On the one hand, it was cool to be recognized. On the other hand, it was eighty-eight degrees outside.

He could clearly see how his family felt about it, though, trudging back to the van with their discount beach towels hanging glumly around their necks. Even Nate seemed to be questioning his allegiances, choosing to sit in the very back instead of in the seat next to Zeke like he always did.

Zeke's stomach knotted up as he buckled in. "Sorry, guys," he said. "I feel like this is all my fault."

"That's because it *is* your fault," Jackie snipped.

Mom cranked the engine, blasting the air, but even it struggled to staunch the sweat trickling down Zeke's temples and pooling under his arms. He really thought the people at the Y would have gotten over that little stunt by now. Forgive and forget, right? At least forget. Sometimes forgetting was easier.

Ahead of him in the shotgun seat, Jackie shook her head. "See? This is what happens when we try to do things as a family. And you wonder why I stay in my room all the time."

Zeke pressed his head to the window, watching all the kids splashing around, trying to dunk their fathers, playing catch with their siblings, seeing how long they could hold their breath. They all looked so happy.

Jackie reached out and rubbed their mother's shoulder. "Sorry, Ma."

Mom frowned at her, then looked over her shoulder at Zeke. "Please tell me you've never been kicked out of the movie theater."

Zeke shook his head. He could probably think of an epic way to make that happen, but he was pretty sure nobody wanted to hear it. His mother put the car into gear. "Then that's where we're going."

"At least there won't be any old ladies in thongs there," he offered, but not even Nate snorted at the joke.

Their mother drove to the theater while Jackie looked up what was playing on her phone. Some special effects–saturated action flick about a giant monster emerging from the deep ocean to save Earth from other giant monsters descending from outer space. It starred one of the Chrises—the super-jacked one—and was starting in half an hour. Zeke couldn't remember the last movie he saw that wasn't on the TV or checked out from the library.

The theater's amped-up air-conditioning produced goose bumps on contact.

"This is heaven," Nate said as they stepped inside. Nobody disagreed.

Zeke looked at the long line of people waiting for snacks, some of them leaving with their arms full of oversize boxes of candy, drinks the size of fire extinguishers. He knew better than to ask for something. After all, this was a splurge; the movie tickets were twice the price of the pool admission. That didn't keep his mouth from watering watching the slushies and nachos go by.

"Hey, you guys want this?"

Zeke snapped back to attention to see an elderly man with a box of Junior Mints in one hand and a punch card in the other. He had crinkled eyes and a head bursting with silver hair. He waved the card around. "It's good for a free popcorn, but I'm probably never going to use it."

"Are you sure?" Mom asked.

"The kernels get stuck in my teeth. Besides, I'm more of a chocolate lover." He shook his box of candy and smiled.

"That's very kind of you."

"Heck, it's just popcorn," the old man said, then moved off to join an old woman who was waiting by the ticket taker. Zeke watched them walk down the corridor arm in arm. In his head he imagined them waltzing and his heart ached.

"See. There are still some good people out there in the universe," his mother said.

Ten minutes later with their free popcorn in hand, the Stahlses found their seats and passed the bucket back and forth between them. With every handful, Zeke could feel the shame of being turned away from the pool receding. Jackie stopped frowning, and the lines in Mom's forehead finally relaxed. It might have just been popcorn, but sometimes popcorn was enough.

Finally their movie started, the camera slowly tracking a giant spaceship hurtling through space. Zeke thought about all those

Friday nights sitting between his parents, watching aliens with rubber masks and flashlight phasers duking it out on the planet Mars, his father grinning like a little boy at how ridiculous it all was.

Zeke leaned over to Jackie. "You can't even see the strings." He knew she would get it. But she didn't even look over at him.

"Just watch the movie," she said.

Kissing Concrete

Zeke woke the next morning with butterflies in his stomach. Not the innocent, hopeful, fluttering butterflies that you might get on Christmas. These were angry, malevolent, demon butterflies with wings like machetes. Hundreds of them, sending sharp pains through his center.

Part of it was probably the entire bag of potato chips that he'd devoured last night while Mom was at work, that on top of a half tub of popcorn at the movies, but the rest was dread. Gordon Notts had said he would be by this afternoon to explain everything, to lay the ground rules for who would be voted the World's Greatest Kid and win the grand prize.

With so much at stake, Mom gathered the family in the kitchen shortly after breakfast for a debriefing.

"As you all know, we have a very important guest coming by today. So we are going to play a game." Her voice was unnaturally calm. Eerily so. Like something out of a horror movie. "The game is called Pretend We Are Not a Dysfunctional Family."

This game already sounded hard.

"What's dish-funk-shinal?" Nate wondered.

"We are," Jackie said.

"Oh. What do we get if we win?"

"Ten thousand dollars," Zeke told him.

"I'll play then," Nate replied. As if he had a choice.

The Pretend We Are Not a Dysfunctional Family game started with cleaning their wreck of a house. It was no small feat. Zeke's mom did what she could throughout the week, barely fending off the Sink of Spontaneously Replicating Dishes and shoving Nate's fleet of Matchbox cars into a corner so you didn't *have* to step on them when you walked through the room. Occasionally she demanded that Jackie pick up all the dirty clothes that seemed to spread over the house like a virus, appearing in unexpected places: a sweatshirt hanging over a lampshade, a bra in the bathroom sink (or in the gutter), a random sock in the fruit bowl with the mushy apple nobody wanted to eat. That wasn't cleaning, though—that was just "staving off the apocalypse for another day." Today, she said, they would *clean*.

Zeke was put in charge of the dusting and vacuuming. After just one room he was already choking. There were cobwebs in every corner. Dust bunnies the size of actual bunnies, and they had clearly multiplied as such. He watched anxiously as his mother flipped the cushions on the couch, hoping the other side was less stained. "You might reconsider," he warned, but it was too late. His mother pulled up the cushion, revealing a trove, including a missing math assignment, a steak knife, a half-dissolved sucker, and a melted chocolate bar.

His mother's face turned red. Zeke decided to go dust a different room. He passed by Jackie, who was on her hands and knees in the bathroom, reeking of bleach. "How do you two manage to pee *behind* the toilet?" she growled at him. "Do you close your eyes and spin around while you do it?"

He decided not to answer that question.

Three hours, six Popsicles, and several stand-in-front-of-the-box-fan breaks later, the Stahlses stood in the middle of the family room, overheated and exhausted. The house was cleaner than it had ever been. The bathroom sink wasn't crusted with toothpaste anymore. Your feet no longer stuck to the kitchen floor. The carpet even had those neat little vacuum lines—including a capital *L* in Jackie's room that Zeke guessed she hadn't noticed yet. The three-bedroom ranch that Zeke's mother and father had picked out together seventeen years ago looked like the kind of place a Not Entirely Dysfunctional Family might live.

"Now we will all just sit very still and not touch *anything*," Mom said.

"Maybe I'll just go outside instead," Zeke said.

"Maybe take your brother with you."

Zeke guided Nate out the front door and sat next to him on the porch. His little brother picked at the edge of the yellowing grass. "Why's Mom acting so weird today? Is it 'cause you're the world's greatest kid?"

Zeke snorted. "Not yet I'm not." He guessed his mother was dealing with the same machete-winged demon flies as he was. "She just wants the place to look nice. She doesn't want people to know what it's really like around here most of the time."

Not that he could blame her. She'd work extra shifts and come home exhausted, hoping for just thirty minutes at the end of it all to sit with a glass of boxed wine, some Advil, and a moment's peace. The last couple of years, everything just got a whole lot harder, and some things she used to have time for slipped away. Like how she used to read them stories at night, he and his brother. Everything from *Nate the Great* to Lemony Snicket. Now their bedtime ritual was like a pit stop at an Indy car race, with her sidling up just long enough to tell you that she loved you and peck you on the cheek. Zeke missed the read-aloud tuck-in times, the twenty minutes of him and Nate and Mom crammed together under one blanket, his mother teasing his hair, doing different voices for each character. He missed how she squeezed his big toe on her way out. *Sweet dreams*, she'd say.

He missed those toe wiggles, though he would never tell her that.

Nate continued to pick at the grass. "Are we really dish-func-tional?" he asked.

"Yeah, probably," Zeke said. "But then, so is everybody a little bit."

"Oh," Nate said, still a little fuzzy on what the word meant. "Are we a little or a lot?"

Zeke shrugged. "Depends on who you ask." *Just don't ask my teachers. Or the principal. Or the school counselor. Or that guy at the Y. Or most of the neighbors.* "Our family's just a little different is all."

"Is that because of Dad?"

Zeke sat back, surprised. He stared at his little brother. "What makes you say that?"

"I don't know. Just seems that way. All the kids at school are always talking about their dads. Greta's dad came in every Friday this year to help with reading. And Brendon Braxton always brags about how he and his dad go fishing every Sunday."

"You don't even like fishing," Zeke said.

"'Cause it's *boring*. All you do is *sit* there. It's not, like, catching lightning bugs."

Zeke smiled. Firefly roundup was one of their favorite pastimes. Not just catching them, but sneaking into Jackie's bedroom at night while she slept, leaving the open jar right there on her nightstand, then tiptoeing back to their room, waiting for the scream when she awoke to find one of them crawling in her hair. "Not everybody likes to fish," Zeke said. What he meant to say was *Nothing wrong with not having a dad*, but it didn't come out that way.

"I know," Nate said wistfully. "Can we go back inside, please?"

"If we go inside, we have to sit still and not make a mess. I'm not good at that and neither are you."

"Well, we have to do *something* or I'll bore myself to death."

Zeke looked around the front yard. Once, they had a basketball hoop, but it rusted out and the backboard fell off so it had to be pitched. They had a basketball to go with it, but Zeke had managed to put a hole in it with the help of several fireworks. He was pretending it was the planet Earth and that aliens were coming to destroy it, just like in all those movies his dad made him watch. He hadn't thought it would actually work.

So that was a no to basketball. But there *was* a garage full of junk: half-used paint cans; a tennis racket with broken strings; a couple of heavy-duty, fifty-foot extension cords; and a ten-foot stepladder.

Zeke started to scheme.

"What's the coolest thing about Spider-Man?" he asked.

"He gets all the hot chicks?" Nate offered, repeating something he might have heard Zeke say.

"I mean, there is Zendaya. But seriously. What does he do that you always wished you could do?"

"Swing through the air?"

Zeke snapped his fingers. He did some rough sketching in his head, the idea taking shape. "How much do you think you weigh?"

"Dunno," Nate said. "Two hundred? Two fifty?"

Zeke guessed him to be about sixty pounds. The Stahlses ran

skinny, despite the nuggets and tots, Popsicles and potato chips. Sixty might work. Those extension cords were strong. "Do me a favor. Sneak inside and get all of the pillows and blankets off of our beds. But don't let anyone see you, 'kay?"

"'Kay. What for?"

"What do you mean, what for? For something *awesome*, obviously. Don't you trust me?"

Nate was the only person in the world Zeke would even think of posing that question to.

As his brother snuck back through the front door, Zeke went into the garage to gather the other supplies, passing by the power tools sporting Scotch tape labels with his name circled and crossed out. He wound an extension cord around his shoulder and grabbed the ladder with both hands.

Nate was waiting for him back on the lawn, a pile of bed stuff at his feet. "What's the ladder for? We going back on the roof?" he asked. "Won't Mom be mad?"

"She will be if she ever finds out." Zeke sized up the front yard. His plan should work. Theoretically.

He gave Nate directions, then he used wire cutters to take a few more strings out of the tennis racket and fed the heavy-duty extension cord through, creating a handle of sorts. He tied one end of the cord to the top step of the ladder—the one you were never supposed to stand on according to the warning sticker—and the other end to the roof rack on the minivan, making sure the line was nice and tight and at a slight angle. He gave the tennis racket a tentative tug. It would have to do. "Is the landing pad ready?"

Nate stood in front of the pile of pillows and bedspreads strategically stationed beside the van. "I think so. What's that?"

"What's it look like? It's a zip line."

It *was* a zip line. But only for really short people who were strong enough to hold tight to an old tennis racket. Zeke handed Nate his SpongeBob bike helmet and helped him buckle the strap. "Safety first," he said, and they both laughed. It was sort of an inside joke.

Nate tentatively climbed the first four rungs of the ladder. It didn't look that tall to Zeke . . . until his little brother was standing near the top. Then ten feet seemed more like a hundred.

"What if I let go before I get to the pillows?" Nate asked.

"Then we superglue your hands to the racket and try again," Zeke said.

Nate nodded as if this made perfect sense.

Zeke held the ladder as tight as he could, a small part of his brain questioning if this was really such a great idea. The extension cord could come loose. The ladder could slip out of his grip. The railing of the minivan could break off. So many things could go wrong.

But another, louder part of Zeke's brain told the smaller part to shut up and just let the kid fly. You can't go through your life waiting for something to happen. You had to seize the moment if you wanted to be great.

"Just try to keep your knees up. And don't let go."

Nate nodded, grabbing the tennis racket with both hands and aiming for the landing pad he'd stripped from their just-made beds. "With great power," he whispered, and then he was off.

Zeke stared, bug-eyed, as Nate slid, slowly but steadily, along the makeshift zip line. It was actually working. He could feel the ladder straining in his hands, threatening to buckle under the weight. *Just hang on. He's almost there.*

It was then that Zeke caught sight of a black van pulling around the corner, letters painted on the side: KABAM.

His concentration broke. His hand slipped. The ladder tilted forward. Nate must have felt the line dip, because he panicked and let go.

The van containing the director of charitable programming at the Klein Agency for the Betterment of All Mankind pulled up to the curb just as Zeke's little brother belly flopped right onto the concrete.

Kerpow.

Pure Greatitude

"Urf."

Zeke was by his brother's side in seconds, one eye on Nate, the other on the two men getting out of the van. "You okay? What did you hurt?"

Nate showed him his elbow and the little raspberry kiss, no bigger than a dime. No tears—the kid was tough. He offered up a mile-long smile. "That was so much better than fishing. Can I go again?"

"I don't think so," Zeke said. " The guys from the contest are here."

"But I didn't even make it to the landing pad," Nate protested. "Can I at least jump in?"

Zeke nodded and watched as his brother launched himself toward the pile of pillows and blankets, arms spread airplane style, making a sound like a bomb going off. He hadn't even said a word about Zeke letting go of the ladder. In Nate's mind, Zeke could do no wrong.

He wasn't so sure about the minds of the two men coming up the driveway.

"Well, would you look at this," Gordon Notts chirped. "The World's Greatest Kid building a zip line for his little brother in the front yard. How ingenious." He was wearing the same white suit, but this time with a yellow shirt and a white tie, looking sort of like an egg sunny-side up. Zeke wondered if it was actually the exact same suit or if he just had several copies. "Ingenious. Did you know about this, Ms. Stahls?"

Zeke saw Notts's startling blue eyes dart toward the door and he turned to find his mother standing there, her own shrewd gaze leaping from ladder to Zeke to Notts to her youngest son lying facedown in a pile of blankets and pillows in the middle of their driveway. Another mother might have registered shock or surprise, but Zeke's mother had been thoroughly desensitized. She simply shook her head.

"Well, I think it's wonderful." Notts beamed as he marched up the lawn. "Just more proof that you belong in this contest. Logan, get a shot of this, will you? Most kids would be on the couch on a Sunday afternoon, sucked into their phones, wasting away the hours, and yet here your boys are inventing clever new ways to make the most of the great outdoors. You must be so proud of Zeke's creativity."

"So proud," Mom echoed. She forced a smile. "Zeke. Sweetie.

Do me a favor and put the ladder away. I'd hate for someone to get hurt." *And consequently grounded for the rest of the summer,* her eyes implied.

Without a word, Zeke untied the extension cord and took the makings of his first ever homemade zip line back into the garage, chalking it up as an almost success. Maybe next time he would find a way to attach the cord to the roof for a steeper incline. Better yet, maybe they could bungee jump off the roof instead. He wondered how many elastic hair bands his sister owned. He figured he would need at least ten thousand.

With everything finally put back where it belonged, Zeke came inside to find his living room full. Gordon Notts and Logan the cameraman occupied the couch, the former sitting tree-trunk straight, vibrating with energy, the latter sort of sprawled with his camera in his lap, looking half-asleep. Zeke's mom sat in one of the other chairs, hands folded in her lap, with Nate cross-legged on the floor beside her. Jackie was missing in action, but Zeke was okay with that. One less thing to worry about.

"There's the kid of the hour," Notts said, standing up and offering Zeke his hand. The man had incredibly smooth palms, manicured nails, teeth that gleamed. "Your mom and I were just talking about how handy you are around the house. She says you help with the cleaning."

"Sometimes," Zeke replied. *Like once every ten years or so. When we are trying to appear normal to outsiders who might give us wads of cash.*

Notts looked impressed. "I'm not sure you realize how admirable that is, Ms. Stahls. Nowadays very few children have chores, and they grow up without any sense of responsibility. But here's your son, contributing to the common good of the household, vacuuming and dusting. I can't think of the last time I actually dusted."

"His brother has allergies," Zeke's mom explained, which was true. Nate *was* allergic to walnuts at least. And sesame seeds. And most vegetables. Though that last one was self-diagnosed.

Notts shook his head. "So he literally saves his own brother's life every time he vacuums. Amazing."

Zeke thought that was kind of a stretch, but he went with it. "What can I say? Family comes first."

This seemed to make Notts happy, judging by the knee slap. "Of course it does. What a heart on this kid." He took a deep breath. "Well, listen, we could go on for days about what a fantastic brother you are, but I'm not the one you have to impress, am I? The competition starts tomorrow, so today we have to go over all the paperwork—waivers, legal agreements, publicity clauses, that sort of thing. But before we get to that, I thought I'd just run down how this whole thing works. There are four other contestants, as you know—though I prefer to call them nominees. 'Contestants' makes this sound like a game show, and it's not. It's more of a platform. A showcase. A chance to remind the world just how fantastic your generation is."

"So it's *not* a competition," Zeke's mother said.

"Oh, no, it most definitely is. When all is said and done, only one kid is going to win the title. But it's not so much a head-to-head thing. See, how it works is, we film Zeke for a couple hours each day, you know, just doing all the wonderful things he normally does—"

"*All* the things?" Zeke interrupted. "You don't, like, film me eating and stuff, do you?"

"That depends. Are you a fantastic eater?"

"I ate seven tacos once," he admitted. Though he paid for it later. As did anyone who needed to use the bathroom that night.

Notts laughed. "Impressive. But no, we don't film *everything*. The voters aren't interested in you brushing your teeth. It's mostly up to Logan here what gets captured."

The cameraman raised a hand, just in case anyone had forgotten he was there, which was easy to do given his quiet demeanor next to Notts's in-your-face personality. Zeke gave him a quick smile and he threw a wink back.

"He'll be the one with you each day, gathering footage," Notts continued. "At the end of the day, my team and I will look it over, edit it down, and create a short video that includes the most memorable parts. The moments that tell your *story of greatness*, that exemplify what makes you such an exceptional kid. Like today with that zip line."

Like today, where you let go of the ladder and almost broke your brother's neck, Zeke thought. *Or a couple days ago, when you tried to cook him in the driveway. Or two weeks before that when you got sent to the principal's office for trying to give one of your classmates* *a heart attack by putting a mouse in her desk.* Zeke supposed those things might be considered exceptional. In a way.

"Once we're finished with all the nominees' videos for each day, we post them to the website. People watch all five videos, decide which kid they think best embodies the idea of *greatness*, and then they vote. One vote per IP address per day."

"So it's sort of like *America's Got Talent?*" Mom offered.

"Sort of," Notts said. "Except substitute 'kids' for 'America' and 'greatness' for 'talent.' Plus this isn't about *one* thing Zeke can *do*, it's about *all* the awesome things that Zeke *is*. Everything he stands for and believes in. Everything that makes him unique."

Zeke tried to think about what those things might be. He had beliefs, sure. He believed that milkshakes were the ideal way to consume ice cream, for example, and that Flamin' Hot Cheetos were overrated. That all cereal should come with marshmallow bits. That little brothers were fun to have around and big sisters were not. That some people couldn't take a joke. That the triple-red shell was the best power-up in *Mario Kart*.

And he believed very strongly that Gordon Notts was still here by mistake. But that was the sort of belief that he couldn't admit out loud. He simply shifted nervously in his chair while Notts continued.

"We repeat that whole process for three more days. Then, after the fourth day of voting, the one with the most votes is crowned the World's Greatest Kid."

"And gets the ten thousand dollars," Zeke said, just to be sure.

Notts nodded. "Plus the satisfaction of knowing that they are setting a positive example for young people all around the world."

"Right. *Obviously.*"

This prompted a little smirk from the cameraman. Zeke seemed to be the only one who noticed.

"This isn't *Big Brother*," Notts said. "We're looking for one or two standout moments each day that show us what an incredible human being you are. It's a three-to-five-minute video, tops. And don't worry. Logan here is a professional. You're in good hands. In fact, he—"

The golden-curled Notts suddenly stopped midsentence, momentarily distracted, as they all were, by the sudden appearance of a young woman in a summery yellow dress.

"Oh. Sorry. Didn't realize you all were here already," Jackie said absently.

Now it was time for Zeke to roll *his* eyes. Even their mother raised an eyebrow. Gone was the pajama-clad, Medusa-haired girl who only an hour ago smelled like toilet bowl cleaner. Jackie's hair was brushed. Her cheeks blushed. Lips glossed. Zeke could smell her flowery body spray from where he sat.

She smiled at everyone. Including him. That's how he knew she must be up to something.

"Right. Mr. Notts, this is my daughter, Jackie. Jackie, Gordon Notts and Logan . . . the cameraman," Mom said.

"Zeke's big sister! Of course!" Gordon chirped, giving her hand two enthusiastic pumps. "A pleasure to meet you. I can only guess that you've been a *huge* influence on this young man."

Zeke coughed into his hand, mostly to keep from blurting out *more like a huge pain in my butt.*

Jackie shrugged. "I've certainly tried," she said.

Her eyes went to the bulky black camera in Logan's lap—the one with the lens cap on—and Zeke realized what this was all about. The dress. The makeup. The fake nice. She was trying to outshine him already. And the contest hadn't even started.

Figures.

"Sorry, sis. They don't actually start filming until tomorrow," Zeke informed her. Most of his apologies to his sister were extra light on sincerity. This one came with zero.

Jackie turned and looked at him, and he saw her cover break, just for a heartbeat. Saw the disappointment flash in her eyes, the falter of her smile. Then she pulled it back together.

"Of course," she said. "I knew that. I was just coming to say hi."

"So you're what? A soon-to-be-senior?" Notts asked, once again showing that he knew much more about Zeke and his family than most of their neighbors. "Big plans for after graduation? College bound?"

"That's the dream," Jackie said. "Michigan maybe. Or somewhere on the East Coast. Thinking of studying music."

91

"We're keeping our options open," Mom added quickly. "Music programs are hard to get into. And you know how expensive college is these days."

Jackie managed a weak smile. "Keeping our options open," she repeated.

"Well, it's always good to have goals," Notts said. He turned his attention back to Zeke, where, in Zeke's opinion, it rightfully belonged. "Speaking of goals . . . we do have one thing we have to film today: your intro video for the website. Can't just leave you as a giant question mark, can we? We need to announce you to the world! Tell you what, I can stay here with your mom and go through all the paperwork, and you and Logan can go knock that out. Sound good?"

It actually sounded a little terrifying; Zeke wasn't sure he wanted to be announced to the world, but he did feel strongly about winning ten thousand dollars. Logan stood up and headed for the patio door, and Zeke followed, taking the longer way so that he could pass Jackie.

"Sorry, sister. No extras on set," he whispered.

Normally she would have bitten his head off. Called him a turd heel or a jerkhole. But she couldn't. Not in front of company.

All she could do was wish him good luck.

It sounded about as sincere as his apology.

They decided to film Zeke's introduction on the back deck. The sun had finally arced over to that side of the house, and Logan said the natural light was better for filming.

Zeke wondered what kinds of houses the other "nominees" lived in. Hailey enjoyed horseback riding. Kyo went rock climbing. Aadya did robotics. They all had hobbies and played sports, so he guessed they were all living in houses bigger than this, or at least in ones without leaky roofs. Picking up all the toys and dirty laundry had made the house look bigger, but Zeke guessed Casa de Stahls still wasn't much to look at by comparison.

The backyard was okay at least, with its wood deck and its little flower garden and the big shady oak his dad had once promised to build a tree house in but never got around to. They never had a swing set either, mostly because there was a nice park with several swings within walking distance. They did have a sandbox, though the neighborhood cats had mistaken it for a giant litter box instead. Not that Zeke still liked playing in the sand at his age.

Unless it was beach sand. That he could certainly go for.

As Logan checked his camera, Zeke caught a pair of spying eyes. Nate had snuck out after them. "Is it okay if my brother watches?" he asked.

Logan nodded. "So long as he stays out of the shot. This one is just you in all of your glory."

Zeke couldn't tell if that was meant to be sarcastic. He had a hard time reading the tone in the cameraman's voice, which was deep and mellow and also sort of detached, as if he had somewhere else he wanted to be. That was something Zeke could certainly relate to. He could think of a hundred places he'd rather be most days.

He motioned to his brother and Nate settled into one of the patio chairs situated behind Logan, looking tiny next to the cameraman who was six foot and change. Zeke only knew of two other Logans. The first was a kid in his grade who drew pictures of dinosaurs instead of doing math. The second was one of the X-Men. This Logan didn't look much like either. He didn't have crazy sideburns or adamantium claws. His black hair was cropped short and his deep-set eyes looked thoughtful rather than intense. He was clearly strong, though, judging by how easily he whipped that heavy camera around. Plus he had a tattoo of a dragon on his right arm. Zeke always wanted a tattoo.

"Almost set," Logan said.

Zeke glanced back through the patio door to see his mother sitting at the kitchen table with Notts, looking through a stack of papers. Release forms. Liability waivers. All that legal stuff. All for a prize that seemed so far out of reach.

His eyes skirted to the sagging gutters, to the compressor sitting by the side of the house, the only one in the neighborhood not humming in the heat. He thought about the yellow-and-pink bike sitting in the garage—Jackie's hand-me-down. He wondered whether there would be enough left in the ten grand to get a new one. And maybe a new one for Nate too, who was using Zeke's old bike, the one with the white *Frozen*-themed basket that had been handed down twice now, with the rusty chain and ripped seat. *Rusty* and *ripped*: two adjectives that described more than a few things around here. Zeke blotted his forehead on his sleeve.

Logan checked to make sure the shot was framed properly, using the Stahlses' rosebushes as background. "Okay. Whenever you're ready," he said.

"Wait, what do I say again?" Zeke asked.

"Easy. Just tell the people who you are and what makes you special, maybe what your dreams are, and then at the end say what you think greatness is. Like . . . I believe greatness is saving the dolphins or something."

Zeke mentally cued the videos he'd watched with his mother two nights ago. Those four perfect kids cheesing it up for the camera: *Hi there. My name is Missy McFlawless and my hobbies include curing heart disease and repairing the ozone layer. In my free time I also groom unicorns and rescue endangered orangutans from the forces of corporate greed. Plus I eat kale and quinoa mixed together with spinach and broccoli. So delicious.*

At least that's what it felt like. Like he was going up against the Power Rangers of Goodness.

"You know what? Let's just wing this thing."

Logan gave him a thumbs-up. Zeke took a deep breath and stared at the camera.

"Hi. My name is Ezekiel Stahls, but my family calls me Zeke. Except for my sister, who calls me pit-stain or cockroach or fart-wad . . . hold on, can I say fartwad? You know what . . . let's start over."

95

Logan readjusted the camera. Gave another thumbs-up. They were rolling.

"Hello. My name is Ezekiel Stahls and I *am* the World's Greatest Kid. I mean, that's not what *I* think, it's what *you* think . . . I mean, it's what you're *going* to think after I reveal my pure greatitude to you . . . Okay. Hold up. Pretty sure that's not a word. Can we try again?"

"You're the boss," Logan said.

Zeke frowned. He definitely didn't *feel* like the boss. He felt like he was drowning. Why was this so difficult? There were eight-year-olds out there who had their own YouTube channels with millions of subscribers. He lived in a world where everybody was on camera, all the time, doing next to nothing and getting attention for it. People posted videos of them opening boxes and making peanut butter sandwiches to huge acclaim. Nobody thought twice about being on camera anymore. All he had to do was introduce himself and say a couple of interesting things about his life. Things that made him stand out.

Except the things that made him interesting were not the kinds of things anyone else would think were all that great. And some of the things that made his life stand out he didn't want to share.

Maybe it would be better to just make stuff up instead. Go all in. Let the audience figure out what was true or not.

Button pressed. Thumbs-up. Rolling.

Zeke struck a heroic pose. "Hiya, America. Zeke Stahls here and I am the total package. I've got an IQ of a hundred and fifty, and I can bench-press twice that. When I grow up, I want to put an end to world unhappiness and perform the first successful whole brain transplant. I also want to stop the ice caps from melting so that the polar bears don't get ticked off and come down here and eat us because, let's face it, that would suck . . ." Zeke stopped, noticing that Logan had lowered the camera. "What? What's wrong?"

"I bench one-eighty," the beefy cameraman offered.

Zeke groaned. "Well, what am I *supposed* to say? Everyone else's video was so perfect."

Because everyone *else* was perfect. At least they seemed like it.

Logan stared back at him. The cameraman's eyes were sea green, like what Zeke imagined the waters off the coast of Honolulu to be. "Sunsets and snowflakes."

Zeke cocked his head. "What?"

"Those are the only two things in my life I've seen that were ever perfect. The rest of us are just doing our best," Logan said. "So how about this? How about you forget about what everyone else said and just do you?"

Just do him. Just be Zeke. Right.

If he only knew for sure what that even meant.

He thought about the question-mark image sitting on the KABAM website alongside the faces of his competition. What made him special? He had no idea. But there was one person, at least, who might. One person who looked up to him for sure.

"Can you give me a sec," Zeke said. "I need to consult with my agent." He waved Nate over, motioning for him to come close, bending down to his ear. "Hey, you think I'm awesome, right?" he whispered.

"You're *pretty* awesome," Nate admitted. "Like an eight and a half."

Zeke figured he should take it. "Okay, so then what makes me an eight and a half?"

"Well, you're good at video games," Nate said. "And blowing things up."

Handy with small explosives? Maybe the CIA would take an interest, but Zeke doubted this was what the Klein Agency was going for. And most kids his age were good at video games. That wasn't going to help him stand out. "And?"

"You know all the words to 'Rap God.' Even the really fast part."

Do the greatest kids in the world memorize Eminem? Zeke wondered. Unlikely. Also, in retrospect, he probably should more carefully monitor the music he listened to around Nate. "Anything else?"

Nate gave it a little more thought. "You always think of cool stuff to do, like the zip line. And the soda bombs. And you let me have whatever flavor of Popsicle I want, even if it's the last one.

Plus . . . you're my big brother," he said, as if that summed up the rest.

Zeke smiled and ruffled Nate's hair and sent him back to his seat. This was why little brothers were better than big sisters. They told you what you needed to hear.

"Okay," he said, standing up a little straighter. "Let's try this one more time."

It took eight more. Nine, actually, if you count the time Logan accidentally forgot to press record, proving that he wasn't a snow-flake or a sunset. But finally they got something they could use. Logan seemed satisfied at least, because as soon as Zeke finished, the man lowered his camera and said, "That one's a keeper."

"Are you sure?" Zeke asked. "We could go again. Maybe I could say something about the children being our future."

"You're twelve," Logan said. "Their future is your future." He started toward the patio door, camera at his side. Nate followed behind, humming Eminem softly to himself.

Zeke stood there for a moment, watching his little brother trail like a duckling. Nate was usually a lot more cautious around strangers, but Logan gave off a vibe that clearly spoke to the kid. He looked like the kind of guy who would take you fishing on a Sunday afternoon. If that was what you were into.

Back in the house, Zeke found Notts and his mother finish-ing up glasses of iced tea, the perspiration on the cups matching the drops dripping from Zeke's brow.

"You're all done? Excellent." Notts beamed. "We will be sure to get your video posted ASAP. I've got to get to headquarters, but Logan will be back again tomorrow to capture some quality footage and get Team Zeke some votes. I'll try to check in as well, just to see if you're having any problems, though I'm confident that there is nothing Ezekiel Stahls can't handle."

Zeke's mom laughed nervously.

"You've got four days," Notts continued. "Four days to show the world—or at least those who visit our website—that you are the greatest kid they've ever seen. I'm counting on you."

You're not the only one, Zeke thought.

Moments later, he and his mom stood together on the cracked cement porch and watched the two men drive away, Logan behind the wheel and Gordon waving through the window. "That man is really weird," his mother said finally. "Who wears a suit in the middle of summer? And that smile. It's like it's *pasted* on."

Zeke knew what was really going through her head because it was also going through his.

"You're still wondering if it's all for real."

Maybe it *was* all a big scam. Maybe KABAM was just a front for some money-laundering scheme, like in a gangster movie. Or maybe the two men were aliens doing reconnaissance to decide if the planet was worth keeping around. Either seemed just as likely as the thought of some organization thinking Zeke could be the world's greatest kid. And Notts definitely looked like he could be an alien in disguise.

"The papers I signed looked real enough," his mother said. "Lots of small print. I guess we will find out tonight when your video gets posted. Or tomorrow, if that man shows up with his camera. How did it go, anyway? The filming?"

"It was hard," Zeke admitted.

"What's not anymore?" She took the last swallow of her iced tea, at this point mostly water, and sighed. "I wish . . . ," she started to say, but she let the rest of the thought melt away.

He had a pretty good guess what she'd wish for anyway.

That night, Zeke took up his usual spot on the couch to watch reruns of *Phineas and Ferb* with Nate. For once Mom didn't have loads of housework to catch up on, so she snuggled in between them. Just the three of them. Jackie boycotted the show, claiming that it hit a little too close to home. Her voice even sounded a little like Candace.

Nate was clearly enjoying the episode, snorting his way through Perry the Platypus's espionage-filled adventures, but Zeke couldn't stay focused. He had the family computer on his lap, and every two minutes he'd press the refresh button on the browser.

Still nothing. The website for KABAM's Greatest Kid contest showed only four grinning faces and the one big black question mark. Maybe there was a problem with the video, Zeke thought. Maybe Logan had forgotten to hit record again that last time.

Or maybe Gordon Notts had changed his mind. That was more likely. Zeke couldn't shake the idea that the contest was already over for him. That Notts had watched Zeke's introduction and decided on a hard pass. Or that some tech guy at KABAM headquarters had found the error, some extra one or zero that had mistakenly pushed Zeke's name to the top of the list. They were probably rerouting Notts's itinerary so that he could go to some other town to tell some more worthy kid that *they* might just be the Greatest in the World. Zeke would receive a phone call tomorrow of the *we regret to inform you* variety.

It wouldn't be the first call like that. It certainly wouldn't be the worst. But it would be bad enough.

"Wait till I tell Mom and Dad about this. You boys are so busted . . ." the television said.

Refresh.

His mother was right. It was ridiculous anyway. World's Greatest Kid. Pffft. As if anyone out there even had the authority to decide such a thing. World's Fastest Runner, sure. World's Best Hotdog Eater. World's Spiciest Chili Pepper. There were measurable ways to decide such things. But greatest kid? Really? I mean sure, Hailey's résumé was probably six pages long already, at age thirteen. And Aadya probably spoke seven or eight languages. But could any of them claim to have dumped a dozen tadpoles in the toilet with a sign on the lid saying *Warning: Amphibian*

Incubation in Progress. Pee at Your Own Risk? Probably not. That was 100 percent Zeke.

Just do you.

Of course, maybe that was the problem.

He hit refresh. Hitched a breath.

There it was at last. His picture. A still taken from the video. Ezekiel Stahls, surrounded by roses, with the octopus wind chime he made in the third grade, now short three legs from an unfortunate baseball-bat-as-lightsaber incident. He elbowed his mother's ribs. "My video's posted."

Zeke's mom blinked herself awake. "What time is it?"

"Not even nine yet. Should I click on it?"

His mom nodded, then shook her head, searched among the cushions and pillows for the remote, and paused the show, catching Candace mid-rant. Nate groaned but then scooted closer, so he could watch too.

This was it, Zeke's last-minute entry into the competition. The video was high quality. The sound crystal clear. Logan did good work.

"Hello. My name is Ezekiel Stahls and I am twelve years old. I live in a small town in northern Indiana with my mom, older sister, and awesome little brother. The people who know me best will tell you that I'm energetic, curious, and above all, creative. I like to try new things and I'm always 'pushing the boundaries,' so to speak. I enjoy playing outside and making up games with my brother. When I grow up, I want to be a ninja. Or a lawyer. Or both. I don't really

know what greatness is, but I hope to find out someday. Peace out."

The video faded to black. Nobody said anything for a moment. Zeke looked at his mother. "It's terrible, isn't it?"

"No. No. Not at all. It's good. It's very . . ." She clearly struggled for the right words. "It's very . . . Zeke."

"Well, that's what I was going for." Next to him, Nate was karate chopping imaginary bad guys, ninjas being cooler than lawyers.

His mother put a hand on Zeke's knee, giving it a little squeeze. "I think we should finish this episode and then tuck in a little early, what do you think? Big day tomorrow, after all."

Big day. Ten thousand dollars. No pressure at all. Zeke nodded. She grabbed the remote and pressed play.

On the TV, Phineas and Ferb's parents finally came home to find that everything was exactly the way they left it. Cartoon logic: no matter how crazy or terrible or messed up life got, it always got right back to normal in twenty-five minutes or less. But nothing ever gets completely back to normal, Zeke knew. Not in real life. And certainly not in twenty-five minutes or less.

As the boys contemplated what kind of trouble they might get into tomorrow, Zeke heard snoring in his left ear.

Beside him, his mother had already fallen back asleep.

To My Dear Family,

Hello from Flagstaff! So named because a bunch of rowdy lumberjacks used a pine tree as a flagpole once, or so the story goes. Did you know that there's an observatory here where Pluto was discovered? Kind of strange when you think about it. Pluto was there all along, but we didn't know it. So in some ways, it's almost like it didn't even exist until some guy spotted it and then it always existed? All in how you look at it, I guess. They say you don't know what you've got until it's gone, but sometimes you don't know what you've got until you look at it just right and realize it's been there the whole time.

I'm picking up one last shipment and then I'm going to get my kicks on Route 66. Your mother knows that song. Tell her to play it for you. I should still be home in time for Zeke's last soccer game, though.

Can't wait. Love you all so much.

Dad

P.S. Why didn't anyone come to Pluto's party?
Because he failed to planet.

Winners and Losers

Turns out it *was* for real. KABAM. Notts. The competition. All of it.

Logan showed up at the door at quarter to ten the next morning, the black van parked on the curb looking like part of an FBI sting. Zeke was in the kitchen making his favorite sandwich—two strawberry toaster pastries glued together with cream cheese. Nate was deeply entrenched in a third helping of Fruity-O's. Jackie was still asleep despite two attempts to wake her. Mom buzzed around the house like a dizzy fly, banging cupboards and pounding back black coffee. She was already running late for work—perhaps by design. Zeke could tell she was nervous about leaving her three children alone with this man she'd only met twice in her life and who had said all of twenty words to her.

"I don't know," she said for the seventeenth time. "He has a *tattoo*. Not that there's anything wrong with that. But still . . . we don't know him. What if he kidnaps all three of you and holds you for ransom?"

Zeke glanced around their one-story house, complete with stained ceilings and holes in the walls. "That would make him the worst criminal ever," he said. Just imagine the note. *Bring me a box of uncooked spaghetti and the loose change underneath your couch or the kid gets it.* "We'll be okay. Jackie knows tae kwon do, remember?"

"She took *one* class. And that was just to see if there were any cute boys. That hardly makes her a qualified bodyguard."

"I can protect us," Nate chimed in. "I can make a flame-thrower. All you need is hairspray and a lighter."

Their mother frowned at Zeke.

"We never actually made one," he protested. The key word being *we.* Zeke made it. Nate simply watched and then cheered when Zeke clomped around the backyard pretending to be Godzilla, nearly setting fire to the azaleas. "Besides, didn't you sign some kind of paper that says they aren't allowed to kidnap us and stuff?"

"I signed a lot of papers," Mom admitted. "But yes, I think there was something about liability. Or maybe that just means I can't sue them if they do. I really don't know. This was clearly a mistake. I should just call in sick."

He knew she wouldn't call in sick. She never called in sick. She was the one who filled in when *other* people called in sick. Still, Zeke appreciated the concern.

"You worry too much," he told her, conveniently ignoring his massive role in that. "Logan seems like a nice guy. Nate likes him." His brother gave a thumbs-up, milk dribbling down his chin. "Go to work. Sell lots of housewares and neckties. I'll work on winning ten thousand bucks. And when you come home, we will still be here, completely unkidnapped. Promise."

Mom's frown lines deepened. She glanced at the clock. "Crap. I'm really going to be late." The attempted kiss on Zeke's forehead was too quick to even make contact.

Logan met them at the door. The cameraman wore blue jeans again, and a white polo shirt with KABAM stitched on it in red. He carried his camera in one hand, a gas station coffee cup in the other. "Ms. Stahls," he said with a nod. "Zeke." He waved to Nate in the kitchen. "What's up, little man?"

"Thirdsies!" Nate replied, pointing at his bowl of cereal.

"Kid after my own heart," Logan said, then turned to address Zeke's clearly frazzled mother. "All good, Ms. Stahls. As Gordon explained yesterday, my job here is to just stay out of the picture and keep the camera rolling. Observe and record. That being said, we also totally respect your family's privacy. If Zeke ever feels uncomfortable, he just says the word and the camera's off. I promise you have nothing to worry about."

Mom nodded, but Zeke could tell she was still on the verge of canceling the whole thing. He did a little hula dance by the refrigerator, just to remind her of what was at stake. He didn't really know how to hula. Mostly he wiggled his hips.

"And how long will you be filming again?" she asked, ignoring him.

"Few hours at most. Gordon just wants to give people a sense of what Zeke's like, what he does that makes him special. It really is like reality television. Except rated G, of course."

"Did you hear that?" Mom said to the boys. "Rated *G*." She checked her phone, groaned, then turned and blew a kiss to Nate before screaming toward the hallway at the top of her lungs, *"Jacqueline Arianna Stahls, get your butt out of bed! The camera guy is here and I'm leaving!"*

Nate apparently took that as instant inspiration to start rapping. "Butt outa bed. Butt on your head. Gonna headbutt you till your butt is dead."

Logan laughed. Mom did not. She tossed her children one last worried look, saving her arched eyebrow for Zeke especially. "Be good," she warned.

"Don't you mean gr—" Zeke started to say, but she cut him off.

"You know exactly what I mean."

Soon the Stahlses' minivan was coughing its way down the street, leaving Zeke and Logan standing by the door.

"So what happens now?" Zeke asked.

Logan shrugged, hefting his camera to his shoulder. "You tell me, kid. This is your show. I'm just along for the ride."

"My show," Zeke repeated softly.

That's when it hit him. Like a concrete belly flop: he really had no idea what he was doing. He should have given this a little more thought, made some kind of a plan, *schemed* a little. After all, in all of those reality television shows—at least the dating ones his sister talked about with her friends—the prospective couples always went places and did things, like snorkeling or wine tasting.

There was nowhere nearby to snorkel, and the world's greatest kid probably wouldn't break into his mother's half-finished box of Franzia sitting in the fridge.

"Don't stress it. Just do what you'd normally do," Logan suggested.

Zeke wasn't sure *that* was such a good idea either.

Think, Zeke. What do great kids do?

Calligraphy and crosswords. Canned food drives and rock climbing. At least that's what the likes of Hailey or Kyo would do. But what could *he* do?

He glanced at Nate, who had taken his third bowl of cereal to the family room to watch more cartoons. *Great kids are great to the people they care about.* For Zeke that was an awfully short list, but it at least gave him a place to start. *They certainly don't let their little brothers just sit around and watch television all day.* He went to the family room and flipped off the TV. Nate flashed him a dirty look.

Zeke noticed Logan had followed him, camera at the ready. "Let's play a game."

"Blindfold dodgeball?" Nate guessed.

Zeke shook his head. One smashed picture frame was all it took for Mom to keep that sport from ever gaining any traction.

"What's the Biggest Thing You Can Stuff Up Your Nose?" Nate suggested.

They'd played that one a month ago. Jackie hadn't been too happy when she had to get the tweezers out to remove the uncooked ziti from Nate's left nostril. "I was thinking Monopoly."

Nate's face scrunched, which didn't surprise Zeke. After all, his little brother had never once won a game of Monopoly out of twenty or so tries. It probably had something to do with Zeke making up the rules as he went along. Zeke's rules for Monopoly usually involved crime syndicates and embezzlement schemes that resulted in him skimming cash from the bank and Nate spending half of his time in jail for snitching.

This time would be different, though. Because this time Nate would be playing with the World's Greatest Kid.

Except Nate had to go and throw a wrench in it.

"Can Jackie play with us? It's more fun with three."

Zeke glanced at the camera, taking it all in, and felt an uncomfortable shiver pass through him. He couldn't purposely leave his sister out, could he? That wouldn't be very great of him. "Of course," he said. "One sec."

He headed toward Jackie's room, Logan following at a distance, and knocked six times. Finally her door opened a crack, barely showing off pale pink walls filled with posters of international landmarks. In contrast to her tidy room, his sister's hair was a tangled nest and she still had sleep in her eyes. She had apparently snoozed through their mother's shouts. The girl could sleep through almost anything. "What?"

"Do you want to play Monopoly?"

Jackie's voice practically dripped with disgust. "Why on god's green earth would I want to play Monopoly with y—"

Zeke's unusually big eyes clearly clued her in. He glanced across his shoulder to where Logan was standing in the hallway.

She poked her head out, saw the cameraman, and immediately pulled it back. Like an upside-down box turtle spying a hockey stick coming its way. "You said Monopoly?" Jackie said out loud, then mouthed, *That game takes for freaking ever.*

Zeke couldn't even remember the last time he and his sister had played Monopoly together. Or any board game for that matter. They used to spend rainy summer afternoons trying to outsmart each other at Connect Four or flatten each other's hands during cutthroat games of slapjack. Mastermind was a favorite as well, even after they'd lost half of the pegs. Jackie never just let him win any of the games they played—even though she had the advantage of being so much older—making him earn his victories, which were few and far between. She never cheated, though. She played tough, but she always played fair.

Right up until she stopped playing altogether.

"Nate wants you to," Zeke said. The next sentence came out haltingly and with a great deal of effort. "I would also like you to." After all, if inviting his sister to actually spend time with him didn't automatically qualify him as the World's Greatest Kid, nothing would.

Jackie smoldered at him from behind her door, but in a robotic voice she said, "What a fantastic idea. You know how much I *love* family game time."

Stop being weird, Zeke lipped.

I'm not the weird one, she mouthed back before shutting the door in his face.

Zeke turned to the camera. "She loves family game time," he repeated.

Logan nodded. "You can tell," he said.

Zeke went to the hall closet and grabbed the game, his eyes glossing over the dusty copy of Mastermind sitting at the bottom of the stack.

It was a full fifteen minutes before Jackie appeared in the family room, having sloughed off her pajamas for a breezy summer dress, her hair corralled into a ponytail, a collection of bracelets jingling around her wrists. He wasn't sure you really needed lip gloss and eye shadow to play Monopoly with your brothers. Then again, hadn't he broken down and actually put on deodorant this morning, only realizing after the fact that the camera wouldn't pick up the sport-fresh scent of Right-Guarded pits?

Of course, only one of them was in a contest to win ten thousand bucks.

"We're ready," Zeke said. But Jackie had stopped in the hall, suddenly frozen by the camera's gaze shifting to her.

"Just pretend I'm not here," Logan told her.

Yeah right, Zeke thought. He understood his sister's discomfort. You can't *not* be aware of someone filming you. The camera was unnerving. Like the Eye of Sauron: constantly watching. Suddenly every move, every word, every look was under scrutiny. Logan had only been here twenty minutes, and in that time, Zeke had gone to pick his nose twice, both times remembering Logan could be recording at that moment, forcing an abort mission, the booger staying buried until he was out of lens shot.

He could tell his sister could feel the eye on her as well.

Jackie smoothed out her dress and joined her brothers on the still nicely vacuumed floor, forming a perfect little family triangle. Zeke finished counting out the starting cash—slipping his brother an extra hundred and hoping the camera caught him in the act. Nate picked the shoe. Jackie the dog. Zeke the battleship. Because it was a freaking battleship.

"Youngest goes first," Zeke said, holding out the dice.

Nate already looked confused. "Really? You always said smartest goes first."

Jackie plucked the dice out of Zeke's hand and placed them in Nate's. "In that case, it's still you," she said, smiling—first at Nate, then at the camera.

Nate rolled. The shoe bounced five spaces and he bought a railroad. So far, so good.

They played normally for a while, circling the board over and over, collecting properties, mostly playing by the actual rules, not Zeke's lexicon of made-up ones. But then Nate landed on Marvin Gardens—Zeke's most expensive property, with three houses already, threatening to drain him of all of his cash, practically knocking him out of the game. "How much?" he groaned.

It was time for Zeke to put his greatness on display. "Only five dollars," he said.

"Really? With three houses? Just five bucks?"

"Yeah, that seems extraordinarily cheap?" Jackie seconded, giving Zeke a hard stare.

"What can I say? I'm extraordinarily generous." He spoke a little louder than normal—just to be sure the camera picked him up. *That's right, America. See how nice I am?*

Jackie wasn't having it. "Oh really? You weren't that generous when *I* landed on you."

That's because I don't want you to win, Zeke thought. She had to know what he was up to. "It's the little-brother discount," he said.

Jackie went quiet for a moment, studying the board. Zeke didn't like the sly look on her face. "I see now," she said. He also didn't like the tone in her voice. She pointed to the dice in front of Nate. "You rolled doubles. Go again."

This time he landed on Jackie's property. Nate cursed his

terrible luck. "Ugh. How much for *that*?" he wondered, eyeing her pair of houses.

"Actually," Jackie said, "there's a big parade in your honor happening on Park Place right now, so *you* get to visit for free."

"Wait. For free? Really?" Nate repeated. "That's awesome!" His face split with a grin.

"It's not *that* awesome," Zeke countered. "I only charged you five when you landed on me."

"Yeah. But that's not *quite* free, is it, Nate?" Jackie said.

"Not quite," Nate agreed.

Zeke threw his sister a piercing look. What was she doing? Was she seriously trying to out-nice him in front of the camera? Was she sabotaging his act of charity? Jackie picked up the dice and rolled, landing on Community Chest, but Zeke got to the card before her. She started to snatch it out of his hand but must have remembered the camera on her, because she instantly pulled back and smiled, speaking between clenched teeth. "What does it say, brother?"

"It says you win second place in a beauty contest. Collect ten dollars." Zeke wasn't lying. It really did say that. She reached for the card again but he leaned away from her. "It also says the player to your *right* won *first* place in the same beauty contest, and *they* collect five *hundred* dollars."

He had to wait a moment for it to sink in—Nate wasn't all that good with his lefts and his rights.

"Wait. That's me," he said. "First place? For a *beauty* contest?"

Zeke shrugged. "What can I say? You take after your big brother." He winked at his sister. "We sometimes play by our own special rules." He handed Nate the tangerine bill, then went for the dice so he could take his turn, but Jackie slapped her hand over them before he could get there, her face suddenly lit up with fake surprise.

"Oh my gosh, Nate, I just realized—you're the shoe!"

Nate looked at his playing piece. Then back at his sister. "Um. Yeah?"

"Well? Don't you realize what this means?" she continued, face full of animated surprise. "According to the *special* rules, if the player with the shoe wins first place in the beauty contest, he or she gets a bonus three *thousand* dollars *plus* hotels on all of his properties."

Nate's eyes blew up to the size of Fun-Time Chocolate Sandwich Cookies. "Really?"

"Really," she said. "It's the Beautiful Brother First-Place Prize Bonus. Isn't that right, Zeke?"

Zeke bristled. He couldn't believe she was doing this to him. On the very first day of filming. In the very first *hour* of filming. Her picture wasn't one of the five posted on the Klein Agency's website. Her greatness wasn't being called into question. And yet here she was stealing his thunder, one-upping him at every turn.

Nate was already reaching for the little red boxes to place on his properties, humming to himself. The kid was rolling in cash now. No way he could lose—which was the goal all along . . . but not this way. Not because of *her*. Thunder thief. Zeke couldn't let her get away with it.

"Hey, Nate. What do you want for your Water Works?" he asked.

Nate shrugged. "I don't know. A hundred?" Apparently, he'd forgotten how much he'd paid for it the first time around.

Zeke nodded and stroked his chin thoughtfully, then he gathered up all of his cash and his properties into a pile and pushed the stack over. "I see your offer, and I present this counteroffer."

Immediately Jackie did the same with all of her remaining cash and properties. "I will match that offer," she said pertly. "Plus I'll let you *keep* your Water Works."

Nate looked at the two mounds of fake money and cardboard deeds piled in front of him. Offerings from two siblings determined to out-nice each other in front of the camera.

"Deal!" he said, raking in his hoard with both hands. He took up several bills and sprinkled them over his lap, making it rain in six different colors.

"Looks like we have a winner," Logan said as the bills came fluttering down.

Zeke glared at his sister across the board. There was no prize for second place.

Nothing But Can

Nate begged to play again—with the special rules, of course—hoping to reprise his blowout victory. Zeke was afraid to say no in front of the camera, but thankfully Jackie claimed she was all Monopolied out. "I'm going straight to my room. I'm not passing Go or collecting two hundred dollars."

Or ten thousand, apparently, Zeke thought. But at least with Jackie crawling back in her cave, he wouldn't have to worry about her trying to steal his spotlight anymore. Unfortunately, on the way out of the room, she finally grabbed her copy of *Elle* from the counter. The one that she hadn't bothered to look at in three days. Zeke figured in ten seconds she'd come bursting back out, brandishing the ruined magazine in his face like he was a puppy who'd chewed one of her shoes.

He turned to his brother, who was cleaning up the game by shoveling everything back in one messy pile—the same way they cleaned pretty much anything. If it's tucked away, stuffed inside a box with the lid shut tight, it's not a problem. "Let's go outside," he suggested.

"I bet it's already hot."

"It's probably hotter in here," Zeke said. *Or it will be soon.*

As Nate went to put on his shoes, Zeke returned the dilapidated box to the closet, wondering what the other four contestants were doing right now, with their own Logans following them around, documenting their greatness. Not playing board games, probably. If he had to guess, Hailey Richter was at horse-riding camp, grooming the Thoroughbred she got for her tenth birthday, probably named something cringy like Meadow or Cotton. Kyo was probably running a 5K. Up a mountain. To raise awareness for deforestation. Aadya was curing the common cold.

And Dom . . . well, Zeke didn't really have a handle on Dom. In fact, he didn't *really* know the first thing about any of them. All he knew was that they were better than him. Or they thought they were better. Or *he* thought they thought they were better. He knew he was making assumptions, but he couldn't help it. Like every other kid he knew, Zeke followed, favorited, and thumbs-upped other people based on only a scrap of video, a chirp of text, a funny meme. That was just how the world worked. Didn't take much to judge someone on. And everybody was qualified.

Zeke looked over his shoulder at Logan and his camera. The cameraman pointed down the hall. "Just going to use the restroom, if that's all right. Gas station coffee goes right through me," he said. "Try not to do anything great in the next two minutes."

Shouldn't be too hard, Zeke thought. He closed the closet door and went to find his brother.

Nate was sitting by the doorway, staring at his shoes, clearly frustrated, face in a full-on pout. The kid was surprisingly good at a lot of things for a seven-year-old: baseball, multiplication, monkey bars. But tying his shoelaces was an ongoing struggle.

Zeke knelt down in front of him and took his brother's hands. "Make bunny ears, remember?"

Dad had actually been the one to show Zeke how to tie his laces. He hadn't forgotten the little rhyme his father sang in his scratchy tenor. He could still hear his dad's voice if he tried, if and when he wanted to try. Zeke helped his brother form the two loops. "Bunny ears, bunny ears, playing by a tree," he sang softly, guiding Nate's smaller hands through the motions. "Criss-crossed that little tree, trying to catch me. Bunny ears, bunny ears, jumped into the hole, popped out the other side and now . . . we take . . . a stroll."

Pull and done.

"See? Not so tough," Zeke said. "Now you try the other one by yourself."

"I can't."

"You can. Just yesterday you were swinging through the sky like Spidey, remember? You can definitely tie your own shoes."

Nate stuck out his tongue in concentration. Zeke recited the lyric again as those little hands looped and twisted and pulled. Finally, after only two tries, Nate beamed up at him. "I got it!"

"You got it," Zeke said. "Told you."

"All set?" Logan stood at the end of the hall. For a moment, Zeke had nearly forgotten the man was in the house. Nate gave the cameraman a smile.

Outside the sun was partially shielded by cotton-ball clouds, cutting some of the heat at least. Across the street, Mrs. Gwon was weeding her flower beds. She did a double take when she saw the cameraman standing by the garage filming the boys. Zeke couldn't even imagine what she was thinking. Then again, it couldn't be too much stranger than the truth.

"Whatdya wanna do?" Nate asked. "Hide-in-seek?"

Nate always called it hide-*in*-seek, probably because he was tiny and could tuck into most anything—the cupboard under the bathroom sink, his toy chest, the laundry hamper. Trouble was he couldn't keep from laughing, so he was always easy to find—Zeke just had to listen for the snorting.

Zeke looked down the street at a basketball hoop eight houses away, much like the one the Stahlses used to have—the one his father had put up the week they moved into the house so he could teach his newborn baby girl how to take a jump shot someday. Now all that was left of it were four rusty holes above the garage door.

Still, it gave Zeke a good idea. Maybe even a great one.

"Hang here for a sec," he said, heading back inside.

Thankfully Jackie was still hiding in her room, so no questions asked. Zeke moved quickly, first pulling the trash can from under the sink, then heading to the fridge, rooting through the crisper drawer, acutely aware of Logan standing ten feet behind him this time. Thanks to his pyrotechnical expertise/ability to blow things up, they didn't own a ball, so he needed an acceptable substitute.

Snagging the best option, he circled back through the garage, found the packing tape right where he'd hidden it from the time he taped cling wrap over the toilet seat, and grabbed the cordless drill and pruning saw from his mother's gardening supplies. Both sported *No Zeke* labels, but he knew the great ones didn't always play by the rules. The great ones make their *own* rules.

On his way back to the driveway, he stopped by the big plastic garbage bin and emptied the kitchen trash. He turned to the camera and conjured a smile. "Technically it was my *sister's* turn to take out the trash, but why wait for someone to clean up a mess when you can just as easily do it yourself, right?"

That had to be worth at least a couple hundred votes right there.

Back in the yard, Nate took in Zeke's armful of stuff. "What's all that for?"

"Basketball," Zeke said.

"But we don't have a basket. Or a ball."

"Not yet we don't," Zeke said. "Sometimes you have to use your imagination."

A lamppost sat in the Stahlses' front yard, only six feet high, but it would have to do. The bulb had actually been burned out for months, but replacing it was near the bottom of a very long list. "Here. Keep this steady."

Zeke flipped the trash can upside down, then used the drill to make a starter hole in its plastic bottom, just big enough to fit the blade of the pruning saw. It took a while to get going, and he nearly took his own thumb off—which would have made his video more dramatic, to be sure—but at last he made the final cut and the plastic bottom came free.

Nate studied it, frowning. "You put a hole in our trash can."

"On the contrary, I just made a basketball hoop," Zeke replied.

He directed his brother to hold the can high above his head, while he taped it to the lamppost using half the roll of tape. In a perfect world, it would also have a backboard, but this was far from a perfect world. The hoop in place, he handed his brother the grapefruit he'd snagged from the fridge while Logan circled around for a better angle.

"I don't even like grapefruit," Nate said.

"Nobody likes grapefruit," Zeke told him. That wasn't actually true. Jackie loved grapefruit for some incomprehensible reason. "Who's it gonna be? Curry or James?"

"King James," Nate said. Zeke wasn't sure why he even asked; Nate was always LeBron.

"Bushes are the three-point line." Zeke pointed. "Driveway's out of bounds. Try not to smash the ball on your first shot."

Nate looked at the grapefruit skeptically for a moment, then he shrugged, squared up, and launched it from ten feet away, giving it the perfect amount of arc. It disappeared into the top of the can, and then plopped from the bottom into the grassy lawn. *Thunk.*

"Nice shot!" Zeke cheered, legitimately impressed, with both his brother's shooting skills and his own ingenuity. "See? Told you it would work." He retrieved the "ball" and heaved up a shot of his own that missed badly, nearly rolling into the street, but Nate snagged it, tossed it back, and Zeke followed with an easy layup.

He turned to the camera and shrugged. "You can't make 'em all."

Then he and Nate shot it out with the rest of the Imaginary National Trash-Canball Association for the championship.

They got most of the game on film—"Enough for the highlight reel," as Logan put it. There were a couple of dunks from Curry and another trey from James. There was no dribbling, of course, and at least one humorous moment when Zeke, forgetting it was a grapefruit, attempted a bounce pass that went absolutely nowhere, followed by a scary moment when Nate's free throw attempt hit the actual glass top of the lamp, somehow thudding off without smashing it.

It proved to be the end of the ball however.

"It's leaking," Nate said, holding the bruised, beaten, and splitting grapefruit up for Zeke to see. Its insides were pure pulp. The game was over.

Almost.

Zeke stared past his brother to the driveway and a memory floated to the surface. A summer day just like this one. Six-year-old Zeke, staring up at the hoop they used to own—so impossibly high up, the big orange ball heavy and sweaty in both his hands, smelling of hot rubber.

And then his father's own hands, huge and strong, hoisting him up with ease so that he was nearly even with the hoop, making the impossible possible. Making him fly.

Zeke crouched down and tapped his back. "Hop on," he said. "Just try not to get any juice in my hair." Without hesitation, Nate climbed aboard. Zeke grabbed him by the ankles, holding tight. "This is it. Three seconds left on the clock. Down by one. King James has the ball. He drives toward the basket, leaps, and . . . slams it home! Lights out! Game over!"

"In your face!" Nate said. Talking trash to the garbage can.

Zeke knelt to let Nate hop off and the brothers exchanged a sticky high five. He turned to Logan. "I don't suppose you could, like, add some cheering in the background for that part. Maybe some cool firework effects or like a big explosion or something?"

The cameraman shrugged. "I just collect the footage. I don't pick what goes in or put it together."

"Right. Forgot," Zeke said. He picked up what was left of the ball and tossed it in the boxwood bushes for the squirrels or ants to find while Nate did a victory dance around the lamppost. Just as Zeke was putting the forbidden power tools away, Jackie called through the screen door.

"Lunchtime."

That was better than *Zeke, get your scrawny butt in here so I can beat you senseless with this magazine you defiled.* Maybe that meant he was in the clear. He licked a drop of sticky grapefruit juice off the back of his hand and grimaced.

Nope. Still just as sour as always.

A Dish Best Served Grilled

Zeke returned from scrubbing basketball guts off his hands to find Logan in the kitchen, his camera aimed in the direction of the dining table. Gordon Notts had said that they weren't interested in watching Zeke eat, but apparently Logan felt otherwise.

Seeing the cameraman, Jackie immediately started apologizing. "Sorry. I'm afraid I didn't make you anything."

"Not necessary," Logan said. "Thank you, though. Looks delicious."

Zeke pulled up a chair. It really didn't look too bad. It was only grilled cheese and chips, but the sandwich was golden and the corn chips were artfully arranged in its orbit. Another plate sported a starburst array of apple slices with an orange at its center, looking like a flower. Something she probably saw on Pinterest. In addition, each place setting had an actual knife and fork—neither of which was necessary—and a napkin tastefully folded into a pyramid. A vase with a single peony picked from the backyard served as a centerpiece, its petals already drooping.

Put a camera in her face and your sister suddenly becomes Rachael Freaking Ray. Leave it to her to try to make a grilled cheese look like a three-Michelin-star meal—the same girl who once served him a bowl of double noodle soup in a drinking glass because all the bowls were dirty. Of course, he didn't have much room to talk. It's not like he ever did any cooking. Zeke started to pick up his sandwich when Jackie cleared her throat.

"Aren't you forgetting something?"

Zeke picked up his napkin and set it neatly in his lap. It was something his mother always did at restaurants. The ones without a drive-thru.

"I meant grace," Jackie said.

Zeke flashed her a look. *Grace? Really?* He couldn't remember the last time they said grace at the table. That had always been Dad's thing—part of his Protestant upbringing, he'd say, along with church on major holidays and a tendency to say *gosh nabbit* when he got angry. Their mother wasn't the religious type, as evidenced by the fact that they hadn't even made the Christmas service for the past two years.

"What's grace?" Nate asked, more or less confirming Zeke's suspicions about how long it had been. But Jackie seemed intent on putting on a show. It wasn't such a bad idea, actually. Gave off that wholesome family vibe.

"It's a prayer of thanks," Zeke said. "For this delicious booty sitting before us."

Nate snorted.

"Bounty," Jackie corrected, then she clasped her hands in front of her. "Dear Lord, thank you for this meal we are about to receive. And thank you for this . . . um . . . wonderful family. Please look out for those less fortunate than us . . ."

"Especially the children," Zeke interjected, feeling like he was already being upstaged again.

"And the sea turtles," Nate added. Jackie raised an eyebrow. "They're in danger."

"Endangered," Zeke corrected.

"That too."

"Fine. And look out for the sea turtles. And please, Lord," Jackie said a little louder now, "help us to be the good people—"

"Great people," Zeke interjected.

"The *great* people we know we can be. Amen."

"Amen, sister," Nate echoed.

Zeke continued to glare at Jackie. No doubt about it: she was still trying to muscle him out of the spotlight, to be better than him. Fine. She wanted to play nice? He'd show her nice. He channeled the judges on all those baking shows his mother loved. "Thanks for making us lunch, Jacqueline." She hated it when he called her Jacqueline. "The marbling on the bread is just beautiful. Is this Wonder brand?"

"Great Value," she said.

Zeke nodded. "Of course. Excellent choice. And these

chips—perfectly salted with just the right amount of crisposity." He popped one into his mouth and chewed thoughtfully.

"I'll be sure to let the good people of Frito Lay know," Jackie said, her voice still full of artificial sweetener. "Nate, don't forget to eat some apples."

"Yes, Nate," Zeke seconded. "It's important to maintain a well-balanced diet." The world's greatest kid would take care of his body *and* be interested in the health and well-being of others. Or so he assumed. He grabbed an apple slice to set a good example, followed by a big bite of sandwich. He closed his eyes. "Oh. Oh wow. This . . ." He held the sandwich up admiringly. "I mean, I've had my fair share of grilled cheeses in my day, but this? It's like you somehow crammed one slice of heaven between two slices of bread." *Now who's the nicest kid around?*

Jackie carefully inspected an apple slice before taking a nibble out of it. "Thanks," she said. "I got the recipe from a magazine."

Zeke was in the middle of his second bite, thinking up another over-the-top compliment, when her reply struck him. He froze, sandwich crammed in his mouth.

"I mean, I was a little worried at first because the recipe called for *two* pieces of cheese and I thought we were going to be one short, but then I managed to find an extra," she continued.

Zeke stopped chewing, mushy lump of grilled cheese mashed against his tongue. He looked at his sandwich—at the thin layer of gooey yellow gluing the bread together.

She wouldn't, he thought.

But of course she would.

"Funny," Jackie continued, looking thoughtful, "how just when you think you're out of luck, you suddenly find exactly what you're looking for in the least likely of places. There's a name for that, isn't there? Serendipity? Or is it karma?"

Zeke was pretty sure he could taste magazine paper now. And were those little bits of glossy print flecked into the middle of his sandwich? What happened to cheese that had been left sitting squished inside of a magazine for three days? Did it grow mold? Some disease-carrying fungus? Had his sister just given him smallpox? Would he break out in hives? Need to have his tongue amputated? Would other people saying grace at the dinner table ask their god to look out for him? *Dear Lord, bless that poor boy stricken with cheese poisoning.*

Zeke set his pathogenic sandwich back on his plate. Jackie looked at him, mocking concern.

"What's wrong? Aren't you going to finish it? There are hungry people all over the world who would be happy to have that. Some of them children. Did you forget about the children?"

Did *she* forget who was the contestant here? Zeke scowled at her, then remembered the camera was on him and quickly set his face back to neutral. No. She knew exactly what she was doing. This was more than just revenge for a stupid prank. This was a willful act of sabotage. And Logan was getting it all on tape.

Zeke stood up, suddenly feeling like he might lose it. "Excuse me. I have to go to the bathroom." He circled around the table until his back was to the camera, then gave Jackie a stone-hard glare.

She smiled sweetly back at him.

"Don't take too long. You don't want it to get cold."

The bathroom was off-limits to the camera, so Zeke knew nobody would see him scrubbing the top layer of his tongue off with his toothbrush. He squeezed another glop of minty toothpaste straight into his mouth and smeared it around just to make sure all the cheese taste was gone, then washed it all down with two glasses of water.

Don't want it to get cold.

You know what's cold? Undercutting your brother's attempt to win your family ten thousand dollars. Hogging the spotlight. *Poisoning a sibling. That's* cold. He couldn't *believe* her right now. He had to put a stop to this before she ruined whatever chance he had in this competition. It was time to have a talk. And it was a talk Zeke did not want captured on tape.

"Jackie, can you come here a sec?" he yelled through the closed door. "I need your help?"

A moment later he heard his sister's voice on the other side. "Did you fall in the toilet again?"

Did she seriously just say that out loud? That was *one time*. It was the middle of the night and Nate had left the seat up. God, she was the *worst*! Zeke opened the door just a hair. "Did you just tell the entire world I fell in the toilet?" he fumed.

"Chill. Logan's still in there with Nate, who's trying to see how many Fritos he can stack on his head. What do you want?"

"We need to talk."

"Yeah . . . forget it. I'm not coming in there with you."

But Zeke wasn't taking no for an answer. He grabbed his sister's arm and pulled her inside, shutting the door behind them. The bathroom was small, and he didn't feel like standing too close to a suspected murderer, so he pulled back the shower curtain and stood in the bathtub, putting a couple of feet between them. "What are you *doing*?" he hissed, making sure to keep his voice down.

"What am *I* doing? What are *you* doing?" she whisper-shouted back.

"What does it look like I'm doing? I'm trying to be the World's Greatest Kid."

"Oh really? Since *when*?"

"Oh, I don't know. Since *yesterday* maybe!" Zeke said. "And you're *really* not helping."

Jackie stuck up a finger. Not *that* finger, though that wouldn't have surprised him. Her face was red. "First off, you can't just become the World's Greatest Kid in one day. That's not how it works. It's not some switch you can just flip off and on. Secondly, letting your brother win one game of Monopoly out of a *zillion* doesn't make you great. It makes you fake nice for like an hour. Third, it's not my job to help you pretend for millions of people that you're something you're not."

Zeke thought *millions* was probably stretching it. But at least

134

his suspicions were correct: his sister *was* actually trying to sabotage him. *If they ask to interview me to tell everybody how "great" he is, I'm not going to lie.*

"Except I'm trying to win this thing. I'm *trying* to be good."

"Right. That's why you smashed cheese in my magazine."

"Better than putting it in your *sandwich!*" Zeke countered. "That cheese was probably covered in Ebola or something." He honestly had no idea how Ebola worked. Or cheese for that matter. He just knew his stomach was rolling.

Just like Jackie's eyes. "Oh, calm down, you big baby," she said. "I threw that magazine away the moment I opened it. Your sandwich was fine."

Zeke paused. Squinted at her. "It was?"

"Of course it was," she said, her voice tight. "I wouldn't do that to you. And you know why? Because *I'm* not like that."

Zeke took that last part straight in his rumbling gut. It was impossible to ignore the emphasis added.

She would never do such a thing.

Only one kid in the house would even *think* of doing such a thing.

Zeke slumped against the back of the tub. "Right," he mumbled. "Okay. I get it."

Jackie frowned. "All right, maybe I was messing with you a little. But come on, Zeke—world's greatest kid? We both know this has to be some kind of fluke. There are kids out there who actually deserve to win this thing. Who actually have a shot at it.

But you—" She stopped suddenly, looked down at the tiled floor.

She was probably right, of course. But at that moment, it didn't matter whether she was right—all that mattered was she said it. And believed it.

Zeke stepped out of the tub and pushed past her.

"Zeke . . ." she started, but he didn't want to hear any more. He tried to forcefully throw open the door, but that was impossible with the two them scrunched in so tight together, like Daniel Timmerman's cheeks in a tight pair of chinos. He could barely crack it enough to squeeze through.

"Zeke, hang on," Jackie said, but he didn't bother to turn around, slinking out of the bathroom, biting hard on his bottom lip as he made his way down the hall, her words echoing in his head.

Some kind of fluke.

He felt the heat under his skin. Okay, so she didn't *actually* try to feed him old, moldy cheese. And he might have even deserved it if she had. And if he was being completely honest with himself, if serendipity or karma or whatever it was that controlled the universe had a lick of sense, that letter from the Klein Agency would have had someone else's name on it, someone more deserving, just like she said.

But it didn't. It was addressed to the parents of Ezekiel Stahls. To him. Which meant he was given this shot, even if it was a long one. The longest, in fact.

But it might be a little shorter if he had his sister on his side.

Hola from Albuquerque, New Mexico, easily one of the best-named cities in the world. Say it ten times fast, I dare you. It was named after some duke named Alburquerque, but somewhere along the line that first R got dropped. Either way, still quirky, Albuquerque. Everything here has peppers on it, by the way, even their hamburgers, which means I'm destined for some heartburn later. Won't have to stop for gas at least—just make it myself!

The photo on this card is of the big balloon festival they have here each year. Hundreds of hot-air balloons, all different shapes and colors. It got me thinking that it's something we should do as a family someday, don't you think? Take a balloon ride. Just float above it all, see what everything looks like from far away. I bet it's gorgeous.

I'll add it to the list.

Be home soon. Love always,

Dad

Some Reassembly Required

Zeke half expected Logan to be right there, ready to capture his sulky, near-tears expression, but thankfully the hallway was empty. The cameraman wasn't in the kitchen either—just Nate and his bushy hair full of corn chips, which he was picking out and eating one at a time as if he were harvesting them straight from his scalp. "Twenty-three," he said. Presumably how many he stacked on top. Or maybe how many he had eaten so far.

"That's great, man. Where's Logan?" Zeke asked.

Nate pointed to the front door.

Terrific. He left, Zeke thought. *He realized I was a hopeless cause and bolted.* Maybe he overheard the argument with Jackie. Or maybe he just finally acknowledged what was staring him in the face—that he was in the wrong place, filming the wrong kid. He probably called Notts, told him that there was no way Ezekiel Stahls could be the one they were looking for. *All he does is break things and bicker with his sister. There's nothing awesome about this kid at all.*

Zeke opened the front door to find he was mistaken, though. Logan wasn't gone. The van was still there, pulled up to the curb. The cameraman was parked on the porch step, reading. Zeke recognized the cover immediately: *Winnie-the-Pooh*. A classic. It was one of the books his mom used to read to them, he and Nate . . . back when she had the time. They had their own copy sitting on the bookshelf in the corner of their room.

The cameraman held his copy in one hand and traced the path of the sentences with a finger of the other. Zeke had never met an adult who read like that. Logan appeared to be taking his time, savoring every sentence. He must have noticed he had company because he gently set the book down beside him. "Sorry. Just taking five."

"Don't need to apologize. That was one of my favorites growing up," Zeke said.

"Growing up," Logan repeated with a chuckle. "Way back in the day."

Zeke could see the humor. But then some kids have to grow up faster than others. "I probably should warn you, though, that one doesn't even have the best character. Tigger doesn't show up until the sequel."

Logan studied the cover for a moment: the stuffed bear surrounded by his friends. "Tigger's the bouncy one, right? The one that's always getting into trouble?"

Zeke nodded. Tigger was his favorite. Followed by Eeyore. That donkey was all kinds of relatable.

Logan scootched over and then patted the step. "Take a load off," he said.

Zeke glanced through the door behind him to see that Nate had moved on from corn-chip-head stacking and was now trying to see how many apple slices he could cram into his mouth at once. Jackie hadn't emerged from the bathroom apparently. She could stay there the whole day for all he cared—he'd pee in the yard if he had to. Wouldn't be the first time.

He plopped down on the cement, still somewhat cool in the shade. They sat for a moment, a foot of space between them, just "taking a breath," as his mother would say. Zeke finally relaxed his fingers. When he'd come through the door, he'd been steaming, fists clenched, but just sitting here, he could already feel his frustration starting to fizzle. Something about Logan was strangely calming. At least when the camera wasn't rolling.

"Everything okay in there?" Logan asked finally, nodding behind him.

"That? Yeah. Of course. Just your usual sibling stuff. Nothing the world's greatest kid can't handle."

Logan smiled. It was clearly a *whatever you say* kind of smile.

"I guess this probably isn't what you expected when you signed up to film me," Zeke added. "I can't imagine what you must be thinking."

The big man shrugged. "I'm not allowed to vote, so you don't have to worry much about what I think." He scratched his chin. "Besides. I know it's not easy, having the camera in your face all the time. Feels pretty weird, I'm guessing."

"*So* weird," Zeke admitted. "I mean, I know Notts said to just be myself, but . . ." Zeke couldn't quite put it into words, that itchy feeling he got when the camera was on him.

"It's hard to be the real you when you know somebody's watching."

Zeke nodded. *Hard enough knowing who the real you is supposed to be period.*

The cameraman leaned over so his whole head was in the sun. Clearly the heat didn't bother him as much. Probably because he had air-conditioning to look forward to back in his hotel. "Your sister . . . you can tell she cares," he said, pausing before adding, "about what people think of her."

"What gave it away? The artfully arranged fruit platter or all the lip gloss?"

"I think it was the napkins. But like I said, the camera makes people act different."

"She's not acting any different," Zeke countered. "She's always been a jerk."

It was meant as a joke. Sort of. He knew it wasn't true. Not always. Zeke stared at the trash can taped to the lamppost. He could remember a time when it would have been him and Jackie out in the driveway playing H-O-R-S-E or chalking out elaborate hopscotch courses, complete with lava pits you had to leap over

141

and puzzles you had to solve. That was before she got her phone and her braces off and her bevy of friends. Before she put the No Trespassing sign on her door, the one that always stayed shut. Before things started falling apart and the distance stretched between them.

"I can relate," Logan said. "I have an older brother. I spent half of my childhood in a headlock and the other half getting rug burns. Siblings are a pain. But then if I ever need anything, he's still the first person I call."

"If I called Jackie, she'd just hang up on me."

Logan laughed. It sounded a little like a sea lion's bark. Husky and hoarse. "I wouldn't be so sure." He looked back over his shoulder again. "She always stays home with you while your mom's at work?"

"It's cheaper than daycare," Zeke said, repeating one of his mother's phrases. Even when Nate was still in diapers, it fell to Jackie to watch them. Of course, it was probably harder then, when his sister was only as old as Zeke was now. He couldn't imagine having to change Nate's diaper. The kid's *farts* could clear a city block.

Logan had this look on his face, something like sympathy, and Zeke was suddenly annoyed again. "She gets paid, you know. And it's not like it's a hard job. We mostly take care of ourselves. She's basically just a stay-at-home lunch lady."

"Well, if that's all she is," Logan said with another shrug. "Though when I was your age, I had to make my own lunch most days. My parents were never home and my brother never bothered—just made me fend for myself. And I can tell you my grilled cheeses never looked so good."

It did look good, honestly. And it tasted good. At least right up until he thought it might kill him. Sometimes you fool yourself into thinking things are one way when they're actually something else entirely.

Zeke's eyes fell on the lamppost turned basketball hoop. "I guess I should probably take that thing down."

"You're probably going to want your trash can back."

"Sure. Except I'm not sure I can fix it."

The cameraman winked at him. "I don't think it's broken beyond repair. Especially not for the world's greatest kid. In my experience most things can be fixed, if you're willing to put forth the effort."

Zeke stood up to get the tape.

Down the Poop Chute

Fifteen minutes and the rest of the roll of tape later, the family had their kitchen trash can again, sitting under the sink with half of a cold grilled cheese sandwich buried inside. At a glance it looked fine—only when you looked too closely could you see the cracks. Like a lot of things, Zeke supposed.

Fixing the trash can had been easier than expected. Fixing how this day had gone so far would be harder.

Zeke asked Logan for a camera-free moment and gently knocked on Jackie's door for the second time that day. He could hear her music playing. Minor chords and major growling as usual.

"Hey, Jacks. I was thinking about taking Nate to the playground," he ventured through the closed door. After all, great kids took their little brothers to the park in the summer—especially when it was actually hotter *in* the house than in the shade of the trees.

Great kids probably also invited their older sisters who they'd just fought with in the bathroom. Not as an apology, exactly—that was taking it too far. This was more like an olive branch.

A branch that Jackie promptly snapped in half.

"Have fun," she yelled over her music.

He waited for her to at least open up and give him the speech, the same one she always gave whenever he and Nate left the house, inherited directly from their mother: *Look after your brother, watch for cars, put on sunscreen, don't do anything stupid—I don't want to hear any sirens.* But her door stayed shut.

"Okay. Well. We'll be back in an hour or so, I guess."

In response, the music just got louder.

Zeke reached for the handle, tempted to just barge in, but when his fingers touched the knob, he froze. He wasn't sure what he'd say to her anyway. And he doubted she would listen.

"She's not coming," Zeke told Nate back in the kitchen. He and Logan were making apple-slice smiley faces at each other, Nate giggle-snorting and practically choking on his. Logan took two slices and turned himself into a walrus, clapping his hands together. It was the kind of thing that their father would have done with them; maybe he did and Zeke just couldn't remember. He tried not to think about it too hard.

Hawthorne Park was only a ten-minute walk along

neighborhood streets. The city park, with its playground, was one of the things that drew his parents to this house. They always knew they wanted a bunch of kids, and those kids would need a wide-open green space to run around. Of course the houses in the rich neighborhoods north of them came with their own clubhouses and play areas, but Zeke didn't mind having to walk to the public space to get his swing on. Besides, all those newer, fancy houses butted right up against each other so that there was hardly any room to launch your sister's decapitated Barbie doll heads with your newly constructed Tinkertoy catapult . . . if you were into that sort of thing.

The community playground was bigger anyway: eight swings and a merry-go-round, plus the giant play structure in the middle—three stories of brown and green plastic shaped like a castle with several towers and plenty of places to hide. Zeke couldn't count the number of games of tag he'd played here, churning up mulch in his attempts to chase down Jackie, who taunted him by running backward on her then twice-as-long legs. Games he now played with Nate, who still had several years of catching up to do.

Though lately, Zeke felt like he was starting to age out of the playground business. The monkey bars just weren't as exciting when you could reach them without jumping, and he could shimmy up the rock wall in three lunges. But he knew Nate still liked coming. Besides, maybe Zeke would find some inspiration here—something he could do that would be camera-worthy. Better than throwing a game of Monopoly, at least, or fighting with his sister.

The park was busy as usual, the swings full, the merry-go-round in perpetual motion, the whole playground a symphony of squeaks and squeals. Kids chased and tackled each other. Parents hid in the shade, tethered to their phones. Zeke spotted a couple of boys he knew from school standing by the exit of the playground's tallest slide and pulled Nate in that direction. "Look. Deshawn and Eli are here. Maybe they'll want to play capture the flag or something." *Plus, how cool will it be when they see me with a professional cameraman recording my every move?*

The two boys didn't seem to notice Logan at first, though. They were too busy looking up at the top of the playground's tallest slide. Deshawn held his skateboard tight to his chest.

"I'm telling you it's possible," Eli was saying, brushing his mop of blond bangs from his eyes.

"I didn't say it wasn't possible. I said you'd be stupid to try it," Deshawn said as Zeke ambled up to them. "Hey, Z. What's up?"

A friendly nod but no fist bump. Deshawn and Eli weren't exactly Zeke's besties, but then Zeke had never stuffed a mouse in either of their desks, so they had no reason to dislike him either. "Just bringing my brother to the park," he said casually. He glanced over his shoulder.

Eli caught the not-so-subtle gesture. "What's with that

WWE-looking dude with the camera?" he whispered.

"Oh him?" Zeke said dismissively. "That's just Logan. He's filming me. You know. For the World's Greatest Kid competition. *Turns out I'm one of the finalists.*" He whispered the last part as if it was top secret intel.

The two boys looked at Zeke like he'd switched to speaking Latin. Deshawn shook his head. "No. Seriously. Who is that guy?"

"I told you," Zeke said, incredulous. "He's from KABAM. It's like this nonprofit thing. They're interested in making the world a better place, so they're running a contest to find the greatest kid in the whole USA, and I'm one of the contestants."

"You?" Deshawn said, raising an eyebrow. "The *greatest kid*?" Zeke shrugged.

"Right. And my mom's married to the pope."

"It's true," Nate piped up. "Logan has been filming us all day. He got me stacking twenty-three Fritos on my head." Nate shook his crown and a couple of crumbs flew free, corroborating at least part of the story.

Zeke moved a little closer. "The winner gets ten thousand bucks," he whispered.

"Ten thousand!" Deshawn shouted. "No cap? How come I'm not in on this? I'm a better kid than you are! What did you even get on your last report card?"

Actually the grades on Zeke's final report card were stellar. It was the comments under *classroom behavior* that left something to be desired. Zeke didn't try to explain how he'd been chosen, though. Mostly because he still had no idea himself. "It's not just about school stuff. It's about the total package."

"And this guy, he just follows you around and films everything you do?" Eli asked. "Then what? It goes on TV or something?"

"Posted to their website. It's not livestreamed or anything, but there will be thousands of people watching and voting. Maybe even millions." Still an exaggeration, but it sounded good and had the desired effect. Deshawn and Eli looked at each other, clearly impressed, then over at the camera. Deshawn flashed a peace sign. Eli flexed his biceps, though there was little noticeable difference.

Suddenly Eli's eyes went wide; he grabbed Deshawn by the shoulders. "Dude, you *have* to do it now. This guy can video it. You could be *famous*."

"Do what?" Zeke asked.

Deshawn held up his skateboard. "Eli wants me to surf down the Rocket." He thrust his chin upward, at the slide beside them. The giant plastic castle had several escape routes, but only one was three stories high—shooting down at an almost fifty-degree angle before leveling out for a long exit into the mulch. All the neighborhood kids called it the Rocket because it was crazy fast, provided your sweaty legs didn't hold you back. Some called it the Poop Chute, because it was rumored that a first grader once soiled his pants on the way down out of pure fear.

Zeke had been down the Rocket a hundred times, of course.

Forward. Backward. Headfirst. Feetfirst. With his sister behind him. With his brother in front.

But never on wheels.

"I told him he doesn't have to stand up or anything. He can crouch the whole way. Just so long as he stays on the board."

"And I told this fool that I don't want to *die*. I'm only twelve. I have an incredibly bright future to think of."

"You're not going to die," Eli shot back. "That thing's like, what? Thirty feet? The absolute worst that could happen is you break your spine and forget how to walk."

"Well, if that's all that's gonna happen, why don't *you* do it?"

Zeke noticed Logan had moved a little closer, getting the conversation on camera.

"You know I've got no balance. But come on . . . it would be so cool. It would be, like, the greatest thing ever," Eli continued.

Greatest. Thing. Ever.

Another exaggeration, obviously, but it *would* be pretty sick. After all, Zeke couldn't quite picture any of the other contestants doing something like this. Maybe the one who called himself Special K. Still, it was the kind of thing that would help Zeke stand out. It was bold. It was dangerous. It was *great* . . . in its own way. And Jackie hadn't reminded him *not* to do anything stupid this time, so really, if he hurt himself, it would kind of be her fault for letting him go without a warning.

"I'll do it," he said.

The other two boys stared at him.

"What?" Eli said.

"I'll do it. I'll surf it."

"Do you even skate?" Deshawn asked. "I've never seen you on a board."

"I've skated a couple of times," Zeke said, though by couple he meant once, and that was skateboarding down the sidewalk, not a thirty-foot slide at a dangerously steep angle. Still, the principle was the same, wasn't it? Keep your balance; don't fall off.

"Yeah. Zeke should do it," Eli said. "Prove just how great he really is."

Logan had been zoomed in on Eli for that last part, which meant Zeke was locked in. The great ones never back down from a challenge. Muhammed Ali. Winston Churchill. Beyoncé. Captain Marvel. All of them stood their ground. He *had* to go through with it now.

"I'm in," he said as confidently as he could manage.

"Okay. But we need to lay some ground rules," Eli continued, though Zeke wasn't sure what made him the expert all of a sudden. "No sitting or straddling the board. Feet on at all times. You can hold on to it and crouch, like I said, though it would be so much cooler if you stood up straight."

"And don't you dare break my board," Deshawn said. "I got it for Christmas."

"Don't break stuff. Check," Zeke said, trying not to think about his own record when it came to that particular promise: a picture frame, the ceiling fan, that wind chime, his pinkie finger, the neighbor's window, a turtle's sense of safety and well-being. It wasn't a great streak, but this time would be different.

He took the skateboard, a checkered deck with white wheels. He gave one of them a spin. Slick as snot. He looked up at the Rocket. The whole trip would take three seconds, max. And that was providing he stayed on. If not, it would be over in less time. "All right. Let's do this."

As he passed by the camera headed toward the ladder, Zeke heard a nagging voice in his head: *You sure this is a good idea?* It was his mother, or Jackie, or some combination of the two. But Zeke couldn't back out now. Did George Washington take one look at the Delaware River and say, *Forget it, I'll just pay more for my tea?* Did Edmund Hillary and Tenzing Norgay see Everest and say, *A little* too *high, don't you think?* Did Amelia Earhart make a U-ey when she realized how far her flight would be and land her plane?

All right. Maybe she wasn't the best example.

It didn't matter. He was determined to surf down the Rocket on this skateboard and look awesome in the process. Logan would get it on video, and the whole world would see just how incredible Ezekiel Stahls really was. Like the hundreds of videos he watched on the internet of people pulling off dangerous and amazing feats, garnering zillions of likes. The votes would come pouring in.

He felt a tug on his shirt and turned to see his brother's pinched face. In his excitement and apprehension, he'd almost forgotten about Nate.

"You're going down *that* thing?" He pointed at the slide. "On *that* thing?" He pointed at the board. "Can you *do* that?"

"Of course I can," Zeke said, trying to sound sure of himself for his brother's sake. *Don't you go doubting me too.* He put his hands on Nate's shoulders. "Just do me a favor and wait for me at the bottom . . . but not in front of the slide, 'kay? I'll be coming in hot."

Nate nodded and went and stood, not with the two boys, but with Logan, who was tracking Zeke through the camera. The camcraman cocked his head to the side, one eyebrow raised, but Zeke gave him a thumbs-up. *You said "just do you," remember?*

Zeke tucked Deshawn's board under one arm and slowly began the three-ladder climb to the top of the castle's tallest tower. The other kids monkeying around saw Zeke with the board and took a step back, realizing something very spccial and potentially paralyzing was about to happen. As he climbed, Zeke noticed a couple of the parents on the periphery looking up at him as well. He wondered if one of them would intervene, shout at him to come down, try to talk him from the ledge, but nobody said a word. Zeke wasn't their kid after all. Or maybe the presence of Logan and his camera made them think that this was all a stunt, that Zeke was a professional. The Tony Hawk of the playground scene. Some hotshot young YouTube sensation with a legion of followers and an energy drink endorsement. Whatever it was, they simply sat and watched. One of them even held up his own phone to record.

Zeke reached the top of the tower and looked down. It was steeper than he remembered. Roller-coaster steep. The ten-inch lip on each side of the slide seemed like a more-than-adequate barrier when your body's pressed to the plastic, but now those ten-inch rails seemed way too short, barely tall enough to keep the skateboard in line, let alone its rookie rider. If he could sit on the board, maybe. But sitting wasn't surfing. Sitting was sledding. Sitting was *sort-of* daring, and *sort-of* daring didn't get your family four tickets to Hawaii.

Zeke ran his hand along the top of the slide, the plastic hot from the sun. He swallowed hard. Maybe this wasn't such a great idea after all.

But then he caught sight of the small crowd that had already formed below. Deshawn holding up his phone, Eli's fingers tucked under his sweaty armpits. Behind them a cluster of younger kids was watching as well. And then there was Nate, looking up at him, squinting up into the sunlight like a bystander in a Superman comic.

Ten thousand dollars or not, Zeke couldn't let the kid down.

"Be careful," Deshawn yelled. Logan nodded emphatically, echoing that advice. But Zeke was about to stand on top of a wheeled plank of wood eight inches wide and shoot down a thirty-foot slide at a bazillion miles per hour with only a small plastic lip on either side keeping him from careening off to his own splattering demise—being careful wasn't an option. He would have to count on being awesome. And lucky. He wiped his sweaty hands on his shorts, and then, for the second time in one day, Zeke whispered a little prayer, this one purely selfish.

"Dear Lord, please don't let me die on the Poop Chute. Amen."

He set the skateboard down, its nose hanging over the edge. The way the slide was designed, he would have to crouch pretty low just to make it through the opening, but that was okay—he wanted his center of gravity as close to the deck as possible. He put both feet on the board, squaring up, testing his balance. It seemed sturdy enough, only giving the slightest wobble. He took one last look around. He wasn't afraid of heights—he'd spent plenty of time goofing around on the roof of his house. But the mulch that covered the playground looked sharp and pokey, nothing like his unmowed grassy lawn. And besides, he'd never tried to skateboard down his roof.

Holding on to the front of the board with his left hand and the overhang of the slide with his right, Zeke gave Deshawn's Christmas present a little nudge, the front wheels hovering now, waiting for Newton's laws to kick in. He could already feel all the tension in his thighs, his knees threatening to buckle. He scooted another centimeter. The board leaning, itching to go. Thirty feet was a lot, more than four Steph Currys stacked on top of each other. Three seconds to get down. Ten heartbeats—at least with the rate his heart was currently going.

And yet Zeke hesitated.

Because the more he thought about it, the more he realized this was a really terrible idea.

After all, even if he made it to the bottom in one piece, what would it prove? That he was great or just fortunate? And what kind of example was he setting? How long would it be before his brother was up here on someone else's skateboard, trying to break his own neck just to impress a bunch of strangers? And how come none of the parents down there were trying to stop him? Didn't they see what he was about to do? He looked again at Nate, who was pressed close against Logan now, one hand gripping the cameraman's shirt.

Zeke took a deep breath. Forget it. Ten thousand bucks was a lot, but certainly not worth dying for. This wasn't happening. He would find some other way to win this thing.

Just as he was about to step off the board and let it go shooting down without him, he felt the fingertips of his left hand slip from the overhang.

The skateboard inched forward a little bit more, just past the tipping point, its nose angling downward, front wheels looking for contact with the hard plastic.

Oh no.

Zeke's stomach dropped. His two bites of non-Ebola-infected grilled cheese instantly started clawing their way back up.

Oh no no no no no.

This was happening whether he wanted it to or not.

Zeke's right hand tore free from the plastic overhang and instinctively found the tail of the board, nails digging into the wood as he crouched as low as possible, doing everything in his power to maintain his center of gravity as the front wheels touched down and board and rider blasted off.

The world suddenly blurred past him.

There was a reason they called it the Rocket. Zeke's life did not flash before his eyes, but only because there wasn't time for it to. There was only time for the one thought, two words repeated over and over in his brain rapid fire: *Hold on hold on hold on.* The world came rushing up to meet him as he zipped down the slide at something close to Mach One, his insides scrambled, every muscle pulled tight. He held on to the board with both hands, feeling his body list one way and then the other, threatening to catapult right over the edge, the sound of wheels rumbling down the slide eclipsed by the sound of Zeke's own screaming and the cheering of the crowd getting closer and closer.

Until that moment, only half a heartbeat long, when he realized he was actually almost there, that the slide was leveling out, that the faces he'd been looking down on were now even with his own. The moment when he realized he wasn't going to die.

This epiphany was followed immediately by a rush of triumph. The adrenaline hitting him full blast. Zeke Stahls. Ultimate Slide Surfer. Daredevil of Hawthorne Park.

He let go of the board and stood up, thrusting both fists into the air.

"I am the grea—"

That's all he managed to get out before both he and skateboard exited the slide, at approximately the same time and at the same speed, but in completely different directions.

One landed on its wheels and skidded to a stop.

The other landed on his face and did pretty much the same.

There was mulch. So much mulch. He was practically buried in it. Zeke blinked, but he didn't dare move, even as the crowd closed in. Everything hurt.

"Dude, that was epic," Eli said, hovering over him. "I can't believe you actually tried to stand up!"

Zeke spit out the piece of wood he'd been chewing on. "I think I broke all the things," he groaned.

"Seriously, man, you okay?" Deshawn asked. "Do we need to call an ambulance?" He held his phone up to capture all of the pain in Zeke's face.

No sirens, Zeke thought. *That's the rule.* He slowly sat up and did a damage check. His head was ringing. And there were scrapes on his elbows and knees, but very little blood. He could move all his limbs and wiggle his toes. His head was still attached to his body. A little bruised but mostly he was just dirty.

He saw a hand reach down to help him up, but it wasn't Deshawn's or Eli's or even Nate's. It was Logan's. His camera was sitting in the mulch by his feet, no longer filming. The big man pulled Zeke up with ease.

"Did you get it?" Zeke asked, brushing himself off. "Please tell me you got that."

"Takeoff to landing," Logan said. The cameraman pointed to Zeke's ear. "You've got a little bit still stuck in there."

Zeke tilted his head and banged on one ear as little bits of wood came loose from the other, as if his skull were full of the stuff. "Was it cool?"

"It was something."

Zeke felt a pair of skinny arms coil around his waist. Nate, cheek pressed to his brother's side, eyes shut. He gave Zeke the confirmation he was looking for. "That was *incredible*," he said.

And then, a little softer.

"Please don't ever do it again."

Suck It, Toad

It was enough for the first day. Probably more than enough.

That's what Logan said when they got back to the house, Zeke wincing from his skinned knees and still somehow finding bits of mulch in the folds of his clothes. They stopped at the van, where Logan loaded up his camera, saying that he would upload the day's footage to the servers and then Notts and the team at KABAM would combine the best bits into a video and post it on the website come evening.

"Don't worry," Logan promised, "they'll only use the highlights."

"Terrific," Zeke quipped, though he wasn't sure what those would be. Losing thousands of fake dollars to his brother? Avoiding a nonexistent poisoning from his sister? Discovering a new use for grapefruit or setting the neighborhood playground slide skateboard speed record? It had certainly been an *eventful* day, but was it a *great* day? He guessed he'd find out in a few hours when Gordon Notts posted the videos for the rest of the world to judge.

And the world would be more than willing to judge, he knew. He just hoped his mom wouldn't ask too many questions about the raspberries on his knees.

As she walked through the door that evening, twenty minutes later than expected, Zeke noticed she reeked of perfume again, but this time the smell was masked by something much more enticing.

"Is that pizza?" Nate asked, jumping off of the couch.

"Not just pizza," Mom said. *"Ambrosia's."*

"Did you get a raise?" Zeke asked. At twenty bucks a pie, Ambrosia's was a major splurge. Like birthday-level bingeing.

"God I wish," his mom said. She set the box on the table and opened it to reveal Zeke's favorite: pepperoni, onion, fresh garlic. The kind of pizza that would transform your breath into a chemical weapon. "I thought we would celebrate your first day as the World's Greatest Kid. Is he still here, by the way? Logan? I didn't see the van."

"He left hours ago," Zeke told her. "Said he got what he needed."

"Probably just as well. Not sure I ordered enough for five. Speaking of, where is your sister?" Zeke's mom turned her voice up fifty decibels. "Jackie! Dinner!"

"Not hungry," an equally loud voice yelled from the hallway.

"It's Brojuh's!" Nate called back, practically drooling over his slice already.

"I'll eat later."

His mother leveled Zeke with a look. "What did you do?"

He tried not to wriggle under her stare. Wriggling implied guilt. "Me? I was too busy being great to do anything. She's just in a mood. You know how she gets."

Ms. Stahls looked like she didn't believe most of that, but she also looked too tired to press it. "So were you? Great?"

"I wess wiw wus hafo wape am fime ow," Zeke said, the pizza already burning the roof of his mouth.

They didn't have to wait long. Halfway through Zeke's second piece, his mom got a text notification from KABAM saying that the first videos were online and day one voting was officially open. For the next five hours, people all across America could make their pick for the WGK.

Zeke ran to the family room to grab the laptop sitting on the table. His mother wiped his greasy fingerprints off the screen with a napkin and yelled down the hall again. "Jackie! Your brother's video is up!"

"Fantastic," came his sister's monotone.

"Don't you want to come watch?"

"I have a phone. And a tablet."

"Don't you want to come watch with *us*?"

"I'm good. Really."

Zeke's mother gave him a follow-up glare. "Seriously, what was it? Do you make more lost sister signs again?"

Zeke suppressed another smirk recalling the posters that he'd plastered all over the neighborhood with his sister's picture on them. *LOST. Reward if found. Goes by name Jackie. Highly temperamental and potentially violent. Not potty-trained. Approach with caution.* He'd lost video game privileges for two weeks.

"That was *so* last summer," Zeke said as he typed in the address for the Klein Agency for the Betterment of All Mankind, clicking on the link to the competition. Sure enough, the page had changed; the introductory videos had been replaced with something that said *Moments of Greatness, Day 1,* showcasing a freeze frame of each of the contestants in action. Zeke's showed him standing at the top of the Rocket.

"You went to the park I see."

"It was scary," Nate informed her. "Zeke almost died."

Another look. Such piercing eyes she had. "What do you mean you almost *died*?"

Zeke made sure his legs were tucked under the table, knee scabs hidden. "Maybe we should just watch the videos." He clicked on the picture of the girl with the rainbow braces, careful to avoid the *Vote for Hailey Richter* button underneath. He didn't know if the World's Greatest Kid was supposed to vote for himself, but it was Mom's computer and he figured he had a good idea of who she was going to pick.

At least he was 95 percent sure.

"We're not watching yours first?" Mom asked.

"I want to know what I'm up against," Zeke said.

That's what he thought, at least. But he was very much mistaken.

Hailey's video didn't start with her riding her prizewinning pony through an emerald pasture like Zeke had guessed. Instead, she was in what appeared to be a library, sitting on a rainbow carpet of alphabet letters, teaching little kids, Nate's age or younger, how to make origami boats, her cheery, singsong voice matching her overanimated gestures. A boy-band tune thumped in the background. Hailey's head bopped with each fold, and as each kid finished their boat, her face exploded with excitement and she gave them a high five.

It was sickening.

In fact, there was a whole twenty seconds of her helping a kid with a cast on one arm. He would fold part, then she would fold part, offering a constant stream of encouragement. *There you go. You've got it. It looks terrific.* Zeke almost gagged. "What kind of parent takes a kid with a broken arm to an origami class?"

"Hush," his mother said.

The video cut to a brief interview with Emily Vorman, children's programming coordinator for the Heartland Public Library, who explained that Hailey volunteered there during the summer, two mornings a week: "She's just so good with the kids. So patient and so kind. They absolutely adore her." The video cut back to Hailey signing the one kid's cast. It zoomed in to show the message. *Get well soon! Hailey*

She dotted her *i and* her exclamation point with hearts. What kind of twisted person *does* that?

The clip finished with her reading a book to her little pod of admirers, a fairy tale, of course. "And they all lived happily ever after. The end." Fade out on the little kids cheering and asking for more.

"Blech," Zeke said.

"I thought it was sweet."

Zeke stared at his mother. "You're kidding, right? It was so fake. She probably didn't even read the whole book, just read the very end for the camera. And you know none of those kids really wanted to be there. Their parents just dropped them off for the free babysitting."

"Don't knock free babysitting," his mom said. "Click on the next one."

Zeke did, and another, different bubble-gummy pop tune kicked in, the video focusing on Aadya's spectacle-framed face before zooming out to show her making something too. Not paper boats, though. This time it was sandwiches. Lots and lots of sandwiches. PB and J or ham and cheese, slapped together and then stuffed into Ziploc bags. Aadya's voice overlapped the music.

"The first and third Mondays of every month, my youth service group gets together in the kitchen of our church and makes two hundred sack lunches, which we then take to all the shelters in the city."

"Wow," Mom said. "That's impressive."

Zeke flashed her a dirty look. She was not supposed to be

impressed by this. She was his mother. She was supposed to be skeptical and irritated like he was. The Ambrosia's was already starting to sour in his stomach.

"It's not much: a sandwich, a piece of fruit, a bottle of water, and a bag of chips. But when you aren't sure where your next meal is coming from, knowing that someone out there sees what you're going through . . . well, I just hope it makes a difference, no matter how small."

At that point, the camera zoomed in to show Aadya writing on a Post-it Note and tucking the note into the bag she was filling. The note said, *Don't Give Up.* She appeared to write a note *for each and every bag.*

There were more scenes of her loading a van, shaking hands with other volunteers, even one of her handing a sack lunch to someone. *Probably all staged,* he thought. Aadya's clip ended with her youth group standing in a circle, hands clasped, saying a prayer. Except they weren't praying for themselves, as Zeke had, standing at the top of the Rocket. They were praying for those they'd just given a meal to.

Welp, there goes the Christian vote.

His mother didn't say anything this time. She didn't have to. What do you say to that? Wish she hadn't fed those people? Zeke silently clicked on the next one.

There was Kyo. Special K. He was sitting in a chair with a game controller in his hand.

Finally, Zeke thought, *a kid who just sits around the house and plays video games all day. Maybe this guy I can beat.*

But then the camera zoomed out little by little to show that Kyo wasn't in his home. He was in *a* home, yes, but it was a *retirement* home. And he wasn't playing alone. There were three others sitting in chairs beside him, all of them clearly in their golden years. The game was *Mario Kart*, and those oldies were totally into it, zooming across the tracks, swaying with every turn. One lady with foot-tall hair seemed to be a particularly hardcore gamer, leaning forward with a scowl on her face screaming, "Suck it, Toad!" every time she launched a turtle shell. She knew what the best power-up was.

They all looked like they were having a great time, Kyo included.

There was another interview, of course—with one of the facility's directors. "The residents love it when Kyo shows up. They don't even bother with the video games unless he's here. Something about him just brings out their youthful side. He understands and appreciates everyone, no matter how old they are." The clip cut to Kyo helping to serve dessert to an elderly man, playing a game of checkers with another, and pushing some old lady in a wheelchair through a garden. It ended with a shot of the woman with the Bride-of-Frankenstein 'do and Kyo bumping fists.

"I bet he steals their Jell-O when they're not looking," Zeke said.

"I bet he doesn't," his mom said.

Whose side are you even on? Zeke shook his head. Libraries

167

and poverty shelters and old folks' homes. Was today National Community Service Day? Did these kids seriously spend every freaking summer afternoon doing stuff like this?

He was about to find out. Zeke clicked on Dom's video.

And found himself staring at a pile of dog poo.

A hand reached down with a little plastic bag and scooped it up. The camera pulled back to show Dom making a face. "If I'm being real with you . . . this isn't my favorite part," he said, then he lit up the screen with his broad smile. "But it's worth it."

Cut to the kid absolutely *surrounded* by puppies. A platoon of puppies. He's literally lying on the grass, engulfed in them. A blanket of wriggling fur, wagging tails, and lolling tongues, Dominic covering his face, laughing.

"Awwww. Can we get one?" Nate begged.

"There is no way we can afford a dog," Ms. Stahls said. "Though they are really frigging cute."

They were, of course. That's what made the whole thing so painful to watch.

The video went on to explain how Dom's mother worked at the local shelter and so he spent a lot of time there in the summer helping to care for the stray animals. There were shots of him feeding and brushing, cleaning out litter boxes, and filling water bottles. There was twenty seconds of him with one dog in particular—a Yorkie who was missing one of its back legs. Because of course it was.

"This is Graybeard," Dom said to the camera. "He's probably

my favorite because nothing stops him. He's only got three legs, but he doesn't let that slow him down. I admire that. I think we could all be more like him."

The video ended with Dom and Graybeard running around in the yard. Then Graybeard leaped into the kid's arms . . . with just *three legs . . . in slow freaking motion* . . . and started licking the kid's chin. Fade out on maximum adorability.

Zeke's mom sighed. "That one's my favorite so far."

"Doesn't count! *He has a three-legged dog!*" Zeke protested.

His mother affected a soothing voice. "Let's watch your video. I'm sure it's good too."

Zeke shook his head. "I don't want to."

"Come on. How bad can it be?"

How bad *could* it be? He wasn't sure, but he knew it couldn't possibly reach the bar that had just been set. There were no geriatric gamers in his video. No tripodal animals. No casts to sign or people to feed, unless you counted his sister feeding him and Nate aesthetically arranged apple slices. For a moment he felt betrayed. Why didn't Gordon Notts tell him what he was really up against? Why didn't Logan say something instead of just letting him play a stupid *board game with his brother* this morning? They lied to him. They said they just wanted to get an honest look at what he did every day. Was this really how these other kids spent their free time? Were there really people like this out there?

Wait . . . were *most* other people like this and he just didn't know it?

While he was groaning, his mother reached over and clicked on his video.

There was music. Not quite as upbeat as the others'. Something vaguely superheroish, though. Hints of Batman, perhaps. A little dark, a little tense. Honestly, it suited him.

The video opened with a shot of the Stahlses' front yard.

"That's our house," Nate said, pointing. You could tell by the peeling paint and the window with the jagged crack in it—a casualty from Zeke's slingshot-making phase. Another broken thing on the list.

Cut to the three of them on the well-worn carpet—Zeke sliding all of his money and his properties to his brother, declaring him the winner. *We sometimes play by our own special rules.* That was followed by about twenty seconds of the two of them playing basketball in the front yard.

"Is that a grapefruit?" Mom asked.

"Three seconds left on the clock. Down by one."

Zeke kept his lips sealed, his eyes focused on the screen, where his brother was wobbling up on top of his shoulders.

"Is that our kitchen *trash can*? Taped to our *lamppost*?"

"Shh. Here comes the good part," Nate said.

"He drives toward the basket, leaps, and . . ."

Slam dunk. But there was no cheering. Instead the video cut straight to Zeke at the top of the Rocket, one foot resting on Deshawn's skateboard, getting ready to launch himself into playground history.

His mother leaned forward, squinted. "Is that what I think it is? Are you about to do what I think you are?" She was full of questions all of a sudden.

From the computer speaker, Zeke heard his own voice again: *"Wait for me at the bottom. I'll be coming in hot."* He cringed at his own line. His mother's hand flew to her mouth as the screen version of her son soared down the slide. Gordon Notts, or whoever pieced together the video, decided to be a little creative with this part, at least, breaking in with the slow motion again and steadily ramping up the volume on the music. As a result, Zeke's mom got a nice long look at her son flying through the air at the end of his run, the expression of pure terror plastered on his face, the eruption of mulch chips caused by his less-than-graceful impact.

The music hit a high note just as Zeke hit the ground.

Terrific. This is what people were going to remember. They'll see everyone else doing all these meaningful, selfless, puppy-covered things, but all they'll remember about him was how he made a Zeke-size divot in the earth. He was going to be a punch line. They would probably make a meme of him. It would say, *Mondays be like* . . . and then show Zeke plowing into the ground face-first. He didn't want to watch anymore.

Thankfully there wasn't much more to watch. Only twenty seconds left.

They were back in Zeke's house, in the hallway this time, the camera peeking around the corner, zooming in on the front door. Nate sat on the stairs, huddled over his shoes, Zeke crouching next to him. The music was gone now, replaced by some off-key singing.

"Bunny ears, bunny ears, playing by a tree. Crisscrossed that little tree, trying to catch me."

The camera zoomed in to show Nate's little fingers pulling his two loops tight. *"You got it,"* video Zeke said.

The clip ended with the two of them crossing the street— Zeke and Nate, their backs to the camera, big brother holding his little brother's hand, keeping a lookout for cars, even though they weren't specifically told to.

Zeke watched his mother, waiting for a reaction. To say something about the busted trash can. Or tell him he owed her for the grapefruit. At the very least he knew she would have to chastise him for the skateboard stunt. Instead, she looked at Nate.

"You tied your shoes," she said.

Nate nodded. "Zeke showed me how."

"Yes he did. Of course he did. And that song. Your dad . . ." She looked as if she might say something else, then thought better of it. She reached over and smoothed Zeke's hair instead, then stood up with her plate and headed for the sink.

She stopped halfway to the kitchen before turning around and coming back to the table. "Almost forgot."

She stood in front of the laptop and scrolled down, casting her vote with a click.

Puppies Are the Worst

Zeke spent the next hour in front of the computer, watching the votes pour in.

Well, not pour, exactly—this wasn't *American Idol*—but there was a steady stream.

Unless your name was Ezekiel Stahls. Then it was more of a trickle.

There was no place for comments, which was probably a blessing, though it meant there was no way of knowing *why* people chose which kid they did—only the counters beneath each picture, ticking up with every refresh. Which Zeke did, every fifteen seconds, his tally inching upward. It was strangely addicting, that tiniest surge of affirmation with every new vote.

And depressing. Because with every refresh, the margin between him and the rest of the pack grew. Each of the other four contenders for the title of World's Greatest Kid had over a hundred votes before Zeke even clocked double digits. They hit the thousand mark about the time he passed one hundred. To make it worse, Zeke knew that a lot of his votes—maybe the majority of them—were from people who just enjoyed seeing him become a mulch muncher. They were pity votes. Or ironic votes. From people who enjoyed seeing other people make fools of themselves. Zeke couldn't really blame them: half the videos he and his brother watched online involved clumsiness, bad judgment, and/or bodily harm. The votes that didn't come from people gawking at his graceless wipeout probably either came from kids in his class or JC Penney's employees. Zeke knew his mother would have talked him up. *You won't believe what my son is involved in.*

The same mother who snuck up behind him and closed the computer after an hour of clicks and sighs.

"Hey. What'd you do that for?"

"Because it's not good for you. There's nothing you can do about it, so just leave it be."

"But don't you want to know?"

"I want to know if Baby Yoda ever gets a lightsaber. That's what I want to know."

So Zeke reluctantly joined his mother and brother on the couch to watch TV, the laptop left closed on the kitchen table. He supposed he could try to steal Jackie's tablet, but that would require her emerging from her cocoon, which she still hadn't done. The three slices of pizza they'd saved for her were barely warm now, grease congealing in the box.

That's when his mother snuck a peek at her phone.

"Expecting a call?" Zeke prodded.

"Just checking Facebook," she said.

He shifted to steal a glance and she moved to hide it, but she wasn't fast enough. She wasn't lying at least. It *was* Facebook. More specifically it was KABAM's Facebook page, where the results of the competition were being continuously updated. Zeke didn't get to study it, but he saw enough to know he was still behind.

No. Not behind. Behind implies the possibility of catching up. Behind suggests you are playing on the same field, running on the same track. "You said it wasn't healthy to keep looking."

"You're right," Mom replied. "I'm shutting it off now." The screen went dark and she set it on the coffee table. They both stared at it for a moment before going back to watch Mando get ambushed by a posse of blaster-wielding thugs. Zeke knew how it was going to turn out; you never bet against the guy in the beskar armor.

Or the kid with the three-legged dog.

"It's only the first day," his mother whispered.

Zeke was pretty sure she was talking to herself.

When ten o'clock rolled around, Zeke followed his brother to their room, feeling spent. Their mom tucked Nate in and then

175

sat on the edge of Zeke's bed, his toes sticking out of the covers. "You can come back out to the family room if you want and turn something else on."

"I'm actually kinda tired," Zeke admitted, still staring at his toes. "Busy day."

His mother frowned. "Being great is pretty exhausting, huh?"

"Wouldn't know," he said. *Trying* to be great was exhausting, though. And watching other people be so much better was more than just exhausting—it was demoralizing. Zeke knew the odds were stacked against him at the start, but he didn't know just how stacked until tonight. He thought of Aadya's Post-it Note. Easy for her to say.

He needed his mother not to worry about it, though, so he mustered a weak smile. "No biggie," he said. "Like you said, there's always tomorrow."

"And tomorrow and tomorrow." She kissed him on the forehead. He wiped it off. "You know I love you, right?" she said.

"Pretty sure you're required to," he mumbled.

"True, but I still do," she stressed. "Completely and forever. No matter what."

Zeke raised an eyebrow. "Even if I were to fall off a three-story slide in a bizarre skateboard-related accident, severing my spine and forcing you to take care of me for all eternity?"

"Even then," she said. "Though if you try a stunt like that again, I'll kill you."

She threatened to kiss him again and Zeke blocked her with

a pillow. Mando wasn't the only one who could hide his face. She paused in the doorway. "You fixed the trash can, right? There's not, like, this giant hole in the bottom of it still?"

"It's as good as new," he said. "Well. It's good enough anyway."

"Good enough is good enough."

After she was gone, Zeke lay in bed, listening to his brother's soft snore like a kitten's purr and trying not to think about the competition, but it was no use. He wondered what the numbers looked like by this point, if Hailey had hit ten thousand votes yet. Or twenty. Or fifty. Wondered if he had even passed three hundred. Wondered how many people even knew about the contest or had any clue what it was for and what possessed them to even place their vote in the first place. What made them experts all of a sudden? He tried to imagine a world before Twitter and Instagram and YouTube. Not having your whole life on display, open to everyone's opinion. Not knowing whether total strangers liked you or laughed at you or thought you should burn in hell.

Of course, the total strangers weren't wrong. Not in this case, at least. Zeke hadn't done anything that matched what those other kids had. Nothing he did today really bettered mankind, and both grapefruit and trash-can kind had come out worse for his efforts.

One thing was made absolutely clear to him tonight, though: his family might as well kiss that money goodbye.

So long air-conditioning. So long roof shingles. So long new shoes for his mother's tired soles. This was it, his chance to fix some things. Really *fix* them, and he could already feel it slipping away.

So long Hawaii.

Beautiful, sunny, coconut-scented Hawaii.

Zeke closed his eyes and tried to picture them—those tropical isles. The glittering sand. The endless blue ocean. His father had always promised to take them all someday. Not to Hawaii, necessarily, a place he'd never been himself—hard to drive a big rig across the Pacific—but to one of the coasts, at least. East, West, didn't matter.

Also didn't happen.

Instead, Zeke was left to conjure his own mental picture. Admittedly most of it came from *Moana*, crashing waves and swaying palm trees and everyone eating pineapples picked right off the trees. For some reason when he thought about Hawaii, he imagined crabs playing the bongos. Maybe he was mixing up his Disney movies, but he could almost hear them drumming. *Bappity, bap, bap.*

No. That wasn't imaginary drumming that he heard. It was knocking. Actual knuckles softly rapping on his door. Probably his mother coming to check on him. But then he saw the slip of paper sliding underneath. He untucked himself to get a look, unfolding the scrap to find his sister's meticulously neat printing—the first note she'd slipped under his door in over three years. He read it in the glow of Nate's night-light.

My room. ASAP.

* * *

She was sitting on her bed when he slunk in, pizza box open in her lap. The clock read 12:05.

"Eating after midnight. Aren't you afraid of turning into a monster?" he asked. "Oh, wait . . ."

"Funny. Sit," she commanded.

Zeke settled into the lime-green beanbag chair in the corner, parts of him clearly still sore from impact. He would never admit it to her, but he actually didn't hate his sister's room. He liked the mix of colors, soft pink and bluish gray to go with the green. A music stand sat in one corner, propping up a black folder full of concertos and sonatas, her violin case resting underneath. Various medals and awards hung from a bulletin board on the door. Her bed was patrolled by a collection of stuffed animals, including Bruce, a stuffed moose that Dad had found in a truck stop in Montana and brought back for her—probably the only stuffy Zeke *hadn't* taken hostage over the years because he knew some things were just off-limits. Her shelves were neatly arranged, her books in alphabetical order by author to prove just how uptight she was. Her desk was tidy too—every pen, pencil, and paper clip in its proper place, accented by a few framed photos of her and her friends. She was smiling in each of them, surprisingly.

The coolest part, in his opinion, were the posters. All of cities and countries she planned to visit someday: Barcelona, San Francisco, Sydney, Taiwan. Like she'd made a bucket list and then splashed the contents of that bucket all over her walls. It would

179

take a lifetime to get to all of those places, he knew. That and winning the lottery.

"How's the pizza?" he asked.

"Still good," she said. "I mean, it would have been better four hours ago, but you take what you can get."

He thought of his grilled cheese sandwich. *Don't take too long. You don't want it to get cold.* "You could have eaten dinner with us," he said, eyeing the one piece left in the box.

"I could have. But I was still mad."

"At me?" He wasn't sure why he was even asking. At this point wasn't that a given?

"Yeah. Mostly," she said, then took a breath. "At least at first. Then I was mad at myself for getting all worked up about it. Then I got confused because I didn't really know what I was mad about to begin with."

"The cheese," Zeke guessed.

"Trust me, it wasn't the cheese. On the scale of your pranks and petty tortures, that one ranks pretty close to the bottom. It was kind of uninspired, no offense."

In his head, Zeke promised to do better.

"No, the truth was, I wasn't even angry, really. I was just . . . frustrated. Or jealous. Or some combination of all of those."

"Because I'm the world's greatest kid?" Zeke had seen the numbers. He knew how far it was from the truth, but he couldn't resist saying it out loud.

Jackie snorted. "Let's not get ahead of ourselves. But that's a part of it." She took up the last slice of pizza, contemplated it, and then tossed it back.

"Waste not, want not," Zeke hinted. Another of his mother's faves.

Jackie handed him the box. That's how he knew she wasn't *that* mad at him anymore. Otherwise, she would have thrown it at him instead.

"It's not just this stupid contest, though," Jackie continued. "I mean, I think that brought it to a head, but it's everything really. The whole situation. Our whole history." She reached for Bruce the Moose and sat him in her lap. "You remember the other day when you were making fun of me because of my math grade?"

Of all the things they'd said to each other the last few days, he didn't think the calculus jab at the breakfast table would be the one to stick, especially not after calling her a butt-crusted armpit-muncher yesterday. "It was just a joke."

"To you, maybe," Jackie said. "But not to me. Because the sucktastic truth is, you're right: I'm not great at math. And it's so aggravating, because I try, you know? I mean I *really* try. I study for hours. I watch all the videos. I ask my teachers for help. I sit next to the nerdiest kids I can find and bug them constantly to show me what they're doing, but I still don't get it sometimes. Then I come home with a B or a C, and Mom gets all peeved and says I can do better. *You can do better, Jackie, you're smarter than this.* But the truth is, I'm already doing the best I can . . . and it still doesn't matter." His sister cast her glossy eyes up to

181

her own unbroken-because-nobody-tried-to-swing-on-it ceiling fan doing its best to cool the room. "Do you see the problem? I go out of my way to be good, like, *all* the time, and it seems like nobody notices. It's just expected of me because I'm older and more responsible. Because I've *always* been good. Because I've *always* taken up the slack. But you . . . you go out of your way to be obnoxious—"

Zeke winced. "Such a strong word."

Jackie arched an eyebrow. "Believe me, I'm being *sooo* generous here," she said. "The point is, because you act the way you do all the time, when *you* do something good, it's like this big revelation. Like this holy freaking moment, and we're all supposed to bow down in awe just because you made it a whole week without being called down to the principal's office."

"Six."

"What?"

"I made it six weeks this last year," Zeke said. "Remember that stretch in October? Counting fall break it was actually seven."

"Right. Fine. We'll call it seven. And do you know how many times I was called down to the principal's office last year?"

Zeke guessed it was probably zero. He wasn't too far off.

His sister held up one finger. "And you know why? So I could pick up my perfect attendance certificate. Because that's what I do, Zeke. I show up. Every day. And maybe I'm not perfect, but I'm there. And I try. And then . . ." Jackie took a deep breath, cast her eyes back up to the ceiling again. "And then this whole competition thing comes along, and I don't know, it just threw me for a loop. I mean, I know neither of us is, like, the world's best kid or anything. But if it had to be one of us . . ."

Jackie leaned back against her wall and closed her eyes. Zeke stared at the poster of the Golden Gate Bridge behind her, one end of its rust-red span reaching into the fog. He couldn't remember the last time his sister had talked to him like this. With all of her shields down. Probably before things got too hard to talk about. He suddenly felt like he should be honest with her in return. He felt like he owed her that.

"It should have been you."

She opened her eyes, looked at him. "What?"

"You're right," he said. "I know you're too old to even enter, but between the two of us, you would have had a much better chance of winning this thing. I mean you're definitely not the greatest kid either—you're bossy and moody and *way* too obsessed with your hair. Plus you don't like rap music or *Rick and Morty* or beef jerky, which doesn't even seem possible. But at least you wouldn't have already screwed it up as bad as me."

Jackie squinted at him. "I have a perfectly healthy relationship with my hair," she said defensively, "and beef jerky is revolting. But I wouldn't say you screwed it up entirely. Yeah, you're behind in the contest—like *way* behind—but on the plus side, you've already got seven hundred likes on YouTube."

She took out her tablet—an iPad wannabe handed down from a friend—tapped and swiped and then gave it to Zeke. There he was, plummeting down the Poop Chute. And there he was a second later sprawled on the ground. Over a thousand views so far. He scrawled through the comments. *Game over, man . . . Red Bull gives you wings . . . Wendy, I can fly . . . This kid should try snowboarding . . .* Most of them were full-out snark. A few bemoaned how dangerous it was. One asked where this poor kid's parents were and why weren't they watching. *Parent,* Zeke thought to himself. *And she was at work making sure the mortgage was paid.*

His sister's tablet in hand, Zeke couldn't help himself. He typed in the address for KABAM, navigated to the contest website, and scrolled to the results.

He frowned. Hailey and Dom had just over six thousand votes each. Aadya and Kyo had well over five.

Zeke was sitting at eight hundred and fifty. More than he thought he would get, but still so far out of the running. He handed the tablet back to Jackie, who glanced at it and then set it on the pillow beside her. "That's pretty bad," he said.

Jackie nodded. "I know. I've been watching it. Watched your clip too. I made the cut, at least, though the family room lighting didn't do my complexion any favors. And I'm not sure that playground stunt did you any either. Not for the KABAM crowd at least."

"It seemed like a good idea at the time."

"Really?" Jackie prodded.

Zeke shook his head, remembering how it felt, standing at the top of the slide, looking down. "No, not really. I actually thought

184

I might pee my pants. But I had to do *something*."

Jackie nodded. "I get it. The camera makes you do funny things."

"Like put on makeup at nine o'clock in the morning."

"I wear makeup all the time."

It was Zeke's turn to give her the *really?* look.

"Yeah, okay. But at least I didn't almost crack my skull open."

You could have come, he thought. *You could have tried to talk me out of it.* Though he probably wouldn't have listened. Old habits die hard. "Did you watch the other videos?" he asked.

His sister nodded somberly.

"So then you see what I'm up against. Those guys are freaking saints. They hang out with old people voluntarily. And they give hugs to puppies. What's better than puppies?"

"Nothing," Jackie replied. "Nothing is better than puppies. These kids—they've definitely got the advantage."

"Puppies!" Zeke repeated. "With missing legs!"

Jackie heaved a sigh, then reached out and swiped the crust from Zeke's hand. He didn't put up a fight. He realized this was the longest he'd been in her room in the last couple of years—invited, at least. It was also probably the longest conversation they'd had without calling each other names. The whole thing felt not entirely dysfunctional.

His sister gnawed on her crust. "No question, these guys have found their angle. They've obviously had more time to plan. They've got resources. If you want to even stay in the running at all, we are going to have to up your game."

We? Zeke thought. Was he about to get an ally?

"These other kids are like professional do-gooders," Jackie continued. "Everything is carefully choreographed. It's like a reverse-Wonka situation."

"A reverse what?"

"Willy Wonka? *Charlie and the Chocolate Factory?*" Jackie scoffed. "Mom and Dad took turns reading it to us when you were little, don't you remember?"

Zeke shook his head. He could remember his mother reading to him but never his father. Probably because he was away so much of the time. Or because Zeke was too young for it to stick. He knew his sister remembered all kinds of things he didn't, though. She carried more of Dad than he did, down to the stuffed moose in her lap.

"Anyway, Charlie was in a competition with a bunch of other kids too, but they were all greedy, whiny, bratty punks and he was this poor, hopeful, earnest little boy—so there really was no contest. I mean, he screwed up and he *still* won because he was really only competing with himself, see? Everyone else flat-out sucked. You, on the other hand, are up against the best of the best. It's like trying to beat Mother Teresa."

I'd like to see Mother Teresa skateboard surf down the Rocket, Zeke thought. "So you're saying in this scenario I'm the whiny, bratty punk?"

"You have your days," Jackie admitted. "But no. You're not

that bad. Problem is, you're no saint either."

It was a fair point.

Jackie chewed and swallowed the last of her crust. She never talked with her mouth full. "If *you* want any chance at all of winning this thing, you need to play the game the way everyone else is playing it. You can't *just* be you. You've got to manufacture opportunities to showcase your greatness."

"I thought you said I didn't have any greatness."

"Yes . . . well . . . I guess we'll have to manufacture some of that too." Jackie scooted to the edge of the bed, eyes suddenly intense. "I don't think we can feed the world or solve the climate crisis on such short notice, but we can at least *try* to get to their level. Let me send some texts and make some calls. In the meantime, there are a couple things we can work on right now, starting with your humblebrag."

Zeke stared blankly at her. "My humble what?"

"You know when someone tells everyone how awesome they are without actually saying how awesome they are? Like if I were to say, 'Wow, this violin concerto is so tough—how did I let my music teacher convince me that I could play Prokofiev."

"What's a Prokofiev?" It sounded like the name of a gun from *Call of Duty*.

"Forget it. The thing is you have to come off as confident but not arrogant. You have to be down-to-earth but also sort of above it all. You have to be like everybody else but also better than everybody else. You have to let people know that you're great, and even let them *know* you know, but without letting them know you know, you know?"

Zeke wasn't so sure.

"You want to stand out, don't you? I'm sorry, little brother, but these are the twenties. Nice guys finish first, but only by letting everyone know how nice they are. You have to have stage presence. What are you wearing tomorrow?"

Zeke looked down at the shorts he had on, only day three on them. "These probably. And whatever T-shirt I can find."

Jackie frowned at him, then went to her dresser and started fishing around in the second drawer, the one above the one where she kept her diary—not that he should know that, or especially know that she had already described her wedding in detail on page ten. It would be a destination wedding in the Caribbean, apparently. Mom was going to walk her down the aisle, and Zeke was only invited if he was muzzled and handcuffed to his chair.

"Here," she said, handing him a black T-shirt with a band's name on it.

"Revisionist History?"

"They're a socially progressive ska band out of Oregon. They also have their own line of fair trade, sustainable, hemp-based beachwear."

That was a lot of words Zeke wasn't entirely familiar with. "And this is going to help me how?"

"Because your 'My Zombie Ate Your Mee-maw' T-shirt isn't

exactly on brand. And while we're working on your image, let's see your smile."

Zeke smiled. Jackie recoiled.

"Oh my god. Why do you always look like you're about to set something on fire?"

"What?"

"You smile like the Joker. It's creepy."

"How's this?" Zeke said, making his grin wider and showing off all of his crooked teeth.

"No. That's even worse. Now you look like Pennywise's demented little cousin. Can't you just smile normal? Like this?"

Jackie smiled at him. He had to admit, she had a nice smile. The kind that made you think of hot chocolate on a snowy day.

Their dad used to smile like that. At least he did in all of the pictures they had.

Zeke fixed that image—the one of his father—in his head and tried again. Jackie nodded. "Okay. Better. Maybe a little on the sad side, but that's okay. It makes you look thoughtful. Try to smile like that when the camera is on you. Also, maybe stop putting holes in things. It gives the wrong impression. You want to be *con*structive, not *de*structive."

She meant the trash can. Probably. Assuming she was talking just about today, at least. Zeke gave her a questioning look. "So does this mean that you think I can still win?"

Jackie hesitated. "I know what you want me to say, Zeke. And I want to say it. I do. But at this point, I'm not even sure that an endorsement from Malala could make that happen."

Zeke frowned. That's what he thought. Of the three of them, he knew Jackie would be the first to be honest with him. And the last to believe in him.

"On the other hand," she added, her tone tilting up a notch. "You *are* trying. Even I can see that. And I, for one, wouldn't mind having a brother who's not a total demon spawn for a couple more days. Not to mention, we kinda need this. *Mom* needs this."

Jackie looked toward her door and the dark hallway that lay beyond, leading to the sofa where, most likely, their mother had fallen asleep in her work clothes.

He recalled Mrs. Crawford: *Do you think you can do that, Zeke?*

Yes. Maybe. He wasn't sure. But it would at least be easier with Jackie in his corner, rather than on the other side of the ring taking jabs at him. "So you're going to help me, then?" he asked, still trying to wrap his head around this turn of events.

Jackie shrugged. "So long as you promise not to do anything too Zekey." She stood up and started pushing him toward the door. "Now, get out of my room. It's late, and you're getting your stink on everything."

"But what about tomorrow?" he wondered. He still had no idea how he was going to be great.

"I told you, let me make some calls. You just work on that smile."

Zeke gave her his serial-killer-clown grin again. On purpose this time. Menacing as can be.

Jackie shuddered. "You're such a freak," she said, and gently closed the door in his face.

Back in his bed, Zeke did as he was told, working his mouth into various smiley shapes, though without a mirror, it was impossible to tell if they were more beneficent saint or deranged lunatic. Probably somewhere in between. Smiling just came naturally to some people, he guessed.

He tried to remember the last time he saw his mother smile. Like, really smile. Not a sarcastic smirk or a forced expression pinched with politeness but a full-out, joy-fueled grin. The kind Nate got when that first can of soda did pinwheels in the street, spewing foam like a geyser, or the ones captured in the photos of Jackie and her friends. A genuine smile with no strings attached.

Come to think of it, he couldn't remember the last time he'd heard his mother laugh either. She'd chuckle at the shows they watched, offer an amused grunt at Nate's antics or one of Zeke's jokes. But to laugh until her belly ached? Until her eyes squeezed tears and her shoulders shook and she ran out of breath? It felt like forever. Not since Dad was around. He was the only one who got his mother to laugh like that. To laugh until it hurt.

We kinda need this.

There was no kinda about it.

Zeke grabbed his flashlight and reached underneath his bed for the treasure buried underneath.

Greetings from Milwaukee, birthplace of the modern typewriter, if a typewriter can be considered modern anymore. This place is famous for its beer, of course—I mean, they named their baseball team the Brewers. Also President Teddy Roosevelt was shot here before giving a speech. The bullet lodged in his chest, but instead of going to the hospital, he gave the speech anyway. Talk about guts. Just goes to show—no matter how badly the odds are stacked against you, you don't give up.

Seeing the sailboats on the lake reminds me that we all need some sand and sun pronto. Start thinking about where you want to go. Galveston. The Carolinas. The Jersey Shore. It's all good. There's nothing like standing on the edge of the water and looking out over the horizon. It makes you believe that things can last forever.

Can't wait to see you.

Love, Dad

P.S. Why can't sailors recite the whole alphabet? They always get lost at C.

Here Kitty, Kitty

The next morning, Zeke knocked on Jackie's door, desperate to know what miracles she'd conjured in the middle of the night.

He'd stayed awake until well past midnight himself, flipping through memories and racking his brain for ways to be great, but inspiration eluded him. Ultimately, he drifted off, a postcard in hand, slipping into a dream where he was on a sailboat skimming across Lake Michigan, the sun at his back, the wind tousling his hair.

And Teddy Roosevelt at the helm.

The former president had sea-foam in his mustache and a maniacal look in his eye, laughing with abandon as the waves crashed. A squall arose, winds ripping at the sails, the churning, frothing sea threatening to capsize their little ship, pulling them into the abyss, but Teddy stayed firm at the wheel. *When you're at the end of your rope*, dream Teddy said, *just tie a knot and hold on tight.*

Zeke woke in a panic, quickly changed into his new socially progressive T-shirt, and crossed the hall.

Except Jackie wasn't answering his knock. And Logan's van was already pulled up to the curb. Zeke gave up on trying to summon his sister and went into the kitchen to find his mother finishing her coffee and Logan with his camera case in one hand and a basketball in the other. He handed the ball to Nate, who was munching through a second frozen waffle.

"Here you go, King James."

Nate beamed back at the cameraman, holding the ball like it was made of solid gold. "Seriously? For me?"

Logan nodded. "Passed a garage sale on my way in this morning and remembered the grapefruit. Figured your mom would rather you eat your food than play with it."

"A girl can only dream," Mom muttered.

Nate abandoned his second breakfast and started dribbling across the linoleum, grinning like it was Christmas morning. *Thunk, thunk, thunk.*

"That's nice and all, but we don't have a hoop, remember?" Zeke said. The basketball didn't look like it would fit through the trash can, and even if it did, he was under strict instructions not to put holes in things for the foreseeable future.

"Sure. But I noticed they had a court at that park yesterday. I figured maybe you guys could play there."

Nate continued to pound up and down the house, occasionally kicking the ball instead of dribbling it. Still, didn't take much to make that kid happy.

"That's sweet of you," their mom echoed. "You *really* didn't have to." She watched as her youngest nearly put the basketball through the kitchen window before chasing it down the hall.

"Life can't always be about have-tos, Ms. Stahls. You gotta sprinkle some want-tos in there, or the have-tos will just drag you down."

It sounded a little like something Dad would say.

Mom stood by the door for a moment in her dark blue business suit, keys in one hand, empty coffee cup in the other, staring at the cameraman as if she suddenly couldn't remember who he was or why he was here in her kitchen. Then she snapped out of it and looked at the clock on the stove. "Oh jeez. Gotta run. Logan, there's coffee in the pot. Help yourself." She blew Zeke a kiss across the room. "Remember: indoor dodgeball has been permanently canceled," she warned. "And no more skate surfing or whatever you call it. And wake your sister up. I don't pay her to sleep. Love you. Be *good*."

Zeke heard the front door slam closed, leaving him and Logan alone in the kitchen. The cameraman, dressed in his standard white company polo, pointed to Zeke's chest. "Revisionist History?"

"They're a band out of Oregon that my sister likes. They're trying to save the world by making swimsuits out of seaweed or something. She thought I should wear it."

Logan shrugged. "The world can always use more saving. Coffee cups?"

Zeke pointed out the cabinet. Logan fished around and pulled out the World's Greatest Mom mug. "We had one of these growing up," he said with a smile. He set it back and fetched another. Nate whipped into the kitchen and wrapped both arms around the cameraman's legs before dribbling away again. Zeke had never seen his brother act this way with a stranger before, though he supposed Logan was getting less strange by the minute. "So how did it go last night?" Logan asked as he filled his cup.

Zeke assumed he meant the video. The votes. The first round of competition. The camera wasn't on yet, so there was no reason to fake a smile, demonic or otherwise. "I'm sure you already know."

Logan nodded. "I know that a thousand people clicking a button don't get to decide what a person's worth."

"Oh yeah?" Zeke snorted. "What world do *you* live in?"

Logan took a sip of his coffee. "Touché."

He set his cup on the counter and opened up his case. Just looking at the camera, Zeke started to itch. Without it, Logan was kind of cool, laid-back, easy to talk to, but the moment he pressed record, it felt like the whole dynamic changed. Maybe it's because those peaceful green eyes weren't looking at Zeke straight on anymore; they were looking through a lens, and somehow that distorted everything, added a layer between them. It made Zeke feel like he was being watched, of course, but that wasn't the same as being seen.

"I mean, I can't blame 'em, I guess," Zeke said. "Like who's *not* going to vote for the kid with all the puppies?"

"Actually I'm allergic to dogs," Logan admitted. "And I've never been good at origami."

He offered a sly wink, and Zeke felt everything in the room lighten a little.

He was about to ask the cameraman what he really thought of the other videos when Jackie burst into the kitchen, her phone to her ear. She had already ditched her pj's for ragged cutoffs and short sleeves, and her hair was banded into a sloppy bun. Still, even without dressing up, it felt like she commanded the attention of the room.

"What? You're kidding? How did that happen? Yeah. Yeah. I got it. Okay. Just chill, all right? We'll be right over." She tapped her phone, flipped her hair, and sighed dramatically. "Oh, hey, Logan. You filming already?"

"Just starting," he said, hefting the camera to his shoulder.

"Well, I'm not sure you want to yet," Jackie said. "Turns out we've got a neighborhood emergency." She held up her phone. "That was Angela. Her stupid cat is stuck up in her stupid tree and won't come down and she's *totally* freaking out. Angela. Not the cat. Well, probably the cat too."

Angela was Jackie's best friend for the last six years. They did everything together, which was fine with Zeke because she was one of the few friends of his sisters who didn't look at him like he was some kind of infectious swamp monster. She and Jackie were planning to apply to all of the same colleges, hoping to room together if the stars aligned—and the scholarships were overflowing. Angela also brought fresh-baked cookies for the whole family whenever she came over, which made her a favorite in Nate's book as well.

"I told her not to bother with 9-1-1 just yet. That help was on the way," Jackie continued.

Zeke stared at his sister, teeth grinding through his frustration. What about the contest? After everything she'd said last night, after all that *we* stuff, she was just going to abandon him to go help her friend with her *cat*?

Jackie stared right back at him, clearly waiting for something.

Zeke cocked his head like *what?*

Jackie raised an eyebrow like *duh.*

He shook his head. She rolled her eyes.

"Help *is* on the way, yes?" she repeated.

Oh. Right. This was the plan. Zeke pointed to himself. "*My* help."

"I mean, you *are* pretty good at climbing trees," Jackie prompted.

It was true. There were very few trees in their neighborhood that Zeke *hadn't* shimmied up, often with a squirt gun in hand, ready to super-soak unsuspecting passersby. But he still wasn't sure. This was her grand gesture? Rescuing Angela's cat? Not exactly saving the world.

Then again, didn't Superman do this very same thing in one of his movies? Spider-Man too? Even Batman probably saved Cat-woman at some point, which was pretty close. Maybe this *was* just the thing he needed. Let Dom pick up poop from his three-legged pooch. Zeke was about to save a poor animal's *life*.

Jackie turned to Logan. "You're welcome to come with."

It was a not-so-subtle hint. *Some serious greatness is about to go down, and you won't want to miss it.*

Logan took the last swallow from his mug and pointed to the door.

Angela Borman lived only ten blocks away. Zeke guessed that was one of the reasons she and his sister had become friends to begin with. That, and Angela had a hot tub in her backyard. Zeke was admittedly envious. None of *his* friends came with a built-in Jacuzzi. Not that the hot tub currently held any appeal; it was predicted to hit ninety again today. If only his brother *had* developed frost breath.

Despite being only a fifteen-minute walk, Jackie insisted on taking her car, a white Ford hatchback she called Snoopy. It was little more than an engine, four wheels, and two doors, but like the family van, it had air-conditioning, and that was reason enough. Zeke fully expected the cameraman to follow in his van, but Logan surprised them all by squeezing into the passenger's side, the camera smooshing his lap, the top of his head brushing the roof. Jackie turned the key three times, the motor protesting.

Rawr-rawr-rawr-rawr-rawr.

"It does this sometimes," she explained. "It's old. But it was all I could afford."

"You make the best with what you got," Logan said.

"That's what I keep telling myself." After two more tries, the engine coughed to life. Jackie patted its dashboard. "Good boy." She checked her face in her mirror like she always did, her hand brushing against the purple rabbit's foot hanging there next to the Ocean Breeze–scented air freshener. She'd had that rabbit's foot longer than she'd had the car. Zeke knew this because he had one too, though his was dyed blue. Their father had bought them at a truck stop on his way home from Colorado or Wyoming or Montana—somewhere way west of the Mississippi.

Zeke had lost his several months ago. Jackie was always better at holding on to things.

Despite running the AC full blast, Snoopy had barely cooled down by the time they pulled into the Bormans' driveway. Angela was waiting for them in the backyard, standing beside a large maple tree. The shade looked inviting; the cat she pointed up to did not.

"Thank goodness you're here!" she said, perhaps channeling her inner Jimmy Olsen. "Thin Mint's been up there for an hour."

The all-black cat stared down at them from twenty-five feet up with her shrewd green eyes.

"That's a big kitty," Nate said, taking in the enormous

200

fuzzball balanced precariously on a branch, belly draping off both sides like saddlebags.

"A lot of that is fur," Angela said. "She's puffed up because she's scared." Thin Mint let out a pathetic meow in confirmation.

"How did she even get up there?" Jackie asked.

"You don't want to know," Angela muttered, soft enough that Logan's camera couldn't pick it up. "I mean, she just climbed up all on her own, I guess," she added louder. "Probably chasing a squirrel or something."

"Looks like she *ate* the squirrel," Zeke said. Thin Mint did not look like a climber. She looked like a sit-arounder.

"Seriously?" Angela said. "Did you guys come here just to body-shame my cat? Or did you come to help?"

Again, it took a hard stare from his sister before Zeke realized this was his cue. "Right. Yeah. Of course. I've got this." He made sure the camera was focused squarely on him, then added, "I'm not going to let your precious Thin Mint down. I mean, I will . . . let her down . . . but gently."

I hope.

Zeke looked up at the maple tree, easily the most scalable of the several that dotted Angela's backyard. Had it been any of the others, Zeke would have struggled to even get started, but this tree was built for climbing.

Almost as if it had been picked on purpose.

Was this what his sister meant by manufacturing moments

of greatness? Had Angela stuck her own cat up in this tree? And if so, *how*? Did she chase her? Did she use a ladder? Did she just grab her with both hands and heave, flinging what looked to be a hundred pounds of cat into the air, hoping it stuck to a branch on the way down?

Also, was it actually anything special, rescuing a cat from a tree if you were the reason the cat was stuck there to begin with? Was that being great, or was that just fixing your own mistakes?

Then again, there was something to be said for doing just that.

"Here, you're going to want these." Angela handed Zeke a pair of gardening gloves with thick leather pads. "She's not declawed. Obviously."

As he took the gloves, Zeke got a look at Angela's inner arms. He could see fresh scratch marks running along them. If that was the price for getting the cat *up* in the tree, what would be the price for getting her *down*? Not that it mattered—there was no backing out now. With Logan's camera trained on him, Zeke was just as stuck in this scenario as poor Thin Mint. "Hold on, kitty. I'm coming to rescue you."

"Be careful," Jackie said, then she stepped a little closer and whispered in Zeke's ear, "Seriously, that cat bit me once. She might have been playing, but blood was definitely drawn."

"And you are just telling me this *now*?" Zeke hissed. "Isn't there some other way I can be great?"

"This was the best I could do on such short notice," she hissed back. "You got any better ideas, go with them. If not, camera's rolling."

Zeke didn't have any better ideas. And the gloves did give off a kind of superhero vibe.

Jackie stepped back, leaving Zeke all alone in the center of the shot. *What's the worst that could happen? The cat claws out my eyes and I fall and break both of my legs?*

He really needed to stop asking that question.

Zeke took a deep breath. "Ten. Thousand. Dollars," he muttered as he grabbed the lowest branch and struggled upward. It had been a hot minute since he'd done a pull-up, not since the fitness test in gym, and he grunted with the effort, finally clambering onto the branch and getting his feet beneath him.

Thin Mint produced another desperate, drawn-out *meeeerooww.* He took it to mean *my hero, you've come at last.* Though it probably meant *get any closer and I will shred you.* Zeke kept climbing regardless. Hand over hand, ginger steps. Eight feet off the ground now, carefully picking his way, making sure the branches could hold his weight, all too conscious of a camera looking up at him and a frightened feline looking down.

"Avengers assemble!" Nate cheered from below. As if there wasn't enough pressure already, there was also his little brother *literally* looking up to him for the second time in two days.

"Zeke is *so* brave," he heard Angela say extra loud. Zeke was pretty sure that line was written into the script as well, that his sister and her best friend had planned this whole thing last night after he'd gone to bed. He wondered what was in it for Angela. Maybe just the chance to get on camera? That *was* a cute outfit she was wearing. Or maybe Jackie had promised her a nice souvenir from Hawaii if they won. A handcrafted ukulele, perhaps. Some Kona coffee beans.

Fifteen feet up. Getting close. The black bundle of floof was almost at eye level now. Zeke was a good climber, and the ascent had been easier than expected, but looking at the feline in distress it hit him: How on earth was he going to get back *down*?

Down was always more difficult by default, as Thin Mint could attest to. But down while carrying a cat the size of a watermelon? A cat with all of her claws and an established history of blood-soaked violence? Thin Mint was still a good six feet away, eyeing Zeke suspiciously, no doubt debating whether to go for the face or the throat.

"Be gentle!" Angela called up, sounding a little desperate herself, perhaps starting to regret her part in all of this. Zeke wasn't sure whether she was talking to him or the cat.

"Don't worry," he called down. "Everything's under control."

Nothing was under control. The branch beneath his feet was narrower than he would have liked, and he could feel it bending under his weight. Thin Mint was within arm's reach at least, though Zeke hadn't tried grabbing her. He wanted to have a conversation first, make sure they were on the same page.

"Okay, cat, here's how this is going to go. I'm going to reach out and grab you and tuck you under my arm and you are going to be very still and not bite or scratch or pee on me, got it? Then we are slowly going to climb back down. No blood needs to be shed this day." He remembered Angela's pinstriped arms. *At least, no* more *blood.*

The cat did not look like she was of a mind to agree to these terms. She gave him a hiss, showing off those sharp, little teeth.

"No . . . *no,* kitty," Zeke said. "That is *not* the right attitude. I'm only here to help."

Thin Mint blinked once and the fangs retreated. Zeke took that as his cue to proceed. He steadied himself and took a deep breath. Down below, Jackie started to offer a play-by-play for the sake of the viewers who would be watching later tonight, ready to cast their vote.

"Zeke Stahls is about to pull off the most daring rescue in neighborhood history. Poor Thin Mint is just barely clinging to that branch. She looks terrified. He appears close enough to grab her. He resets his balance. Leans over, reaches out, and . . ."

Zeke hoped that the cat would see his outstretched hand as one of benevolence, attached to the arm of a hero who meant her no harm.

She saw it as a bridge.

A bridge that she quickly scrambled across to find his shoulder, which, apparently looked like as good a place as any to drop anchor, because that's where she promptly buried her claws.

A dozen tiny little needles hooked into Zeke's flesh, Thin Mint clinging to his shoulder with her front paws and scrabbling against his chest with the back ones, those rearfoot razors leaving scratches even through his sister's borrowed shirt.

"Ow ow ow ow ow ow ow."

"Meeerrreoooowowow!" Thin Mint echoed.

With his left hand, Zeke clamped down on the big black fuzzy monster Velcroed to his chest, holding her as tight as possible, hoping to calm her with his touch, but her claws somehow just dug in even deeper. It felt like someone massaging his shoulder with a cactus.

"Don't fall!" Jackie called up.

"And don't you *dare* drop her!" Angela commanded.

Easy for you to say, Zeke thought to himself. They didn't have a hissing, squirming, needle-toed hairy ball of pain trying to bleed them to death. Somehow Zeke managed to maneuver down to the next-lower branch, using only one hand, the other one still holding Thin Mint against him, the cat emitting a low growl that sounded like a chainsaw idling. An actual chainsaw would probably be less dangerous.

Feet dangling, searching for purchase on another branch, toes scraping, settling, right hand grasping, little brother gasping, big hunk o' cat clawing, clinging, growling, yowling as Zeke fumbled his way back down. Thin Mint readjusted her position, making a brand-new set of holes in Jackie's shirt, sinking through to the skin underneath.

"You're almost there!"

Almost there. Zeke chanced a glance at the camera, imagining the audience who would later marvel at his backyard heroics. He took a deep breath in relief, slightly loosening his hold.

Thin Mint took that as a sign. Seeing that she was finally within leaping distance of the welcoming grass, she used Zeke's chest as a springboard, getting one final stab in before making the jump. The sudden pain caused Zeke to slip from the branch that held him.

The cat, of course, landed on her feet.

Zeke did not.

He didn't land at all, in fact. His feet slid out from underneath him and he sprawled, flailed, and fell, leaves brushing his face, twigs snapping beneath him, headed groundward, belly first.

And then suddenly, serendipitously, he was caught. A knob jutting out of the very lowest branch had somehow snagged his shorts in the back, almost like a clawed hand taking hold at the last possible second, leaving him suspended like a piñata.

The camera followed Thin Mint for a moment, darting—or at least ambling quickly—back into the house, Angela hurrying after her to make sure she was okay. Then it swiveled back to Zeke, helplessly hanging, arm bloodied, a crown of leaves in his hair.

Zeke offered up an awkward smile. The smile of a deranged killer clown dangling from a tree by his shorts.

Wondering if being great always had to hurt so much.

* * *

It took two of them to get Zeke free, Logan setting down his camera to offer his assistance, letting Zeke climb on his back while Jackie unfastened his shorts from the branch. Zeke was glad the camera was off. It was embarrassing enough that it had captured his graceless fall—seeing the rescuer being rescued would only add insult to injury.

And there were definitely injuries, though they were all minor. Jackie directed him to Angela's bathroom to clean up the scratches on his arms and his chest. He'd certainly had worse, though combined with the scrapes from yesterday's wipeout at the park, it was becoming apparent what toll this competition would take on him.

At this rate I'll be dead by Thursday, he thought. But at least he'd saved the cat. Zeke couldn't think of the last time he'd done something so plainly nice for someone not named Nate.

That, he realized, could be part of the problem. How much of what he'd just done was for Angela and her cat and how much was done for Logan and his camera and the contest? The little pulse of pride that had been swelling inside of him deflated just a bit. He caught his reflection in the bathroom mirror. He certainly didn't look like much of a hero. Just a scrawny, gray-eyed, twelve-year-old boy with slightly sunburned cheeks and scratched-up arms. Not to mention he was now the only kid he knew who'd ever been given a wedgie by a tree. He could only imagine what he looked like, hanging there, arms and legs extended. It reminded him of how his father used to grab him by the back of his shirt and his waistband when he was little, swooping him up from behind and then spinning him around like a carousel. It was fun when he did it. It would always cause his underwear to ride up but was worth it for the chance to fly.

Zeke shook the memory away, then dislodged a leaf from his hair.

By the time he emerged from tending his wounds, everyone was huddled by the uninviting hot tub waiting for him. Logan's camera was poised for his return and Angela had corralled Thin Mint and was cradling her like a furry infant. She stuck Thin Mint's face right in Zeke's so that their noses were touching. The cat looked like she wanted to have him for lunch.

"Minty has something she wants to say to you, don't you, Minty?" The cat stared at Zeke grumpily while Angela dropped her voice a whole octave. "Thank you, Zeke. Thank you for saving me from that terrible tree."

Thin Mint growled softly. The kitty equivalent of rolling one's eyes. Zeke patted her gently on the head.

"It was nothing," he said, wondering if that counted as a humblebrag, then stole a quick glance at the camera and added, "It's what anyone would do." Perfect. Confident but not cocky. Approachable but also above it all.

A look passed between Jackie and her best friend. A slight nod from Zeke's sister followed by a headshake from Angela. A hard stare. A harder stare back. Jackie cleared her throat. Angela frowned and sighed. She turned to Zeke.

"Also I . . . um . . . want to give you this," she said, "for being so courageous."

Then, with the camera rolling, she kissed him. Just on the cheek. A quick and dry, blink-and-you'll-miss-it sort of thing. And the blood that wasn't bubbling up from the scratches on Zeke's arm suddenly rushed to his head, making him even dizzier than before.

Put In One's Place

The kiss (such that it was) would have likely made a perfect coda to Zeke's day-two clip, but it turned out Jackie's plan for manufacturing greatness didn't stop with saving Thin Mint from the clutches of an evil maple tree. After a prolonged off-camera discussion between Angela and Jackie, the content of which Zeke could only guess, the three Stahlses plus one cameraman squished back into Snoopy and rumbled off.

In the opposite direction of their house.

"Where are we going now?"

"Have to run by the store real quick," Jackie replied. "We're out of Popsicles, and *somebody* used up all the soda."

Logan glanced behind him. The cameraman had only been with them a couple of days, but he already knew which body *somebody* referred to. "We were doing science experiments," Zeke explained. Nate made a fizzy explosion sound with his mouth, getting spit all over the car window.

"Is it okay if we make a quick stop?" Jackie asked Logan.

The cameraman shrugged. "If it's good with Zeke."

Zeke nodded. He could tell his sister was up to something. Jackie never took them with her to the store if she could help it. She used those jaunts as an excuse to escape, some brother-free "me time" wandering up and down the aisles, no doubt dreaming of her life a year from now, in college somewhere miles and miles away—that is, if she could get her math grade up and score enough free cash to help pay for it.

Which meant this trip to the grocer had to be part of her scheme somehow. Though how she expected Zeke to reveal his true greatness at a Kroger was beyond him. Maybe she had planted an old lady there who needed help carrying her bags to the car. Better yet, maybe she'd staged a robbery ahead of time and Zeke was about to stop it. *That* would be cool.

Jackie nudged the volume on the radio, just in time for a news update. A somber voice relayed details of a shooting in Michigan, growing wildfires in Nevada, missile strikes in Eastern Europe. All stories Zeke had heard a hundred times before, and his heart sank a little. *This is what Notts was talking about*, he thought.

The radio broadcast said nothing about a fat black cat rescued from a tree. In the grand scheme of things, his little act of heroism simply didn't matter.

Zeke stared out the window at all the passing billboards

advertising fast food and prescription drugs and wondered how it was all supposed to balance out, or if it ever could. Was it even possible to do enough good in the world to cancel all the bad? Was Notts right, and you just didn't ever *hear* about the good things happening? Maybe the good stuff just didn't pack the same punch. It was the terrible and tragic stuff that stuck with you.

"Could you put on some music instead?" he asked.

Jackie changed the station and found some Cardi B.

Two songs later, she pulled into the parking lot and put her plan into motion. It wasn't crowded, there were dozens of available spaces, yet she managed to pick one with a shopping cart barring her way and proceeded to smack right into it with Snoopy's black-bumpered nose. It rolled a foot or so but was still taking up a third of the space. "Ugh," she groaned. "Why can't people just put their carts back when they're done?"

"So frustrating," Logan agreed.

Zeke waited for her to throw Snoops in reverse and choose one of the spots that wasn't blocked by a cart, but she did no such thing. Snoopy rattled. Jackie idled. Logan coughed. Nate asked, "Are we there yet?"

Jackie caught Zeke's eye in the rearview mirror, right above the rabbit's foot.

"Let me guess: You want me to move it?" he asked.

"Would you?" she returned a little too sweetly.

Reluctantly, Zeke unbuckled and Jackie leaned her seat forward so he could squeeze out. He grabbed the misplaced cart and torpedoed it into the nearby corral, relishing just a little the sound of it crashing into the back of the next one in line. Zeke turned to see Logan retrieving his camera from the now-parked Snoopy, not quite in time to catch this minor act of kindness.

"See? Not like it's that hard," Jackie said, getting out of the car as well. She gestured around her. "And yet just look at this place."

Zeke looked around. His sister was right. It was the Wild West of grocery store parking lots, with rogue carts loitering wherever their pushers had abandoned them. Zeke just caught Jackie's coy smile.

One cart was a minor act of kindness. But thirty carts . . . well, that was just thirty minor acts of kindness, but they added up. His sister was a genius. She'd set him up again. A hanging curveball. Zeke only had to swing.

"You know what?" he called. "You guys go ahead. I'm going to stay out here and put the rest of these back, I think."

"Really?" Jackie asked. "*That* is a great idea."

"I know. I just thought of it." Zeke smirked at her. She glowered back. *Don't push it*, her look said. *Our alliance is fragile.*

Nate naturally wanted to stay and help round up the loose carts with Zeke, but Jackie bribed him with the promise of a candy bar of his choice if he came into the store with her instead. The two of them disappeared hand in hand, leaving Zeke to his next manufactured moment of greatness.

He waited to make sure Logan was filming, then he started

with the carts closest to him. As he pushed, Zeke narrated for those watching, in much the same way he'd seen the other contestants doing yesterday.

"It's not *that* big of a deal, I guess," Zeke said. "But it is frustrating how many people don't bother or don't care. What is it, like, five seconds out of your day? And yet we've all watched someone just leave their cart right in the middle of the road, blocking spaces, making a mess for someone *else* to deal with."

He briefly pictured the dirty dishes he'd left stacked in the sink that morning ready to greet his mother when she got home, then pushed the thought out of his head.

"If you ask me that's what's wrong with the world today. Everybody assumes someone else will come along and fix the problem, whatever it is. Nobody takes responsibility."

He pictured the pile of dirty laundry in his hamper, falling out of his hamper, scattered around his hamper, shoved under his bed. How three days from now it would all be neatly folded and smelling like a springtime breeze, waiting in a basket by his door, as if by magic. He pushed that thought out of his head too.

"And yet, if everybody just put their own cart back, if they just did what they should, then the world would be a better place."

Oh yeah. Gordon Notts was going to eat this up. Still, Zeke wondered if maybe he was spreading it on a little too thick. He decided to lighten the tone.

"Besides, being responsible doesn't mean you can't have any fun," he said, and hopped on the back of the cart he'd snagged and gave it a kick, riding it toward its pen.

He could remember Jackie doing the same thing with him when he was younger—Zeke riding inside the cart with his hands on an imaginary steering wheel like a NASCAR driver, Jackie perched behind, providing all the momentum, even making engine sounds to drown out the shouting of their mother telling them to slow down and watch for real cars. Sometimes the cart would tilt back and they'd pop a wheelie, Jackie pushing down with all her weight. Other times she'd lose control and they'd smack into the curb, but even that was worth the ride.

She used to be a lot more fun, his sister.

Zeke wondered who showed *her* how to ride on the backs of shopping carts. It wouldn't have been their mother—she worried too much. It could have been one of her friends, of course. Or maybe she just figured it out on her own.

On the other hand, this seemed exactly like something Dad would do.

With a satisfying clash of metal on metal, another wayward cart was wrangled. Logan was still right behind him, getting it all on tape. Zeke scanned the lot for more to be corralled when he caught something. An actual crime in progress.

Zeke pointed to the transgressor—midforties, sporting sunglasses and a Thin-Minty paunch, pink cheeks, and a buzz cut, practically lifting up his empty shopping cart to stow it on the grassy curb beside his car. The cart corral was only six parking spots away—Zeke counted. It looked like more effort to *not* put it where it belonged. Logan trained his camera on the perpetrator for a moment, then focused back on Zeke.

"This is exactly what I'm talking about." Zeke was on his high horse now, as his mother would say, and would not be dragged off. He watched the man climb into his red pickup, engine starting. He would wait for the villain to leave and then he would put the cart back where it belonged like he had all the others.

But as he watched the man buckle up, something inside of Zeke started to wriggle. Sure, he *could* put the man's cart back for him. He *could* clean up this mess. But would that really change anything? Wasn't this how it all started? Today it's shopping carts. Tomorrow it's littering. By the end of the week that man's company could be dumping toxic waste into the rivers, killing the fish and polluting the drinking water, and all because he thought he could get away with it. And why not? After all nobody ever stopped him.

Until now, that is.

The World's Greatest Kid wouldn't let that happen. Hailey, Kyo, Dom, Aadya—they wouldn't stand aside and let this guy drive off without doing *something*. Even though it would be easier, so much easier, to just let it go.

Zeke stole a quick glance at the camera. Logan looked up and flashed him a questioning look—an *are you really thinking what I think you're thinking* kind of look.

I'm totally thinking what you think I'm thinking, Zeke thought. He took a deep, determined breath and then jogged over to the curb where the abandoned cart sat, muscling it down, even though a voice in his head begged him to leave it there until the man was gone. *This could end badly. Your mother wouldn't approve.* And yet he did it anyway, steering the cart so that it sat right in the middle of the row.

Directly in the path of the perpetrator.

Zeke let go of the cart and stood beside it, facing the truck, which had stopped less than ten feet away. He glanced behind him to see that Logan had come several steps closer. The man in the truck waited for a moment, probably expecting Zeke to move. Instead he shoved his hands into his pockets, a clear indication that he had no such intention.

It was a cart fight at the Kroger corral.

The man honked once, the bleating horn even scarier than a fat cat's hiss. Zeke jumped, his heart thumping hard, but he still didn't move the cart out of the way. *This man is going to run you over. You're about to be the World's* Flattest *Kid,* he told himself, but still he kept his feet planted.

The man in the truck rolled down his window, stuck out one sun-reddened arm in exasperation. "Excuse me, you mind moving your cart so I can get by?" His tone was less than friendly, just barely in the area of forced polite.

Yes, Zeke thought to himself. *Just move it. That would be the smart thing. Hard to spend ten thousand dollars when you've been turned into a hood ornament.* But this wasn't about the ten thousand dollars or the trip to Hawaii. At least it wasn't about *just* that. This was about that feeling in his chest. A sudden itch that he'd seldom felt the urge to scratch before.

"You mean *your* cart?" Zeke said.

"Excuse me?"

"This is *your* cart. *You're* the one who didn't put it back where it belonged."

Through the windshield Zeke could see the look on the man's face. He knew exasperation when he saw it. The driver motioned with his hand. "Okay. Fine. Will you please move *my* cart so I can get by?"

He said please, Zeke told himself. *He asked nicely. That's enough, isn't it?* But even as he thought this, a counterthought occurred—that sometimes being great was about *not* giving in. It was about refusing to do what you're told or even politely asked. If Zeke moved now, then it would be no different than if he had just waited for the man to drive away. If he moved now, he lost.

This is what his mother must have meant when she used the phrase *principle of the thing.*

Zeke felt his hands clamming up. Sweat hung from the tip of his nose. Logan was standing less than ten feet away now. The driver laid on the horn again.

"Move the damn cart!"

No more pleasantries; we were on to cursing now. Zeke's legs Jell-Oed beneath him, but he locked his knees and kept his eyes fixed on the driver. "The corral's right there," he yelled back. "Move it yourself."

Did that really just come out of his mouth?

The man put the truck into park and then threw open the door, shaking his head as he stepped out, slamming it shut behind him. The sound rattled Zeke's spine. He instinctively retreated one step, then two, as the man came forward with angry strides, hands already in fists. Out of the corner of his eye, Zeke saw the camera drop to its operator's side, no longer recording. Logan took two steps of his own toward them when a voice suddenly stopped everyone in their tracks.

"You!"

The driver froze only a few feet away. Zeke turned to see his sister stomping through the parking lot with Nate scrambling behind, a grocery bag swinging in each hand and cold blue fire in her eyes. "Yeah you. What the hell do you think you're doing? Get away from my little brother!" she hollered. Her nostrils flared. Zeke had seen her angry a thousand times—so much more in the last couple of years. But he had never seen her quite like this. He could practically see the heat coming off of her in waves.

The man put up his hands. "Whoa. Hang on now. I was just asking him to move this cart is all."

Zeke noticed Logan was right behind him now, and Jackie right beside. Even Nate had caught up, wedging himself between his siblings. The man looked from Logan to Jackie. No doubt the cameraman looked like he could bust through a brick wall like a bulldozer, but Zeke was pretty sure it was his sister the man was most afraid of.

"No. No way. You do *not* get out of your car and threaten my brother like that, understand? He's just a kid."

Zeke stole a glance at his sister, but she didn't return it—she was boring holes straight through the sunglasses and into the skull of the man confronting her. He looked like he wanted to say something else, to fire back, but he was clearly outgunned here. Even Nate had his arms crossed in defiance.

"Whatever," he mumbled. "You people are all crazy." The man dismissed them with a wave of one hand, then turned to get back into his truck, probably with the intention of throwing it in reverse and backing his way out of the parking lot.

But he wasn't getting away that easily.

Jackie cleared her throat. Or maybe it was a growl. "Aren't you forgetting something?" She shoved the cart in his direction. It rolled to a stop a foot from the truck's bumper.

Zeke held his breath, certain that he—that they—had pushed it too far. That fists were about to fly. But then the man jerked the cart toward him, shaking his head as he slammed it into the corral. Only then did Zeke step aside, the others following. The man climbed back into his pickup with a scowl.

It was over.

Better still, they'd won.

Zeke didn't miss the middle finger pressed to the window as the truck screamed out of the lot and onto the road, though.

He turned to Logan. "You seriously stopped recording? Are you kidding me? That was so awesome!" The words spilled out in a rush. "He was like, *no way I'm putting back that cart*, and I was like, *just do it loser*, and he was like, *make me*, and then Jackie came storming out of the store with that look on her face . . . exactly, that's the one, and . . ."

He stopped. Because that angry look wasn't being leveled at the man who was long gone. His sister's eyes were fixed on Zeke this time. The grocery bags shook in her hands. Her whole body seemed to be vibrating in fact.

"Do you think you could stay out of trouble for, like, five minutes?" she snapped. "Do you think that's at *all* possible?"

Zeke stood there, stunned. "What are you talking about? I was doing exactly what you wanted me to!" *For a change*, he almost added. But his sister didn't appear to be listening. Or at least she didn't want to hear it.

"Just get in the car," she said, sounding suddenly so much like their mother.

Zeke looked over the parking lot, everything finally right where it belonged, and wondered what he'd done wrong. Nate licked some chocolate off of his fingers, then reached up to take his brother's hand.

One Good Turn

They listened to the radio the whole way home. The radio and Nate, who felt the need to give his sensationalized take on the shopping cart showdown.

"I thought he was going to kill you," he said softly. Which actually made twice in two days Nate thought he might become suddenly brotherless. Three times if you counted Zeke's topple out of the tree that morning.

"At least I would have died for a good cause," Zeke whispered back. He was joking, though that didn't keep him from imagining how it would play out. Ezekiel Stahls: shopping cart martyr. People would hang flowered wreathes on corrals around the country to honor his sacrifice. There would be a holiday to celebrate his courage, sponsored by Walmart. Kids would get a day off from school. He knew better, of course. Very few people are ever remembered that way. As heroes.

"I can't believe we almost got in a fight. I can't wait to tell Mom."

"We didn't almost get in a fight," Jackie said sternly from the driver's seat, though Zeke was pretty sure they almost got into a fight. "And you don't need to tell Mom anything. She's got enough to worry about." His sister's mood had done a complete one-eighty. Her voice was terse, her grip on the steering wheel tight. She turned the volume up, presumably to drown out any more conversation on the matter, and Zeke kept his mouth shut. Out in Nevada, the wildfires continued to spread.

Back at home, Jackie put away the handful of groceries, lingering in front of the freezer, trying to cool off. Zeke asked Logan for a few minutes camera-free, wandering into his room and grabbing an armful of dirty clothes. He couldn't recall if he'd ever done his own laundry before. He wasn't sure of the process—his mother always said fairies were involved, as in *don't worry, I'm sure the fairies will come and take care of it like always.* Now, of course, he knew she was teasing him.

"One less thing to worry about," he said to himself as he dumped the clothes into the machine. He followed the instructions on the back of the detergent. There was a setting for "deep wash" and another for "extra rinse" and he hit them both. His sister wasn't making it up—boy stink was a thing. He added a second capful of detergent just to be safe.

As he came back into the kitchen looking for Logan, he saw Jackie standing stove side all by herself, emptying a second can of soup into a pot.

"Little warm for soup, don't you think?"

"This is what I found, so this is what we're having."

She was clearly still miffed about something.

"Where's everyone else?"

Jackie stirred. "Nate took a Popsicle and his basketball and went out back. I think Logan's on the front porch again."

His sister looked tired. She *sounded* tired. Most of the anger had drained from her voice, but that left something almost worse: a sound of resignation. Zeke hated it when his mother's voice got that way—beat down, broken. He wasn't used to it coming from Jackie. She was always the annoyed one, the sarcastic one—eyes rolling up to the ceiling, not down at her feet.

Zeke stood in the middle of the kitchen, hand resting on the old, scarred table that had lived in this house longer than he had. The table where he and Nate carved their initials with a flathead screwdriver—underneath, of course, where nobody could see. The table where his father used to serve up stacks of steaming Sunday-morning pancakes riddled with chocolate chips. It was the same table where his sister had served Zeke over a thousand summer lunches just like this one, often ignoring his groaning because he'd wanted something else. He could only ever remember thanking her once—out of a thousand such lunches—and that was yesterday, when the camera was on him.

He knew what he should do.

"Hey, Jackie," he began.

The spoon went around and around. "What?"

Zeke started to say it, had his tongue already curled around the word as he thought of her standing in the parking lot staring down that man, ready to fight. But something in her voice stopped him. The expectation that whatever he was about to say was something she didn't want to hear. Or maybe his expectation that she would automatically second-guess him, thinking he was just making fun of her somehow.

Or maybe it was that the word itself just seemed too small. Like trying to sate your thirst with only a sip of water.

"Nothing. Never mind," he said.

Jackie went back to making her little soup whirlpool. Zeke was nearly to the hallway, headed for the front door, when she stopped him.

"I'm not always going to be there, you know."

He turned and looked at her, though her eyes were still fixed on the pot.

"Next year. When I graduate and go to college—"

"*If* you go to college, you mean," Zeke interrupted. After all, there was barely enough money in the checking account to keep the fridge full.

"*When* I go to college," Jackie corrected, "I won't be here to bail you out anymore. To clean up after your mess. And Mom . . ." She paused.

"What about Mom?"

Jackie finally looked at him. He knew this look. It was her *why don't you grow up already* look. It would get its own chapter in his book. "She can't do it all by herself. She's exhausted. You see it, don't you? It's just too much for her sometimes."

Zeke looked down reflexively. "*I'm* too much, you're saying."

Jackie grunted. "It's not always about you, you know."

"What's *that* supposed to mean?"

But his sister just shook her head. "Never mind. You wouldn't understand."

She went to the pantry and took out a box of Valu-Time Snack Crackers—so cheap they couldn't even afford the *e*, his mother joked—and set them on the table along with a pair of overripe bananas. No fancy arrangements today. No gourmet sandwiches. No wilting flowers. She was apparently done trying to make things look better than they really were.

"Lunch will be ready soon. Tell Logan there'll be plenty this time."

Zeke left the kitchen before the soup started to simmer.

He fumed as he made his way down the hall.

Not always about you, you know.

Right. Like she should talk. Truthfully, he hoped she *did* get into college. Maybe she could get a scholarship to somewhere as far away as some of those posters on her wall. Maybe even out of the country. He heard Oxford was a good school—wasn't that in England? She could always come home for Christmas.

What was her deal, anyway? Last night, and even this morning, she seemed so ready to help. It was a tag-team effort—Zeke and Jackie, the Stahls siblings against the world. Besides, the cart thing was all *her* idea. It wasn't his fault that guy stormed out of his truck and nearly went Vin Diesel on them.

Okay. Maybe it was *partly* his fault. But it was partly *her* fault too. For a minute, he'd thought things had shifted between them, maybe even gotten closer to how they used to be, and then she went and gave him another one of her condescending, you-just-don't-get-it lectures.

Not always going to be there. Fine. Go then. Sooner the better. Who knows, maybe if he won this contest, he'd use some of his prize money to buy her a fancy luggage set.

Of course, to do that, he'd have to win. Which he wasn't sure how to do. Especially without her help. Which, of course, made her right about what she said. About him needing her around.

Which only irritated him even more.

A little kick of breeze made the air outside cooler than the kitchen. Zeke found Logan right where Jackie thought sitting on the porch in the same spot as last time with the same book in his hand. The camera sat in the grass a few feet away, its glass eye aimed at the house. Zeke was happy it wasn't in Logan's hands. He didn't feel like being recorded right now.

"Lunch'll be ready soon," he said. "Hope hot soup sounds good to you on this balmy summer day."

"I'm good, thanks," the cameraman said, licking his finger

and turning the page. He looked to be a little over halfway through the book now. "How's the arm?"

He meant the scratches—bubbly red reminders of why cats shouldn't climb trees and why local neighborhood boys should wear long sleeves and not their bossy sister's stupid band shirts when rescuing them. "They don't hurt unless I touch 'em."

"I find that's true with lots of things." The cameraman scooted over once again, and Zeke took the spot next to him. He could hear the *thunk* of the basketball being tossed against the back of the house. "Your sister okay?"

Zeke frowned. Back to her again. "Sure. Why wouldn't she be?"

Logan shrugged. "Nothing. Just . . . you know . . . it got a little hairy back there in the parking lot."

"Come on. It wasn't *that* big a deal."

"Really? 'Cause you looked a little scared. I know *I* was scared."

Zeke had a hard time believing that. "Four against one. Pretty sure we could have taken him."

"Pretty sure your sister would have eaten him alive," Logan admitted. "She looked about ready to call down the lightning."

"That's how she always looks," Zeke said. Logan laughed even though Zeke was only half kidding. "Guess it *was* kinda dumb. Making such a big fuss over a stupid shopping cart."

"I don't know," Logan mused. "Sometimes you gotta start small—do what you can, where you can. Cart here. Cat there.

You can't fix the whole world overnight."

Right. Tell that to Hailey Richter, Zeke thought. *Tell that to Aadya and Dom.* He was pretty sure at least one of the other contestants was working on the solution to world hunger this very minute while he sat on his can waiting for his soup to heat up.

He didn't want to think about it right now. The contest. The camera. The votes. The money. He just wanted five minutes without the pressure. Five minutes of normal. He nodded at the book still sitting in the cameraman's lap. "How is it so far?"

"It's funny," Logan said. "And sweet. Not much really happens. Sorta like life that way, I guess."

Sure, like life. Not much happens. Until you try to put all the shopping carts back. Or find yourself standing at the top of the Rocket balanced on a skateboard. Or hanging from a tree branch. Until you get a letter in the mail. Or a phone call in the middle of the night. Then a whole lot happens at once. Then everything can change.

Zeke nodded toward the book. "Kind of a strange choice. I pictured you more as a Stephen King kind of guy."

"Really? Not Shakespeare?" Logan asked.

"I've never read Shakespeare."

"Me neither," Logan admitted.

"Really? Didn't they make you read Shakespeare in high school?" Zeke could still remember Jackie having to memorize a speech of Lady Macbeth's last year—something about stabbing a king to death and then trying to wash all the blood from her hands. She made a very convincing murderer, he thought.

"I didn't really do much in school," Logan admitted. "At least not the stuff I was supposed to."

Zeke ran his finger along a crack in the cement. "Same."

"I was good at fixing things, mostly. Tinkering. Using my hands."

"Sounds a lot like my dad. He was good at fixing things too."

Zeke felt a burning in his chest. He realized this was the first time he'd mentioned his father to Logan. He expected the cameraman to press him on it, ask all the questions that people who didn't know better always asked—the somber nod, the hand pat—but instead Logan studied the clouds for a moment, then asked, "What about you? What subjects are you good at?"

"Not fixing things," Zeke said, thinking of all the warning labels plastered across the tools in the garage. "I'm good at math, I guess. And science. And starting underwear-removal-based revolutions."

"We all have our talents," Logan said. "And our limitations." He looked at his book. "Me, I don't think I'm quite ready for Shakespeare yet. I like books like this because they're easier when you're still getting the hang of it."

Zeke leaned back, head cocked. *Getting the hang of it?* He thought back to the first time he caught Logan sitting on this porch, brow furrowed, scanning each line with the tip of his finger. He squinted up at the cameraman. "Wait . . . do you . . . I mean . . . can you not read?" He hadn't meant for it to come out quite so astonished, like some kind of accusation. Thankfully Logan didn't seem to take offense.

"Told you I wasn't the best student. I faked my way through most of my classes. I mean, I *can* read. Enough to get by. It's just hard. Sometimes the words get jumbled up in my head or turned around, or I just don't recognize them. Like take this one here . . ." The cameraman opened the book to the page with the folded corner and pointed to a word about halfway down.

"*Trespassers*," Zeke said, thinking of the sign his sister used to have.

"That's what I thought." Logan nodded and pointed to another one. "And Woozles?" he said tentatively.

Zeke remembered the Woozles from back when his mother read him this story. They were the imaginary creatures that Pooh and Piglet supposedly hunted, though it turned out the two were simply chasing their own footprints, going around in circles. "I'm pretty sure that's just something the author made up. Kind of like Poohsticks."

Logan made a face.

"Don't worry. Not what it sounds like," Zeke assured him. What the cameraman was describing—the jumbling, getting things mixed up—it sounded like a learning disability. One of the kids in his class last year had dyslexia and sometimes got extra time for tests and things. Of course there were times even Zeke found himself muddling through the reading he was assigned. He preferred it when his teacher read aloud to the class, that way he could just lose himself in the story. Like all those nights snuggled up in his bed, his mother perched on the edge, the lamplight falling on the pages of whatever adventure they were caught up in, Zeke forcing his eyes to stay open so that they could get to the next chapter.

He looked again at the book in Logan's hands. "You know, if you wanted . . ."

He let his sentence trail off. It was a stupid idea. And awkward. After all, he'd only just met this man a few days ago.

"If I wanted what?" Logan asked.

"No. Nothing."

"Go on. Don't leave me hanging."

Zeke shrugged. "I mean just, if you wanted, we could, like, read some of it together. Taking turns. That way I could be here, you know, if there's another word you need help with or whatever. I mean it *is* one of my favorites. Or at least used to be."

Logan smiled, revealing the faintest pair of dimples peeking from beneath his beard. "I'd like that a lot actually," he said.

"Really?"

"Really." He handed Zeke the book.

Zeke cleared his throat. "Just so you know, I'm not very good at the voices. That's sort of my mom's thing. She does a really good Rabbit."

"You don't have to do the voices, if you don't want to."

"No. Trust me. It's better with the voices. They just might not be all that great is all I'm saying."

"Don't worry," Logan said. "I'm not allowed to vote."

He pointed to where he'd stopped and Zeke started to read, slowly getting drawn back into a world that he still remembered from when he was Nate's age. It felt a little weird, admittedly, sitting on his porch, reading out loud to this grown man. But not in a bad way. Quite the opposite. It wasn't the same feeling that he got when he handed a hissing Thin Mint over to Angela or when he pushed one of the rogue carts back to where it belonged. Those times felt forced somehow, like he was following a script. They felt like things he did because he *should* do them.

This felt different. Maybe because the camera wasn't in his face. Or maybe because he really liked this book and was starting to like the man he was sitting next to as well. He thought he might finish one paragraph and then hand it over, but instead he got caught up in the story and finished the page and then the next.

"Suddenly Winnie-the-Pooh stopped, and pointed excitedly in front of him. *'Look!'*"

Zeke paused and glanced over at the cameraman, who was leaning back against the railing of the porch, his fingers laced behind his head, eyes closed, smiling up at the sun. Zeke thought he might be asleep, but then Logan cracked one eye.

"Keep going," he said. "You're doing great."

Zeke turned the page.

By the time Zeke went back inside, Pooh had realized his foolish mistake, discovering that he'd only been tracking his own paw prints. He could see now why Hailey Richter volunteered to read aloud to kids at the library—it was actually kinda fun. Maybe she wasn't such a try-hard after all.

Or maybe she was, but maybe, in certain circumstances, that was an okay thing to be.

He came into the kitchen to see Jackie had set out four bowls. Nate was already sitting down, eyeing his soup with unbridled contempt.

"Just three of us, I think," Zeke said.

"Logan doesn't want any?"

"He said he was going to take off. Said he probably got enough footage for the day. Plus he had something he needed to take care of."

Zeke didn't bother to mention what they'd been doing on the porch. He didn't know if Logan's struggles with reading were the kind of thing he wanted shared with the rest of the world. It felt sort of like a secret between them, and Zeke was actually good at keeping secrets—though admittedly most of them were his own and were of a primarily confessional nature.

"Thought that counts." Jackie shrugged and sat down, taking a cracker and soaking it in her soup. She was clearly still upset, though at least she wasn't yelling or lecturing or giving Zeke dirty looks. He'd take what he could get.

Nate felt differently. "This soup is too hot," he whined.

"Then wait for it to cool," Jackie said.

"How is anything s'posed to cool in here? It's a jillion degrees."

"Toss an ice cube in it if you want."

"Or stick it in the freezer and make a chicken soup Popsicle," Zeke suggested.

"Really?" Nate asked.

"No. God. That's disgusting. Don't listen to your brother."

"Yeah. Don't listen to me. I never know what I'm talking about."

"That's not what I said."

"It's what you meant."

"Whatever," Jackie sighed. "Just eat your lunch."

Nate made tiny waterfalls with his too-hot soup instead. "We should get ice cream."

"I don't have money for ice cream," Jackie said, which was a lie. Zeke knew his sister actually had close to five hundred dollars stashed in her sock drawer, though she probably didn't know he knew. What she was saving it for, he wasn't sure—five hundred bucks probably didn't even get you a one-hour lecture at Northwestern or some of the other schools she was looking into.

She wasn't the only one with a wad of cash either; Zeke had close to forty hidden inside his old soccer cleats in his closet, leftover birthday money from an aunt and uncle he never saw but who never neglected to send him a card filled with a little cheddar. Forty bucks could buy a lot of ice cream, he thought.

Just imagine how much ten *thousand* could buy.

"It's too hot to *breathe*," Nate groaned.

"Why don't you complain about it some more?" Jackie said. "See if that helps."

"It's too hot to complain!"

Zeke leaned over to Nate. "You know, we could just ditch our clothes and walk around in our undies." Sort of the opposite of going commando.

Nate nodded eagerly; Jackie shook her head vehemently. "No way. I don't care how hot it gets in here, you two are keeping your pants on, got it?"

Nate groaned and torpedoed his spoon into his bowl. "You're no fun."

It looked like Jackie was about to try to argue this point—or maybe to just give up and go storming back to her room—when a sudden bang from outside caused all three of them to freeze. It sounded like the hood of a car slamming shut. The crash was followed by a high-pitched humming, like the drone of a swarm of bees. *That* was followed by a low hissing noise.

The hissing was coming from inside the house.

No. Not a hissing, exactly. More like a *whooshing.*

"Do you hear that?" Zeke asked.

"Forget hearing. Do you *feel* that?" Jackie asked back.

They all three turned to the air vent set into the floor. Zeke *could* feel it. The current slowly seeping from between the metal slats, reaching out with chilly invisible fingers.

"Oh my god, is that . . . ?"

"It can't be," Zeke said. "Can it?"

They all scrambled out of their chairs and crowded around the vent, feeling the deliciously crisp blast of artificially refrigerated air tickling their arm hairs, licking the sweat from their slick necks.

"Oh yes, baby, come to papa," Zeke exclaimed.

"It's like making out with a snow angel," Jackie said, tendrils of her hair whipping in the manufactured breeze.

Nate tore off his shirt and fell over the vent like a beached whale. "Get your own vent," he said. "This one's mine."

As Jackie tried to pry her littler brother off, Zeke went to the living room window and peered out. There was their supposedly busted condenser sitting in the mulch by the side of the house, humming happily along for the first time in over a week. Either someone had fixed it, or it had miraculously just decided to work on its own, and Zeke wasn't sure he believed in miracles.

He heard a car door close, the sound coming from the front of the house this time and he knew. In his heart he knew.

I was good at fixing things.

He made it to the porch just in time to see the black van pull away from the curb and slowly make its way down the street.

Salutations from NYC! The Big Apple. The City That Never Sleeps. Home of my personal favorite hero, the wall-crawler himself. The photo on the front isn't Spider-Man, of course. It's Lady Liberty. Did you know that she originally started out a lovely copper brown, but time and the elements have turned her green? Also I hear she sways sometimes in the wind, but she hasn't been knocked down yet. Really worth seeing in person.

Zeke, I think you would like New York. It's full of energy, just like you, everyone always on the move. And, Jackie, there's music everywhere. You hear it just walking down the street. I'm thinking maybe you can grow up and play for the New York Symphony one day.

Westward bound now, which means I'll be home before you know it.

Love, Dad

P.S. Why do smart people move to the Big Apple? Because they're bookworms!

K Is for Klepto

When she came through the door that evening, Zeke's mother squealed. A stretched-out sound like a leaking balloon, stopping in the entryway, eyes like dinner plates, sensing the world had fundamentally shifted somehow—and not in a direction she was used to.

"What am I feeling right now?" she asked.

"*That*, Momma, is called *cold*," Nate replied.

And it was. Almost freezing. As soon as Logan left, the Stahls kids jacked the thermostat down to sixty-five, a compromise between Jackie's economical suggestion of seventy-two and Nate's suggestion of negative a hundred and forty. It took a while, but the house was now chilly and crisp. Zeke had goose bumps on his earlobes. It was delightful.

"Did hell freeze over?" His mother seemed quite serious.

"We think Logan fixed it," Zeke said.

"Plus he gave me a basketball," Nate added from his spot in

front of the TV, forgetting that she had been there for that part.

"Then that man is my new favorite person. Those sharks at the repair shop were going to charge me four hundred dollars to get it running again." Their mother collapsed onto the couch with the added weight of a ten-hour shift. She spread her arms like a high priestess welcoming her god, letting the cold air tickle every part of her. "Where's your sister?"

"Where else?" Zeke said.

He hadn't seen Jackie since lunch. After Logan left—taking with him any need to keep up appearances—she slunk back into her cave, door shut, music cranked. She didn't even warn the boys not to get into any trouble. They could have been building death rays in the kitchen for all she knew, though really they spent most of the afternoon watching videos and playing *Minecraft*, Zeke trying not to think about his standing in the competition, the thousands of votes separating him from the rest.

Hopefully that would change soon. Cats and carts. Zeke Stahls to the rescue.

His mom sighed, then leaned over and started massaging her stocking feet. A *really* great kid—the absolute greatest—would probably volunteer to rub them for her, but Zeke would have to be eight quadrillion votes behind to go there.

"You wouldn't believe the day I had at work. First, I got chewed out for being late. Then this woman came in and wanted to return seven hundred dollars' worth of clothes with no tags and no receipt. She said she went on a diet and lost fifty pounds so they didn't fit anymore. Then she started yelling at me when I wouldn't give her a refund. Like it was our fault for not making clothes that magically shrink to match your body. I swear, some people just assume they are the center of the universe."

Jackie's voice crept into Zeke's head: *It's not always about you.*

Except he *was* the one the camera was following.

"How about you? How was your day?" Mom asked. "How'd the filming go? All great things I hope?"

I wouldn't say they were all *great*, Zeke thought, recalling how he'd dangled from Angela's tree by his shorts. He really hoped Gordon Notts or whoever was in charge cut that part. He needed all of the selective editing he could get.

He glanced at the clock sitting on the mantel, next to the silver framed photo of his parents on their wedding day. Zeke always liked that picture. He especially liked how they were staring at each other and not at the camera, as if it wasn't even there. "In a few minutes you can see for yourself." He fetched the laptop and joined her on the couch, Nate squirming in beside him. The website was already pulled up, revealing the five photos with the current tallies beneath them. Hailey in the lead. Dom a close second. Puppies were clearly not insuperable. Hailey had freckles, though. That probably helped.

"Jackie! Your brother's video is almost up!" Mom yelled, then shook her head. "I swear, that girl. She better have not been hiding in there all day long. I pay to watch you."

For a moment, Zeke was back in that parking lot, barely

standing his ground against that fuming, red-faced man, his sister charging up behind him. "You got your money's worth," he informed her. "Today at least."

"It's up!" Nate said, pointing at the screen. The countdown clicked to zero, informing anyone visiting that voting was open again. A refreshed page also showed links to new videos beneath each picture. This time Nate didn't give away any spoilers.

Instead of starting with Hailey Richter and moving down the line, Zeke clicked on his own portrait first this time. He was greeted by a close-up of his face, looking determined.

"If you ask me that's what's wrong with the world today . Everybody assumes someone else will come along and fix the problem, whatever it is."

"Wow. Look at my boy, dropping the wisdom bombs," Mom said.

The video cut directly to Zeke starting up the maple tree, cat included. Some dramatic music swept in, low strings and thudding timpani accompanying the video as Zeke scrambled up the branches. Amazing how much cooler he looked when accompanied by an orchestral score.

"Wait, is that the Bormans' house?" Mom asked. "Is that their cat? That thing's huge!"

"The camera adds a few pounds," Zeke said. That same camera followed him up the tree, zooming in to show him clutching the frightened feline to his chest, Logan perfectly capturing the anguished expression as Thin Mint sank her claws into Zeke's shoulder. Such is the price of greatness.

Mom actually gasped when the cat sprang free and Zeke tumbled downward, the music crescendoing, but then the video froze at the moment the branch snatched him, a cliffhanger of sorts—suddenly cutting to the parking lot and a tracking shot of Zeke finding carts and shoving them back where they belonged. Video Zeke turned to the camera this time: "It is frustrating how many people don't bother or don't care."

"You went to the grocery?" Mom said, clearly missing the point. "I hope you remembered we needed milk."

"Popsicles," Nate informed her. "And a Kit Kat."

And very nearly a broken jaw, Zeke thought. Because there he was, his video version, pushing that cart in front of the red pickup truck. He could sense his mother tensing up beside him as the music swelled and the man stepped out to confront them. Zeke held his breath again, waiting for that moment—his sister storming in to save the day—before he remembered that Logan had lowered the camera at that point. The footage jumped directly to the man pushing the cart where it belonged before climbing back into his pickup and driving away.

Zeke watched his mother's face, her furrowed frown, her scrunching brow. She was clearly not impressed with his parking-lot heroics. "Did you seriously confront that man? Do you have any idea how dangerous that was? He could have assaulted you. He could have shoved you in the back of his truck, driven you to his house, and thrown you in a pit in his basement." She'd

244

seen a movie where that happened once; now it was one of her ongoing worries. "Honestly, Zeke, what were you thinking?"

What was he thinking? He was thinking he was doing the right thing, if not necessarily the smart one. Though if it won them ten thousand bucks, it would be both.

"Where was your—" his mother started to say, but her question was interrupted by another cut in the video, one that even Zeke didn't see coming. An awkward shot of the Stahlses' front porch, poorly framed and low to the ground, angled in such a way that you couldn't even see all of Zeke's head and only half of the person he was sitting next to. It definitely had that found-footage feel. Though you could, at least, make out what Zeke was holding. And could easily pick up the sound of his voice.

Or voices.

"'I see now,' said Winnie-the-Pooh."

Zeke stared at the screen, confused.

"Is that Logan? I can't tell," Mom asked. "Are you two *reading* together?"

Zeke didn't respond. He just watched and listened to himself tell the story, wondering how this even happened. Had Logan forgotten that the camera was on? Was this an accident? It certainly seemed that way, given the awkward angle and lack of focus and the fringe of grass at the bottom of the frame. It surely had to be a mistake.

Though even if it *was* recorded by mistake, Logan still decided to upload it, and then someone at KABAM, probably Notts, had decided to put it in the video for the whole world to see. Zeke felt an uncomfortable flutter in his gut. He barely caught what his mother said beside him.

"That's a great Piglet. Much better than the one I used to do."

He was about to say something about it—about not even knowing they were on camera—when the video jumped again to the Bormans' backyard, everyone lined up to greet the emerging hero. Zeke's voice cut in one last time.

"And yet, if everybody . . . if they just did what they should . . . then the world would be a better place."

On-screen Angela leaned in for the kiss. You could see the color rushing to Zeke's cheeks.

"Besides, being responsible doesn't mean you can't have any fun."

"Ew. Not this part again," Nate said, covering his eyes. "It was bad enough the first time."

The video froze on the kiss, capturing Zeke's smile, before fading to black.

It really was the perfect ending. But that wasn't the moment that stuck with him. Zeke's mind was still back on that porch, seeing him and Logan sitting together, swapping the book between them. The sinking feeling in his gut grew stronger. The cat. The carts. The game. The slide. These were all moments he expected to see, expected to share. But *that* moment, the one with Logan . . . Zeke hadn't been thinking about Hawaii or KABAM or the drooping gutters and stack of bills. He'd only been thinking about how nice it was, the two of them, sitting in the shade, wandering through the Hundred Acre Wood. Seeing it in the video seemed to lessen that somehow. Took away the magic.

It felt contrived. It felt cheap.

"That wasn't supposed to be there," Zeke mumbled. "That part on the porch. I didn't know he was filming."

"Well, I think it was sweet," his mother said. "I didn't know you still liked reading out loud."

No, Zeke thought. *Neither did I.*

"And that kiss," Mom continued. "I thought your head might explode!"

Zeke blushed, suddenly wishing she'd stop talking about it. His hand went for the touchpad, ready to click on Hailey's picture and see how many endangered black rhinos she'd somehow saved today, when his mother's phone rang.

The caller ID said it was Gordon Notts.

She sat up straight, moving the laptop from her lap to Nate's. "Hello? Hi, Mr. Notts. I'm fine, thank you. Yes, we just finished watching Zeke's in fact. Well, yes, of course. Sure, I'm proud. Well, that part *was* a little scary. I wouldn't say *just* like Tiananmen Square. Yes of course, he's right here. Hang on." She set the phone down on the couch and put it on speaker.

"Zeke, my boy," Notts's voice boomed, still sounding like a circus ringmaster. "Glad I caught you. Thought you might be patrolling the streets, looking for more pets to save."

"No. One was enough for today," Zeke admitted, glancing at the scarlet lines on his arms.

"I'm pretty sure that cat counted as two at least," Notts said, laughing at his own joke. "Listen, the reason I called is . . . well, there's just no good way to say it: our little competition has recently encountered a bit of a setback."

"Setback?" Zeke repeated, suddenly uneasy.

"'Fraid so. We just learned that one of our contestants was not who we thought he was," Notts continued.

Zeke and his mother exchanged looks. He knew what she was thinking. Same thing he was. *If for some reason this letter has reached you in error. . . .* He felt a lump in his throat.

"It's such a disappointment . . ."

Goodbye, beach. So long, grand prize.

"But I feel like I should be the first to tell you . . ."

That you're a loser and you'll never be great at anything.

"That Kyo Sasaki is out of the competition."

Zeke opened and shut his mouth a few times, trying to summon his voice. "Wait. Did you say *Kyo*?"

"I know," Notts said. "Hard to believe, but apparently, he's been dipping his biscuits into everyone else's gravy, if you get my drift."

Mom shook her head. She looked just as confused as Zeke was. "Um . . . not really," she admitted.

"He's been stealing," Notts clarified. "From the elderly. At the home. They caught him pocketing some poor lady's diamond earrings this morning. Just terrible."

Zeke was stunned. Kyo? Special K? The kid with the gelled

hair and soft brown eyes and the confident grin? The kid who said, *I think greatness is making the most of the gifts God gave you?*

Gordon Notts sighed. "Sort of a reverse Robin Hood situation. He's been doing it for a while, apparently, ever since he started volunteering at the retirement center. He takes the residents back to their rooms and while their backs are turned, he helps himself to whatever's lying around. Of course, most of them just assumed they misplaced whatever it was he took, so they didn't bother to report it. But the lady with the earrings was positive it was him, and sure enough, they found them in his pocket."

"So wait . . . what does this have to do with Zeke?" his mother wanted to know.

"Oh, nothing directly," Notts replied. "I'm just calling the other contestants personally to let them know that Mr. Sasaki has been disqualified. I mean, there's no way he could possibly continue. This isn't the World's Greatest Juvenile Delinquent contest."

No. That I might have a chance of winning, Zeke thought. Though admittedly, Kyo was in another league as far as that was concerned. Zeke would never steal from old people. Hide their dentures in their gelatin maybe, or replace the tennis balls on their walkers with squeaky dog toys while they weren't looking. But he had never stolen anything in his life. Even his sister's big wad of cash lay untouched in her sock drawer. And her diary was always put right back where he found it. That was borrowing. And sneaking. And invading privacy. But it wasn't *stealing.* There was a line, and Kyo had jumped right over it.

That's when it dawned on Zeke what this all actually meant for him. For the contest. For the prize.

He was now one of the *four* greatest kids in the world.

"I'm honestly embarrassed," Notts continued. "Obviously we need to be a little more careful in vetting potential contestants. I know I said the computers don't make mistakes, but I suppose the algorithm can't account for everything, you know what I mean?"

This time, Zeke knew exactly what he meant.

"I've got some other PR guys here telling me we should just cancel the whole thing, but I refuse. The rest of you kids are true gems—shining examples of all that is still bright and good in this gloomy world. The show must go on, as they say. Just do me a favor and don't do anything you could get arrested for, okay?"

That was nothing Zeke hadn't heard from Mom on a dozen different occasions. "I won't," he said, which is what he always told her too.

"Fantastic," Notts said. "Because you're going to just love Hawaii, Zeke. The beaches are to die for. Or so I've heard. They look gorgeous on YouTube, at least. Also, just to give you a heads-up, part of tomorrow's schedule includes a video interview with yours truly. No big deal, just a few questions that I ask each of the participants, just so the voters get to know you a little better. It'll be ten, fifteen minutes tops. I'll have Logan connect us. Cool?"

"As central air," Zeke said.

Gordon Notts laughed. "As central air. Hilarious. See you tomorrow, Zeke. Keep up the great work!"

And with that the director of charitable programming hung up.

Zeke and his mother sat in silence for a moment. Finally she said, "That man is like a game show host crossed with a used-car salesman."

"Crossed with a caffeinated chipmunk," Zeke added. And to think that tomorrow that man was going to interview him. Just one more thing to worry about.

Though it could be a lot worse. Kyo Sasaki was probably being "interviewed" right at this moment by men and women who wore blue suits instead of white ones. Zeke reached for the laptop and clicked on Kyo's picture. A window popped up informing them that the video was unavailable. He suspected if he tried to vote for Kyo he'd get a similar message. *Well, I beat somebody at least.*

Zeke hit the refresh button and noted that his tally had already gone up by twenty votes in just the short time they'd been sitting there. Twenty people out there thought he, Zeke Stahls, was the World's Greatest Kid.

Or at least the best of the options still available.

One more click made it twenty-one.

Belize It or Not

Dinner was just the three of them that night. Chicken and rice with a side of applesauce—extra cinnamon on Nate's because he was "just spicy like that." Jackie stayed in her room, insisting she wasn't hungry for the second night in a row, though the one time she did emerge was to grab a strawberry yogurt and the last of the potato chips.

"That's all you're having?" Mom asked. "There's still rice left. Or I can make you something else."

"You don't need to make me anything," Jackie said. "I'm fine."

Zeke was fluent enough in teenager to know that *I'm fine* never meant *I'm fine*. He just wasn't fluent enough to guess what it *did* mean most of the time.

Jackie tried to slink back down the hall, but Mom wouldn't let her sneak away so easily. "Did you watch your brother's video?"

Jackie glanced at Zeke. "Of course," she said. "He did great."

Her *he did great* sounded a whole lot like her *I'm fine.*

"Wanna watch TV with us?" Nate asked, patting the one remaining spot on the couch beside him, though it was more like half a space. They could always scrunch if they needed to. At one time, five of them had squeezed on this couch, though Nate was barely toddling and easily fit on his father's lap. "The baking show's on. The one where they talk funny."

Zeke saw his sister stare at the empty space. She had a look—like when you want something at the store but you're not sure you can afford it. Or you know you'll only regret buying it later. "Thanks. But I've got the SAT coming up in a couple of weeks. Gotta get that math score up. And there are some scholarship applications I can already start filling out for next year."

She started to leave, again, but Mom stopped her, again. "Hey, Jackie?"

"Yeah, Mom?"

Zeke waited for his mother to say something about college. How she was sure Jackie would nail the SAT this time, or maybe how any school would be happy to have someone as smart as her. How proud she was to see her daughter working so hard to make her dreams come true.

Instead she said, "The next time you're at the store, be sure to pick up some milk, okay?"

Jackie's mouth twitched. She glanced at Zeke, then dug her chin into her chest. "Right. Got it," she said softly.

Zeke watched her go, heard her door click shut. He thought

about the one moment that didn't make it on the video because the camera was down and wondered if he should say something. The one moment his mother didn't even get to hear about because they weren't supposed to tell her. Because Jackie told them not to. Because their mom already had enough on her mind.

On the TV, some poor lady's cake collapsed as she took it out of the oven. She looked totally distraught. *What a bloody cock-up,* she hissed. Nate laughed. Snort giggle snort.

"It's not that funny," Zeke murmured. "She worked hard on that cake."

His mother gave him a sideways glance.

"I'm just saying. She tried."

The woman with the botched confection was naturally the one they kicked off. The judges told her it was a good effort and that she showed a lot of promise, but in the end, everybody else's cake was just better than hers.

We're sorry, but this is where your journey ends.

Of course the actual winner of the show only received a bunch of flowers and a cake stand, so it wasn't as if there was a whole lot at stake. Mostly, he imagined, it was a matter of pride—wanting to do your best. Or maybe just being afraid of royally screwing the whole thing up.

The lady on the TV had done her best.

But that didn't change the fact that she was going home.

* * *

That night, Zeke lay in bed and listened for the knock on his door. He watched the sliver of light underneath for the shadow of a slip of paper, summoning him to his sister's sanctuary. They still had two more days of filming after all. Two more chances to prove to the world that Zeke Stahls deserved that all-expenses-paid trip to a tropical paradise and the giant check that came with it.

They needed it more than Hailey Richter at least, who could afford ice-skating lessons *and* whose house had a finished basement—complete with a room that apparently was just for *making hats.*

Because that's what she did in her second video. Zeke had watched them all after Notts's call and then again after the baking show. Hailey's clip opened with an ice-skating lesson where she pulled off something called a lutz, which sounds clumsy and awkward but looked graceful and beautiful. Then she took viewers on a tour of the craft room in her basement where she knitted winter caps for impoverished children, part of the Lids for Kids program that she started at her school. All of her hats had one of those fuzzy little balls on top. "I know it's only June, but if I get started now, I can make close to thirty hats before winter," she said. "After all, no one deserves to be left out in the cold." Even Zeke had to admit it was a good line.

Like Hailey, Aadya started her video by showcasing her talents, bowing to the camera in her crisp, white gi before breaking a board with some kind of jumping spin side kick. It actually reminded Zeke a little of Hailey's lutz, if a lutz ended with a move that could knock your head off. Then the girl with the two braids helped her sensei lead a class on how to stop bullying without resorting to violence. "Your words will always be stronger than your fists," she said, though Zeke had been a lot more frightened of the fists of that man in the parking lot today than the curses he shouted or the middle finger he flipped.

For his second day, Dom took a kid to the park, much the same way that Zeke took Nate on his first, which made him a total copycat if you thought about it. Difference was, Dom's companion happened to be part of a mentorship program through the YMCA. He also had muscular dystrophy.

No fair, Zeke thought, though the instant it popped into his head he felt terrible for thinking it. Watching the two of them laugh and play together only made him feel worse. The video ended with Dom giving his mentee a high five.

At least nobody cured cancer today, Zeke told himself, then felt bad for thinking that too.

Jackie was right: these kids knew what they were doing. It was all carefully choreographed, perfect scenes staged specifically for the camera. Though he wasn't sure he had much room to talk anymore; Thin Mint definitely didn't get stuck in that tree on her own. Still, it was frustrating. No matter what he did, they always seemed to find a way to outdo him. All except for Kyo, of course. He did himself in.

Zeke wondered if they were like that when the camera *wasn't* trained on them, these other contestants. Were they really this awesome twenty-four seven? Or were they more like Kyo and his dipped biscuits? Did Hailey ever badmouth the other kids at her school behind their backs? Did Aadya cuss her parents out when they weren't around? Had Dom ever been sent to the Choices and Consequences room for putting vinegar in the hand sanitizer dispenser?

Were people only good when they knew someone was watching them?

Zeke thought back to that moment on the porch, he and Logan reading together, and his stomach knotted again. Sometimes they were watching even when you thought they weren't.

His eyes flicked to the clock on his desk. Almost midnight. Voting would be closing soon, today's tallies added to yesterday's. Zeke knew he'd made up some of the ground he'd lost, but not near enough. Even with Kyo out of the running, he still needed a major popularity boost to get back in the race.

Which meant he still needed his sister's help. Desperately.

Zeke pushed off the covers and went to his door, opening it as quietly as possible—but not quite quiet enough. Nate pulled himself up on his elbows in his neighboring bed and rubbed his eyes. "Where're you going?"

"I have to ask Jackie something. Go back to sleep."

"Ask her what?"

If there's any way we can still win this thing. "Don't worry about it. Just go back to sleep," Zeke said, knowing his loyal sidekick wouldn't disobey a direct order.

Zeke waited for his brother's head to hit his pillow, then shut the door and crept across the hall. He knocked lightly, careful not to wake their mother, who had actually managed to drag herself from the couch to her bedroom this time, the glass of wine she'd poured sitting half-full on the kitchen counter. "Jackie? You awake?" he whispered. No answer. He knocked a little harder. "Jackie. It's Zeke. Open up. We've got some serious planning to do." He pressed his cheek to the doorframe. "Kyo's out, but those other three are still way ahead of us. We've got to think of something really amazing for tomorrow. Plus, I keep screwing up my smile. And I probably need to borrow another shirt 'cause this one has lots of tiny little holes in it and maybe a little blood . . . and are you even listening to me?"

Nothing. Zeke took a deep breath. Desperate times call for desperate measures. He put his hand on his sister's doorknob and turned it slowly, conscious of all the unwritten rules he was violating. In the little bit of moonlight that peeked through her thin curtains, he saw her lying perfectly still in bed with her back to him, out cold, the covers pulled to her chin. Bruce the Moose sat cradled in her arms, staring at the door. *I'm watching you*, his glassy eyes seemed to say.

She looked younger to him, all curled up, that stuffed animal tucked between her elbows. He could remember only one time when she'd held him like that. A little less than three years ago.

There was a thunderstorm, the window-rattling kind, the rain sounding like machine-gun fire against the roof. The television had said something about a tornado watch and their mother had called to check up on them, to tell them to hunker down and stay away from the windows, so they went into Jackie's room, because it was the smallest and only had the one. They crammed together in her twin bed—this same bed—Zeke on one side, four-year-old Nate on the other, Jackie in the middle, one arm wrapped around each of them, doing her best to convince the boys that they weren't about to be sucked up and blown away, *Wizard of Oz* style. They'd had enough terrible in their lives recently, she reasoned, and the universe didn't kick you while you were down.

She was right. Eventually the rain passed. Eventually their mother made it home from work to find them packed tight under the covers. She didn't bother waking them. Just let them be. That would never happen now, he guessed. But seeing Jackie's face in the moonlight made him wonder.

Zeke was about to hiss her name again, maybe even tiptoe across the room and give her a gentle brotherly nudge to wake her up, when he noticed her usually bare carpet wasn't bare anymore. It took a moment to even register what he was seeing.

Her posters. The ones of all the places she wanted to see when she was older. Sydney and San Francisco. Barcelona and Belize.

They'd all been torn down.

Her bucket list contents lay flat on the carpet, exposing their blank white backs. They weren't ripped to shreds—this was no product of uncontrollable teenage rage—but she obviously hadn't taken much care in their removal either. Zeke could still see some remnants of their corners taped to the walls. He imagined her circling the room, yanking each of them down with one swift stroke like the fall of an executioner's ax, letting them drop where they may. And now they all lay on the floor, leaving barren, ugly walls.

Zeke stood in the doorway and stared, legs frozen but heart beating hard in his chest. He thought of the little wooden chest hidden beneath his bed. All the postcards with all of their possibilities. So many promises made. So many boxes left unchecked.

Why would she do this? he wondered. *Is this because of me somehow?*

He looked again at all the posters on the floor. Blank sheets with nothing to say. All except one. Barcelona was the only poster that had fallen faceup, revealing a beautiful church that looked more like a Disney princess castle, a place that only existed in make-believe.

A girl can only dream.

Only.

Bruce the Moose continued to glare coldly at him from his sister's arms, and Zeke was suddenly overcome by guilt and shame. For sneaking in here. For seeing something he probably wasn't meant to see. For shouting at her earlier. For wishing her away. For so many things.

He couldn't stay here any longer. He quietly backed out of the room, softly shutting the door behind him.

* * *

When he pushed open his own door, he found Nate sitting up in his bed, hands folded in his lap.

"What are you doing still awake? I thought I told you to go back to sleep."

Nate shrugged. "I know. I was doing recon."

"You mean you were eavesdropping," Zeke said. He wasn't mad. How could he be? He'd taught the kid everything he knew about spying. They called it recon because it sounded less devious that way. "What did you hear?"

"Only that you needed her help with the competition. So is she gonna help you or not?"

Zeke shook his head. "I don't know. She was asleep. Plus she's . . ." He struggled with the words.

"A fart-breathed, poop-eating, dingle-head?"

That actually wasn't what Zeke was going to say for once. He motioned for his brother to scoot and make room, settling down on the bed next to him and cradling his chin in his hands. "Seriously, dude. I don't know what I'm going to do. This contest. Those other kids. There's no way I can catch them. I'm in way over my head."

"Maybe I could help," Nate said with a shrug. "I have good ideas too, you know."

Zeke turned and smiled at his brother. "What . . . you think I don't know you have good ideas?"

"I mean, not as many as you," Nate said softly.

"Oh yeah? Who was it that said we should make snowmen out of whipped cream and then eat them?"

Nate pointed sheepishly to himself.

"Right. And whose idea was it to put sugar in the saltshaker?"

"Sugar fries are fire."

"They're the best. And who thought to make fake poop out of the brown Play-Doh and leave it on Jackie's pillow last week?"

"That was you," Nate said.

"No, sir. You *made* that log. I just showed you where to drop it." In an act of retaliation, Jackie had stormed out of her room and deposited the doughy turd in Zeke's bowl of Fruity-O's. Sometimes he guessed he had it coming.

Zeke bumped his brother's shoulder with his own. "You really wanna help?" Nate nodded. "Okay then, mastermind, show me what you've got."

Nate grinned and slipped off the bed, rummaging through a pile of books, dirty laundry, and Matchbox cars. He came back with an oversize tome with an obnoxiously shiny cover: *Guinness World Records*. He plopped the book down on the bed and began thumbing through the pages.

"Where'd you even get this?"

"School book fair," Nate replied.

"Seriously? Mom let you buy this?" Not that their mother was against them owning books—they had ten full shelves in the family room and another five in here—but most of those came from library sales. This glittery thing looked a little out of their price range.

"Micah's meemaw bought it for me," Nate explained. "She saw I only had enough money to buy a smelly pencil so she told me to pick out a book instead."

"And you picked out the most expensive one you could find?"

Nate's grin skewed a little to the wicked side—still taking after his older brother. "It was twenty-five bucks," he whispered.

"Nice." Zeke looked down to see a photo of a guy with a jackhammer stuffed halfway down his gullet. A *jackhammer*. "Wait, he seriously *swallowed* that thing?"

"Pretty cool, huh?" Nate said.

"And this guy did twenty-seven pinkie pull-ups in a minute?" Zeke could barely do one pull-up using all ten fingers—his struggle up Angela's tree proved that. He took over the page flipping, reading the captions highlighting all sorts of people who were the greatest in the world at what they did—even if what they did was totally ludicrous or pointless or downright disgusting. "Most people lifted and thrown in two minutes? Fastest time to drink a gallon of lemon juice? Most slam dunks by a rabbit? You're trying to tell me this guy got his picture in the book just by sticking *spoons* to himself?" He was starting to understand why his brother tried stacking Fritos on his head yesterday, at least.

He could also see where Nate was going with this. There was more than one way to get noticed in this world. More than one way to stand out. These guys were all great . . . in their own pecu-liar way. And they didn't have to save the world to get there. One made it into the book just by guzzling mustard. Another did it by completing a marathon on a pogo stick. Not that Zeke could even finish a marathon on the two spindly legs God gave him, but he could surely find *something* he could do. "So, what? You're saying we just make up ridiculous records and then have Logan film me trying to set them?"

Nate shrugged. "I mean, it was just an idea."

Zeke looked back at the door. He doubted Jackie would approve of this plan. After all, there wasn't a whole lot of charity or nobility involved in growing the world's largest mustache or seeing how many grapes you could eat with your feet.

Then again, they'd tried taking the high road and Zeke was still thousands of votes behind with only two days left to close the gap. He knew he couldn't beat the likes of Aadya or Dom or Hailey at the game *they* were playing, but there was more than one way to define greatness, right? And wouldn't it really be up to the viewers to decide?

He glanced at the cover of the book again. *Mind-blowing feats*, it said. *Superhuman achievements. Stories to inspire.* He could inspire blown minds with his superhuman achievements, why not?

"I think it's an awesome idea."

"Really?"

"Better than anything *I've* got," Zeke admitted, though that wasn't a hard bar to clear.

Nate beamed. Zeke grabbed his notebook and pencil from the desk, thumbing past the page that said *Manifesto of Ezekiel Stahls*. At the top of the next blank page he wrote *Stahls Brothers Path to Greatness*, underlining it three times.

"Okay," he said. "What should we try first?"

A Series of Unfortunate Attempts

The latest path to greatness turned out to be a bumpy one.

In retrospect, the nuggets of inspiration generated after midnight by a sleep-deprived seven-year-old running on Popsicles and a book about wacky world records *might* not have been the most thoroughly thought-out, despite that kid's pure-as-gold intentions. In retrospect, a man swallowing a jackhammer should not always be adopted as a role model.

In retrospect, Zeke should have just stuck another cat in a tree. Or maybe just *planted* a tree—*that* would have made sense. But it was day three, and he was desperate, so he followed the dizzying path all the way to its explosive, and perhaps inevitable, conclusion.

Zeke waited until his mother left for work—fifteen minutes early this time, so as not to incur her boss's wrath again—before collecting the materials they would need to put their plan into action. By the time Logan arrived on the front step, Zeke and

Nate had everything laid out on the counter. The cameraman fetched himself a cup of coffee and sipped it while surveying the odd assortment of items spread before him. "What's all this?"

"*This* is what greatness is made of," Zeke said.

"It's made of Legos?"

"It's made," Zeke said, "of ingenuity, courage, and determination. Today we are going to attempt things that nobody has ever seen before. Feats to inspire the masses. Deeds that will go down in history."

"Breaking records and taking names," Nate added with maximum sass.

"That's right, little brother. Today, I, Ezekiel Stahls, will join the pantheon of men and women who have pushed the limits of human achievement, triumphed over adversity, and conquered their deepest . . ." Zeke stopped and eyed the cameraman. "Shouldn't you be filming this?"

Logan took a slow sip from his mug. "What's with the applesauce?"

"That's for the push-ups."

"And the office chair?"

"It goes with the pickles, obviously," Zeke said.

The cameraman scratched his chin. "You ask your mom about all of this? Or your sister?"

Zeke glanced down the hallway to make sure Jackie hadn't slunk out of her room yet, because Logan was right: there was a good chance she would put the kibosh on the whole thing as soon as she saw it. "I'm allowed to eat applesauce," he said defensively.

Logan put his hands up. "Hey, it's your show. I'm just here to—"

"Observe and *record*," Zeke finished for him, doing little to hide the snark. *Even when I don't know you're doing it.*

Logan gave Zeke a sideways look, then put his mug down, took out his camera, checked the charge, and centered the lens on Zeke. "Okay, kid. Stage is yours."

Zeke took a deep breath and started over from the top: minds blown, records broken, people inspired—the whole time channeling his inner Gordon Notts, minus the bow tie and the obvious orthodontia, really hamming it up. "Because let's be honest," he said to the camera, "anyone can make a sandwich or pick up dog poop or even fold an origami boat, but to be *truly* great, you must set out to do the unexpected, the unparalleled . . . the *impossible*." He grinned straight into the camera—to the thousands of viewers that he imagined would be watching tonight. Watching and hopefully voting for him in all of his amazingness.

Logan grunted. A kind of dismissive half laugh that no doubt was picked up on camera.

He better cut that out, Zeke thought. He turned to Nate, who nodded, his little round face deadly serious, and handed Zeke a black marker. Zeke brandished it like it was Excalibur and he'd just been made king.

"For my first challenge, I shall draw my own self-portrait"—*pause for maximum dramatic effect*—"using only my feet"—*let it simmer*—"while doing a headstand"—*now give them the kicker*—"on top of a pile of toy bricks!"

Ta-da.

"Ooh," Nate said, mouth like a donut. "Aah." It helped to have a plant in the audience.

Logan still looked skeptical.

The feet-drawing feat was inspired by something they'd seen in the book, but the LEGO was Zeke's brilliant twist, the reasoning being that any dope could stand on their head and draw themselves with their toes. The World's Greatest Kid would take it to the next level. The WGK would take it to the extreme. *Let's see you try this, Hailey Land-a-Lutz Richter.*

While Nate dumped the bucket of bricks in the corner of the kitchen, carefully spreading them out to ensure maximum exposure, Zeke uncapped the black marker and wedged it between the piggy that went to the market and the one that stayed home. Between the same two toes of his other foot, he gripped a blank sheet of paper torn from his notebook, then he got down on his hands and knees, facing the wall.

Out of the corner of his eye he saw Logan lower his camera.

"What's the matter?" Zeke asked. "Did the battery die or something?"

"No. It's just . . . I have a nephew who's really into those things. And whenever I visit, I always almost end up crippling myself just walking across the living room. They're brutal on the feet. Can't imagine what they're gonna do to your head."

"Greatness often requires sacrifice," Zeke retorted. He was pretty sure he heard that in a movie once. And he really didn't need his cameraman second-guessing him.

"Yeah. Okay. But this isn't really . . . you know . . ."

"Isn't really what?" Zeke challenged.

Logan seemed to chew on his words for a moment, then he sighed. "Forget it, kid. You do you." It wasn't the first time he'd offered this advice, but it sounded much less encouraging this time around. Still, he brought the camera back up to his shoulder and gave another thumbs-up.

Ignore him, Zeke thought to himself. *He's just a camera jockey. What does he know about being great?*

With a nod of encouragement from Nate, Zeke gently lowered his hands and head to the stud-studded floor and awkwardly turned himself into a human tripod, the edges of the Lego already pressing into his palms and scalp. He tried not to wince as he hoisted up his lower half, extending his legs using the wall for support, somehow keeping the marker and paper stuck between his toes. Logan was right. It was brutal. It felt like the normally smooth linoleum was now made of spikes. Or glass shards. Or covered in little piranha with razory teeth. He could feel one particularly jagged brick already digging into his skull, threatening to bury itself deep into his brain. *I'm going to be a permanent blockhead*, he thought. He would have laughed at his own joke if he wasn't in so much pain.

"I will now . . . *ow* . . . attempt . . . *eee* . . . to draw . . . *aaah* . . .

my own portrait . . . *hss* . . . while upside . . . *ooh* . . . down."
His voice came out breathless and strained. The headstand alone
would have been uncomfortable with all the rushing blood, but
the plastic burrowing into his scalp made it a hundred times
worse, so much so that Zeke could feel the tears welling up. And
yet, with his left foot barely holding the sheet of paper steady, his
right foot somehow Picasso-d its way through a deformed facsim-
ile of a human face, though at the angle he was at, Zeke had to
mostly guess where each feature should land on the page. Nose
here. Eye there. A squiggled mouth. Those awkward triangles
were intended as ears. There was no time for detail—every passing second he could feel the bricks burrowing deeper, threatening
to give him lasting brain damage.

He could only imagine what Jackie would say to that. *What's
there to damage?*

After a minute of pointed torture, Zeke sketched what
he hoped was a swoosh of bangs, completing his self-portrait.
"And . . . voilà!" he grunted through clenched teeth. He made
sure the drawing was facing the camera, holding the pose for
three seconds before collapsing, Lego skidding across the floor.
With Nate's help, he pulled himself to a more comfortable,
upright position, blocks tumbling out of his hair—except for the
one piece that had attached itself to his scalp and had to be pried
loose. He could see the dots imprinted in his palms, and there
was a long black slash of marker across his left foot where he'd
nearly lost his balance and drawn *on* himself instead of drawing

himself. But still, he'd pulled it off.

Sort of.

Zeke blotted the tears from his eyes and held up his misshapen self-portrait for the camera, seeing it clearly for the first time. It gave off strong, rotting jack-o'-lantern vibes. A very kindergartener-coloring-while-having-a-seizure aesthetic.

"It looks just like you," Nate said, which was exactly what he was instructed to say, except given the results, it sounded more like sarcasm. Logan added another all-too-audible grunt.

All right, Zeke thought, that didn't turn out quite as amazing as he'd hoped—but he felt pretty safe in saying that he was the only human being to have ever attempted such a feat. And until somebody came along and did it better, that made Zeke the greatest block-head-standing-foot-sketch artist the world had ever known.

And he was just getting started. Next up was a true test of physical strength and endurance: the Blind Push-up Applesauce Broom Bash National Anthem Challenge.

Zeke and Nate had devised this one together. The internet was full of videos of people attempting all kinds of push-ups—one-handed push-ups, clapping push-ups, snapping, sideways, reverse, cup-stacking, Rubik's cube–solving, one guy even did them with a goat on his back, making him the GOAT of goat push-ups—but it wasn't until they saw some famous actress do them while eating mashed potatoes that they truly got inspired.

Zeke knew how to eat after all. His mother always said so.

Of course they didn't have any potatoes, mashed or otherwise, so they had to substitute what was left of the applesauce. And it wouldn't be enough to just eat while pumping his arms. That had been done before, with everything from M&M's to Taco Bell.

To do it blindfolded and humming while your brother beats you with a broom, though? This is how legends are made.

Zeke set his deranged self-portrait on the counter and grabbed the broom, handing it to his brother. "Remember. Not too hard," he whispered in Nate's ear. "It's mostly for show." Nate nodded and gave it a couple of good practice swings, looking a bit too much like Aaron Judge for Zeke's liking. He turned somewhat nervously back to the camera. "I will now attempt to set the world record for doing push-ups and eating a bowl of applesauce blindfolded while humming the national anthem and getting hit with a broom. Don't try this at home, kids." Though he guessed some of them would anyway; that's just how the internet worked.

Logan stepped back to get a better angle and Zeke could see the cameraman was still frowning. Zeke just ignored it. He rubbed his hands together and slapped his biceps the way Olympic athletes always did, then he dropped back to his hands and knees, face hovering over the clear plastic mixing bowl his brother had set there. They'd scraped enough applesauce from the jar to fill it halfway. How many push-ups would it take to clean the bowl and get through the song? He figured he was good for twenty, maybe twenty-five. He wondered how many Aadya could do. Probably a hundred at least. The difference was, she wouldn't have even thought of doing *this*.

There's probably a good reason for that, a voice in his head whispered.

He ignored that voice too. "I'm ready," he said.

Nate brought out the "blindfold"—an old black T-shirt that they'd cut into one long strip—and tied it around Zeke's head, which still smarted from all the biting plastic bricks. "*Bunny ears, bunny ears*," he sang. He got it on the first try. The blindfold worked perfectly; Zeke couldn't see a thing.

"Here we go," he said. He began to pump and slurp.

He had to navigate mostly by smell, feeling the edge of the bowl out with his nose before plunging in with his face, the applesauce cool and sloppy wet against his chin. He got his first mouthful and pushed back up, his whole body tensed, just knowing that broom was waiting in his brother's hand, ready to strike at any moment. Better Nate than Jackie, at least. She'd beat him senseless.

Zeke started to hum as he pushed, reciting the lyrics in his head. *Ooh, say*—grunt—*can you*—slurp—*see.*

Thwack.

The first hit got him across the shoulder. It didn't hurt, really. Just took him by surprise. Zeke kept going. So did Nate.

By the dawn's—thwack—*earl*—grunt—*ee light*—slurp, swallow, thwack—*what so proud*—thwack—*ly we*—slurp—*hailed*—thwack—*by the twi*—grunt—*light's*—thwack—*last*—slurp—*gleaming.*

Zeke could feel the applesauce dribbling down his chin, dangling from his nose. He made it through the ramparts streaming with only twelve push-ups, but when the bombs burst in air, he felt his grip on the linoleum start to slip and got too deep, accidentally snorting some sauce. Unfortunately this was the same moment Nate chose to wallop him across the back of the head, making Zeke cough-choke and lose his balance, his already-wobbly arms giving out, sending him face-planting in the bowl and getting applesauce up to his eyebrows.

Nate continued to beat him while he was down. The kid was only following orders.

Come on, Zeke. You're better than this. Do you really want to go down in history as the only kid to have ever drowned in a bowl of applesauce? Get up! Show them what you're made of! The great ones don't quit!

Choking, coughing, snorting, Zeke somehow managed to push himself out of the bowl, still humming, desperately trying to give proof through the night. The song was almost over. The bowl almost empty. With four more trembling, sauce-gobbling push-ups, Zeke made it to the home of the brave, then collapsed to his side, exhausted, sticky, and spent. He ripped off the blindfold, rolled to his back, and thrust his cooked noodle arms to the sky.

He saw Logan standing over him, the camera shifting from Zeke to the bowl and back again.

"You left some," he said.

Zeke tried to glare at him but couldn't. There was applesauce running into his eyes.

With two challenges down, Zeke asked for a break to get the smell of cinnamon out of his nose. Logan told him to take as long as he needed—he would just sit in the kitchen with Nate and finish his coffee.

A moment later, Zeke stood at the bathroom sink, one hand holding a used tissue, the other massaging the array of sore spots on his scalp. He was kind of a disaster. There was applesauce gluing his eyelashes together. He could still see little LEGO polka dots in his palms. He thought of the questioning looks Logan had been giving him all morning and frowned at his reflection.

"Seriously? Is it even worth it?"

It would be if he won, no question. But that was a big if, and he was afraid he was only making it bigger. That was the problem with choices and their consequences. Sometimes you made the first not knowing what the second would be. Last night this all sounded like a good idea. A way to separate himself from the pack. To be unique. To redefine what it meant to be great.

Turned out it was just a good way to get applesauce in your hair.

Zeke blew his nose. It was mostly snot.

His head really hurt.

You can't stop now. We need this, remember?

They needed this. The money. The trip. Just-picked pine-apples and fancy luaus with fire twirlers. White, sandy beaches and endlessly crashing waves. There's nothing like standing on the edge of the water and looking out over the horizon.

Or so he'd been told.

Come on, Zeke. You've got this. Stop sniffling, go out there, and show the world what you're made of.

Zeke dried his hands and stepped out into the hall to see Jackie's door was still shut tight. Thank god his sister was such a heavy sleeper. He made his way back to the kitchen to find Logan rinsing out his coffee mug. "Where's Nate?"

"Rolling the desk chair out onto the driveway," Logan said. "Almost asked him why, then figured I probably didn't want to know."

Probably not, Zeke thought. He looked at the camera sitting on the counter. Logan followed his gaze. "Don't worry. It's not on."

"You sure about that?" Zeke snipped. Normally he wouldn't talk to an adult like that, with so much added salt, but Logan had it coming. Or Zeke thought he did, at least.

The cameraman stared into the empty mug for a moment. His voice softened. "Listen, kid. I'm sorry if last night's video took you by surprise. The whole porch thing. I honestly thought I'd shut it off. But when I saw the footage . . . I don't know. I just figured it might help your cause, show another side of you, so I passed it along. I had no idea if Notts would even use it."

"Well, he *did* use it. And it *didn't* help," Zeke said. "I'm still thousands of votes behind."

"Right. And you think this"—Logan waved his hand to indicate the pile of plastic bricks, the applesauce-crusted bowl, the deformed self-portrait—"is going to make up the difference?"

Zeke shrugged. He honestly didn't know what it would take. More than he had to give, probably. But he still had to try.

"Don't get me wrong," Logan continued. "I bet lots of people out there will get a kick out of watching . . . whatever this is. I'm just not sure it's what the competition is really about. I think you might be missing the point."

"What point?" Zeke snapped, tossing his hands up. He could feel all his anger and disappointment and doubt swelling and swirling together. "You say just be yourself, so I do, but then that's not good enough. So then I try to be like the others, but that's not good enough either. What does everybody want from me? You've seen what I'm up against. Those guys—Aadya, Hailey, Dom—they're great at *everything*. And I'm not great at *anything*. I mean, just look at my face!"

He meant the one he'd drawn with his feet. It was sitting on the counter, grimacing at them, but the cameraman kept his eyes locked on Zeke's.

"Maybe the better question is, what do you expect of yourself?" Logan set his mug in the dishwasher. Then he added Zeke's mother's cup and Nate's cereal bowl for good measure. He picked up his camera and started down the hall to the front door but stopped halfway. "By the way, you might not care, but yesterday, on the porch . . . I thought your voices were fantastic."

The cameraman disappeared through the front door, where Nate was waiting, leaving Zeke alone in the kitchen. With a heavy sigh, he grabbed a towel and wiped up the floor where some of the applesauce had dripped, then rinsed the bowl out in the sink. He glanced at the drawing with its unlevel eyes and crooked mouth. Everything jumbled and awkward and out of place.

What do you expect?

But then he heard Gordon Notts's voice in his head. *The show must go on.*

Zeke crumpled up the picture and tossed it in the trash.

When he stepped outside, his brother was waiting for him in the driveway, standing dutifully behind the office chair, holding a jar of dill pickle spears in one hand and Zeke's cheap digital watch in the other. Logan hefted the camera to his shoulder, capturing the World's Greatest Applesauce Snorter as he came through the door. Zeke stared defiantly into the lens.

"I, Ezekiel Stahls, will now attempt the impossible. I will eat that entire jar of pickles in under three minutes . . . while perpetually spinning in circles."

Logan didn't laugh or snort or cough this time. He just kept the camera's eye focused on Zeke. Observe and record.

Zeke sat down, took the jar from Nate, and unscrewed the lid, pulling the first pickle free, dripping with vinegar. It was only then that he realized his stomach was already half-full and wasn't completely on board with this idea. There were a dozen spears in the jar. That worked out to one every fifteen seconds. For a moment he hesitated, hands full of pickle, head full of doubts.

But then he pictured those sparkling Pacific waters, the ones his father never took them to. He thought of his sister's posters, lying facedown on her floor. He imagined the smile on his mother's face when he handed her the check for ten grand. If there was still any chance, any chance at all . . .

He looked at his brother and nodded. Nate started the timer and gave the chair a push.

Zeke took the first bite. Then the second. Crunching his way to greatness as the whole world spun around him.

Two minutes and six seconds later he exploded.

Hello Beautiful Family,

Greetings from Yellowstone, our country's very first national park. That big white cloud on the front of the postcard is actually steam coming from Old Faithful. Yellowstone is home to over half of the world's active geysers, though this one is by far the most famous. Funny how one geyser becomes the geyser that everybody talks about and wants selfies with while all the other geysers just become jealous wannabes. Not sure how that happens, but it always seems to.

I didn't actually get to see Old Faithful go off of course, but I can tell you that the park is beautiful, even from a distance. We really will have to get out to Wyoming as a family sometime. They also have Devils Tower and the Grand Tetons (I know a joke about those, I'll tell you kids when you're older). Maybe we rent an RV, take the whole summer, hit all the big sights. Be nice to be on the road with the people I love for a change.

Miss you. Love you. Be home soon.

Dad

P.S. Here's one I can tell. What did the man say when he fell into Old Faithful while all his friends just stood around and laughed?

You geyser killing me.

Better from a Distance

This is the way the recording ends: not with a bang, but a hurl.

It was number seven that got him. Honestly, he was surprised he even got through half the jar. After three he could feel his stomach revolting. After five everything was starting to turn upside down and inside out. Following orders, Nate continued to push and Zeke's gut continued to spin and churn and gurgle until, halfway through number seven, he dropped both jar and spear, gripped both arms of the chair, leaned forward, and let her rip.

Kerplurrrrrch.

It was impressive, in its own way. Nate said he'd never seen puke fly so far before, arcing like a rainbow because of the spinning. A chunky orange and green rainbow. Except there was no pot of gold waiting at the end, just a broken pickle jar leaking juice onto the driveway.

Of course Logan captured it all on camera. That was his job after all. And he was good at his job. "And on that note," he said, dropping the camera to his side.

Zeke didn't respond. Just rushed back into the kitchen, afraid there might still be more on the way.

Minutes later, he wiped the last of the pickle juice from his chin, guzzled a cup of water followed by half a can of soda, and changed into a shirt that didn't smell like the wrath of dill. He walked dizzily, the world wavering with every step. His stomach cramped and his scalp hurt and his eyeballs felt like they might pop out of his head at any moment.

There was a lady in Nate's book that could do that, make her eyes bulge out like little balloons. It wasn't great, really, just weird and disgusting, but then he didn't have a whole lot of room to talk: he'd just tossed pickle chunks in one last failed attempt to be incredible at something.

And to top it all off, he still wasn't done filming for the day. There was one thing left on his plate: the interview with Notts. Zeke could only imagine how that was going to go. *So what have you been up to, Zeke? Well, Gordy, I got up to seven, but then I went right back down to zero in a hurry.* He was dreading it, even though he knew it was his last chance to salvage the day's footage. To at least *look* like he still belonged in this competition.

Just try not to blow it, he told himself. His stomach clenched again. Poor choice of words.

He found Logan in the backyard, the same spot where they'd

recorded Zeke's introduction only three days ago—though it felt more like thirty. A laptop sat on the patio table, its screen facing the deck chair Zeke was motioned toward (thankfully not one of the spinning kind). Nate sat cross-legged on the deck, rolling his basketball from one hand to the other. He was still wrinkling his nose, no doubt reliving his recent trauma; Zeke's puke bazooka had only missed his poor brother's feet by inches.

"Feel any better?" It was the kind of question someone would ask to be polite, but Logan sounded genuinely concerned.

"I guess," Zeke said, scraping his tongue against his teeth.

"If you need a couple more minutes . . ."

Zeke shook his head. "No. Let's just get this over with."

Logan's deeply furrowed forehead looked all too familiar; Zeke's mother almost always looked like that nowadays. "You're the boss. Here's how it'll go. Notts is going to pop up on that screen and ask you a few questions. All the contestants get the same ones. I'll just stand here behind the computer and record your answers, then it all gets spliced together and tacked on to tonight's clip. Speaking of clips." The cameraman walked over and attached a wireless microphone to Zeke's collar. It looked like a fuzzy black bug. "Just like a celebrity."

"I don't *feel* like a celebrity," Zeke mumbled. He felt more like the inside of a grapefruit that had been slam-dunked onto a cement driveway over and over again.

"Everybody's a star in somebody's sky, kid."

Logan resumed his place back behind the computer, camera at the ready. Nate rested his chin on his ball. Though it was a little cooler today than usual, Zeke was already sweating through his fresh T-shirt. He shifted from one cheek to the other and tried to keep his stomach from gurgling. It was strange: he'd been on camera for more than two days now—literally had Logan following him around, recording his every move—yet staring straight into that glass eye still made him itch. And it would only get worse. Gordon Notts wasn't exactly the kind of guy who puts one at ease.

Like a genie summoned by a mere thought, the black screen on the laptop suddenly came to life and Notts was there, still dressed like Colonel Sanders's lanky, beardless twin. "Why, hello there!" he chirped, his voice amplified by an external speaker, though everything about the man was at max volume already. His white suit gleamed. His smile blinded. He was wearing another bow tie—blue with yellow rubber ducks bobbing across it. His hands flitted around him like hummingbirds. If there *was* a top, Gordon Notts was never anywhere but over it. "Zeke, my boy! So great to see you!"

Zeke held up a hand. "Hey," he said, with as much enthusiasm as he could fake. He could still smell pickles. And cinnamon. Not an ideal combo.

"Logan—we ready to roll on this? I'm in a bit of a crunch. The Richters had to reschedule their interview for earlier. Hailey has clogging lessons this afternoon."

Of course she does, Zeke thought. *Because what kid doesn't want to take clogging?* Richter didn't even sound like an Irish name.

"All set on my end," Logan said, then he looked at Zeke. "You good?"

Maybe it was just his current state of mind, or everything that had happened so far this week, but this seemed like a loaded question. One without an easy answer. Zeke nodded anyway.

"Perfect. Let's roll in five, four, three . . ." Gordon Notts licked the fronts of his pearly whites and adjusted his ducked-up bow tie. "Hello out there, all you do-gooders. This is Gordon Notts, director of charitable programming for KABAM, and I'm here with the one and only Zeke Stahls, semiprofessional slide skater, pet rescuer, and cart coraller and overall terrific guy. How are you today, Zeke?"

Zeke hesitated. Truthfully, he was exhausted. And anxious. And damp. His clammy hands shook, and his gut was making all sorts of terrible burbling sounds. He could still taste vomit even though he'd brushed his teeth twice already. He was irritated at Logan, worried about his mother, confused and concerned about Jackie, and mad at himself for losing his briny second breakfast on camera. And somehow Gordon's beaming face only made it all worse.

He couldn't say all that, of course. He had to choke it down, force a smile. Preferably not the demented one. "I'm fine," he said, taking a page from Jackie's book. "I mean, great. I'm great."

"Of course you are!" Notts said brightly. "Because the world is full of greatness, isn't it? Every day, people like you doing incredible things, bringing color and light and wonder to the world."

You want to see some color, you should check out our driveway, Zeke thought.

"And tell me, Zeke," Notts continued, "what does it feel like to be thought of as one the greatest kids in the world?"

Zeke wiped his forehead on his sleeve. What did it *feel* like? Honestly, it felt ridiculous. Now even more than ever. Yeah, there had been a couple of moments—standing up to that jerk in the parking lot, cradling Angela's clawing cat, even managing that last push-up—where he'd felt a flush of pride. But mostly hearing those words—*world's greatest kid*—just made him think of that mug tucked away in the kitchen cabinet. The one with the crooked letters he'd scrawled himself.

I feel like a fake. A phony.

Except he knew that wasn't the right answer either. He tried to remember Jackie's advice. *Be confident but not arrogant. Down-to-earth but above it all. Like everybody but better.* His eyes gravitated toward her bedroom window, wondering if maybe she was peering at him from between her curtains, but there was no sign of her. He was on his own. He looked back at the camera.

"Well, I guess the best part has been seeing all the great things everyone else is doing," he said. "I mean the other kids in the competition are all just so awesome. And I know there are a bunch more out there just like th—" Zeke stopped and corrected himself. "Just like us."

"Oh, I doubt there's anyone quite like *you*," Gordon Notts quipped.

Zeke squirmed even more. What did he mean by *that*?

"It has to be tough, though," Notts continued, "always striving to be your best all the time when it would be so much easier to just be average. Ordinary. Why do it? What motivates you?"

You know perfectly well what motivates me, Zeke thought. He glanced at Nate, still leaning on his basketball, the one Logan found at a garage sale. The one they had to take to the park. How much did a new hoop cost? Like the one they used to have? You can never get back everything you've lost, Zeke knew, but you could get back some things. If you tried.

"I don't know. I guess it *feels* good. You know. Inside."

"Well, of course, it does!" Notts said, face aglow. "Just knowing that you are striving to be your best self while making a difference in the world, that's all any of us can ask for. Though let's be honest, ten thousand dollars wouldn't hurt. Speaking of which . . . if you *were* to win, what would you do with the cash prize?" On-screen, Gordon Notts craned both eyebrows in anticipation.

Zeke tucked his sweaty hands under his thighs, hesitating, mulling it over. It wasn't as if he didn't have an answer. What would he do with the ten-thousand-dollar prize? Buy that hoop, probably. And a PlayStation. And an iPhone. A moped, perhaps—if his mother would let him. And a crossbow, though he knew his chances at a moped were better.

Also maybe some new underwear. Because the elastic on most of his was starting to give out. And a new pair of shoes so that when he handed the pair he was wearing down to Nate, they wouldn't already have holes in them. And a pair for Mom too, the ones with that new, bouncy foam in them, so her feet wouldn't hurt so much after a second shift. And a book of car wash coupons for Jackie so Snoopy could get a much-needed bath.

Then there was that LEGO set that Nate had been drooling over for Christmas and didn't get. And those supersoft towels that his mother had spent forever admiring in the store, rubbing them against her cheeks. A full set to replace the ratty ones that had been washed a thousand times over.

And also that hole in the wall that still needed patching.

And the lawn mower that wouldn't start.

The pipe leaking through its duct-tape bandage.

The chair with its broken leg.

All the things that were barely standing, barely working, held together with tape and glue and good intentions. He would fix them all.

If he could.

"Zeke?" Notts's face peered out from the screen. "Ten thousand bucks. Don't spend it all in one place now."

Zeke nodded. He knew what his competition would say, of course. They would probably give all the money to charity. Maybe Hailey would buy more poofy balls to stick on her hats. Maybe old Graybeard could be fitted with a doggy prosthetic leg, if such a thing existed. If not, Aadya could probably use her prize money to help her invent one.

That's what *they* would do. But what would *he* do? What *should* he do?

"I'm really not sure," Zeke admitted. "I *was* going to fix our air conditioner . . ." Suddenly Zeke realized: He'd been so worked up about the filming and the competition, he'd never thanked Logan for his miracle work. "But now I don't have to." He managed a smile. The kind of sad one, not the deranged one. Behind the camera, Logan smiled back. "I guess . . . I guess I would just try to make people happy somehow."

"Then it would certainly be money well spent," Notts chimed in. "Provided you win, of course. And the competition continues to be fierce, so I'll remind our viewers to get their votes in and support KABAM in spotlighting the best of humankind. Because we *all* have the potential to be our best selves." He reached up and tweaked his bow tie. "Okay, one last question. And I have a feeling I already know what your answer's going to be, but I'm going to ask it anyway. Zeke Stahls, we are starting to discover how great *you* are, but none of us is *born* great. We all have people who show us the way. Who is the person *you* admire most? Who is *your* hero?"

Zeke stiffened in his seat. The question took him by surprise, though he couldn't say why. Of course the World's Greatest Kid would have role models; he just hadn't given it much thought before. Not like the ten thousand bucks, which he'd been thinking about constantly.

His hero. He squinted up at the gauzy clouds brightened by the sun, then glanced over at his little brother, who was answering the question for him by making web-shooters with his hands. *Pick Spidey. You know he's the best.* Of course Zeke knew that if it ever came down to him or Spider-Man, Nate would choose Zeke.

You pick the one who's there for you. Who shows up. Every day. For real.

Which meant the answer was obvious.

"Mom," he said. "My mom is my hero."

"Your mom, really?" Notts sounded genuinely surprised. "And why's that?"

"I don't know, because she's amazing? She works full-time—more than full-time, in fact—and she still takes care of us three kids. Plus she's funny. And smart. And sweet . . . well, most of the time, she's sweet. And she's creative. She makes all of our Halloween costumes from scratch." Zeke didn't bother to mention it was because she refused to pay for the store-bought ones. "She also makes a killer white bean chili. And a great cinnamon crumb cake. Plus, unlike *some* people, she never once locked me in the closet because I was being annoying." Zeke stared into the camera for a moment as if to say, *you know who you are, Jacqueline Stahls.* "Oh, and when she hugs you, it's like being wrapped in a thick, fuzzy blanket—you're suddenly warm all the way through. Most importantly, she's always there when I need her. So yeah. She's the one for sure." Zeke nodded twice for emphasis.

On-screen, Gordon Notts squinted back at him.

"So not your dad, then?"

Zeke swallowed hard, tasting the leftover bile on his tongue. He felt his heart press tight against his ribs. "My dad?"

"Don't get me wrong," Notts said, still smiling, "your mother is a remarkable woman, to be sure, everything she's done. Everything she's been through. But your father. I mean . . . *that's* quite a story, isn't it? Tragic, of course, but *so noble*. I would think he would surely be an inspiration to you."

Quite a story.

Zeke looked down at his unraveled shoelaces and resisted the urge to bend over and tie them. He got a glimpse, a flash of memory: he and his father sitting on the front porch, his dad's deep voice reciting the rhyme, his heavy hands patiently guiding Zeke's own. *Crisscrossed that little tree, trying to catch me.* It was a memory he seldom shared. Like most of them. Locked away for safekeeping.

"I'm not sure what you want me to say," Zeke mumbled.

He never knew what to say. They hardly ever talked about it, the four of them. They hardly ever talked about *him*. It was easier not to. Mom would say something every once in a while, but even that was always in passing. A chuckle or sigh accompanied by a *your father used to say* or a *you know your dad always thought*. Then she would go quiet for a second and stare at the floor or out the window, waiting for the moment to pass.

People always asked of course. They couldn't help it. Teachers. Neighbors. Kids at school. Then came the pitying looks, the creased foreheads, the gently patting hand. *How terrible. I'm so sorry.* It got exhausting after a while. Having to explain. Having to relive it. Better to keep it tucked away. Better to keep it boxed up.

Except Notts knew. He'd found out somehow. And now he was sharing it with the world.

Zeke crossed and uncrossed his feet.

"He was a truck driver, wasn't he? Your dad?" Notts prodded. "Must have been tough with him on the road all of the time."

Zeke nodded meekly. It was tough. Harder on Mom, of course. Jackie too, because she was older, closer. The days without him seemed to drag on. But then, finally, you'd hear the sound of the pickup rumbling up the driveway, and seconds later he'd be there, walking through the door with souvenirs in hand. Key chains with Zeke's and Jackie's names on them. T-shirts with funny slogans. A lucky rabbit's foot. A stuffed moose. He'd walk in with an *I'm home* holler, his arms stretched out in invitation. Zeke would come bolting down the hallway, ready for liftoff. And everything—the time away, the missed soccer games and violin recitals, the boring Sunday mornings of only cereal and frozen waffles—it would all be instantly forgiven.

All he had to do was walk through the door.

"He was on his way home, wasn't he?" Notts said, his forehead creasing. "That night?"

That night. Truthfully Zeke didn't know exactly what happened that night. It was a story pieced together like a jigsaw puzzle. A text message. A call into dispatch. Police reports from the scene. News articles afterward. The details didn't change the ending—that was always the same. Zeke continued to stare at his shoes. Notts pressed on.

"He was driving down the highway when he saw a car stopped on the side of the road. This would have been, what, about three years ago?"

Almost exactly three years ago. The end of June. Summer break. Not as hot as this one but hot enough. Zeke had been asleep when it happened, his mother having just finished their bedtime routine. Reading aloud and wiggling toes. Even when she told him—because she told them all that night—he didn't completely get it. *What are you saying?* he asked her. *When is he coming home?* It didn't make any sense at the time.

It still didn't make any sense.

Because he shouldn't have even stopped that night. That was the first thing. It was company policy to radio in if you saw a problem but to stay on your route, keep to the schedule, hit your deliveries. But the Stahlses weren't always known for their strict rule following.

Zeke cleared his throat, struggled to find his voice. He still didn't look up, speaking in something close to a mumble. "He texted Mom, saying he'd be a little late. That he was gonna help some guy with a flat tire."

She texted back with a smiley face. She told him to be careful. That's how the story went.

It had been raining. Not the house-shaking storm that made

Zeke and his brother curl up in Jackie's bed that one night, but a steady downpour that slicked some parts of the road with standing water. They never found out who it was their father helped, though the police could tell by the tracks that someone had driven off, presumably on a spare tire that Andrew Stahls had helped change. It wouldn't have taken him long, Zeke knew. Like Logan, Zeke's father was good at fixing things.

Whoever it was, they were lucky. Most people wouldn't have stopped to begin with. Late at night. In the dark. In the rain. Most people would have driven right on by.

Wouldn't they?

"So he pulled over to help some stranger, and then what happened?" Gordon asked.

And then.

Zeke felt his throat tighten. He looked over at Nate, who was hugging his basketball close to his chest now, blinking up at his big brother. He'd heard this all before. He was so young at the time. Too young to process it. For Nate the story *was* the memory; there was no separating the two.

"Then this other car . . ." Zeke began.

Going too fast. In the rain. In the dark. Skimming the shoulder. Its driver exhausted, just trying to get back home himself. He said he didn't see Zeke's father standing by the side of the road, silhouetted against the truck's flashing hazards. Zeke could imagine the screaming brakes, the tires desperately digging for traction, the car swerving out of control. He tried not to think of the sound it made. The impact. Tried not to picture his father lying on the cold, wet ground.

She told him to be careful. She told him.

"By the time the ambulance got there . . ."

Zeke's voice trailed off. He really wanted to tie his shoes, but he couldn't move. He stared at the laces hanging loose, stained with grass and dirt.

"Wow," Notts said after a moment, his voice reverent. "Your poor family. Such a terrible tragedy. And yet . . ."

Zeke looked up sharply.

And yet?

He knew just what Notts was going to say. He knew because it had been said before. A hundred times before. But Notts was wrong. They were all wrong. There was no *and yet*. That was the whole story. No coda. No epilogue. No moral. His father pulled over late one night and got hit by another car while standing on the side of the road. It crushed his ribs and broke his heart, and he bled out next to a cornfield a hundred miles from home the end.

Zeke bit hard on his bottom lip.

"I mean, you must be so proud," Notts continued. "It made the local papers. I know. I've read them. Good Samaritan, father of three, heroically helping someone in need, going out of his way to—"

Zeke couldn't take anymore. "No."

"Sorry?" Gordon Notts looked startled.

"He's not a hero," Zeke said louder, his throat aching, like it was full of slivered glass. "My dad wasn't some fireman who pulled a baby from a burning building. Or some soldier who died on the battlefield. He was a truck driver who stopped to change a tire. He was in the wrong place at the wrong time. That's it. *That's the whole story*."

"But you have to admit, it was still a great—" Notts began.

"No it wasn't!" Zeke snapped, shouting now. "It wasn't great or noble or admirable. It was stupid. If he hadn't stopped, he wouldn't have been there when that other guy went off the road. It wasn't his responsibility. *We* were his responsibility. Us. His family. And he just . . . he just . . ."

Zeke paused, his hands trembling. A voice in his head told him to let it go, shut the box and stuff it back under the bed, but he couldn't. He couldn't fit it all back inside. He didn't dare look at Nate or at his sister's window, just kept his eyes fixed on the computer screen, on Gordon Notts's shocked face. "I mean, so what? So what if he doesn't pull over? So what if he doesn't help? That guy with the flat tire has to wait a half hour for a tow truck? Big freaking deal! He would have gotten home eventually. They *both* would have. But instead . . ."

Zeke thought about the postcards. All the places they were meant to have gone together, all the sights they were supposed to have seen. He thought about the dining room table with the extra chair that they bought not long after Nate was born. The couch where they used to sit and watch all those old B-movies—*Attack*

297

of the Killer Tomatoes, Plan 9 from Outer Space—laughing at the terrible special effects.

Those Sunday morning pancakes. Waking up to that smell of bacon and knowing his dad was home for the whole day. That he'd take them to the park and push them in the swings and then maybe get ice cream after. That they wouldn't have to watch out the window for his return.

Crawling around the inside of his father's rig, looking at the berth where his dad sometimes slept and the pictures he had taped there. A wife and three kids. More than any man could ever want, he used to say. More than any man could ask for.

All of that, left behind. And for what?

For what?

Zeke's eyes burned. He brushed off tears with the back of his hand. He caught a flicker of movement. Logan, shutting off the camera.

"I think we're finished here."

There were rules. Not that Zeke was a stickler for them in general, but there were rules about where the camera could follow him. Not into the bathroom, obviously. Not into the bedroom, at least not without his permission.

He wasn't so sure about the roof.

So when he heard feet coming up the ladder behind him, his first thought was of Logan and his camera, and he refused to turn and look because he didn't want the whole world to see his face just then, tear tracks merged with trickling sweat, snot smeared across his cheek, the red spiderwebs in his eyes. He couldn't put on a phony smile right now.

But he didn't need to worry. The person whose voice called from the top of the ladder had seen him cry before.

"You're not supposed to be up here, you know."

"You never tried to stop me before," Zeke said with a sniff.

"That's not true. I have, in fact. Several times. You just ignored me. Like you always do. With everything. Eventually I just figured I'd wait until you fell and broke something and then at least I could laugh and say I told you so."

Jackie climbed up onto the roof and crouch-walked across it. Zeke gave her a quick sideways glance as she sat down beside him. From this vantage point, you could spot two or three missing shingles. You could easily see the patches of dead grass in the front yard where Mrs. Gwon always let her dog pee. The leaning mailbox from where Snoopy accidentally nudged it with his rear. All the little gaps and imperfections.

Jackie sat with her knees bent, careful to not let her bare skin touch the rooftop. "You know it's, like, ten degrees hotter up here."

"Nobody asked you to come," Zeke snipped.

"Also not true. Your little minion did. He came barging into my room and told me what happened. He said you were doing your interview with Notts and got upset and stormed off."

"I didn't storm off," Zeke muttered.

"He said stormed. He said you yelled at the guy."

Okay. Maybe he stormed a little. But it was justified. Or mostly justified. "He wanted to talk about Dad," Zeke muttered.

Jackie let that one sit for a moment. She wrapped her arms around her legs, leaned forward, and balanced her chin on her knees. "Oh," she said. The *oh* was like her *fine*. It came preloaded. It came weighed down. "What about him?"

"Notts wanted to know who I admired."

"And you said Dad?"

"No. *I* said Mom. But I guess he knew already. About the accident." Zeke picked at the tiny grains on the roof shingles that looked a little like sand.

Jackie sighed. "God, I hate having to tell that story. Everybody wants to hear it. And they always think that your telling them will somehow make *you* feel better."

"But it doesn't," Zeke said.

"No. It never does," she agreed. His sister squinted up at the sky. "I mean, what's there to say? It just sucks. *You* know it sucks. *I* know it sucks. It sucks for Mom, who's had to do everything by herself for the past three years. It sucks for Nate, even though the kid can barely remember anything about him. Think about it too hard and it pulls you down. You start to sink."

Zeke nodded. Doesn't hurt too bad as long as you don't touch it. So just don't touch it.

Except sometimes you can't help it.

Zeke clenched and unclenched his fingers. "It makes me mad sometimes," he admitted. "Just thinking about it. At him. At the whole world. Almost like I'm blaming him. Is that terrible? Does that make me a terrible person?"

Jackie took a moment. Then she shook her head.

"Some days I'm so pissed, I don't know what to do with myself," she said. "So I lock myself in my room, crank up my music, and just try to breathe."

"Or you tear down all your posters," Zeke said.

Jackie glared at him. "How do you know I took my posters down?"

Zeke decided to exercise his Fifth Amendment rights, but his silence still incriminated him.

"You can be such a creep sometimes, you know that?"

He knew—he just didn't want to admit it. "Why'd you do it?" he pressed.

Jackie shrugged. "I don't know. I just couldn't stand to look at them anymore. All those places—they seem so far away. And with everything that's going on—Mom and you and Nate. The money. The house. I mean, I'm not even sure I can go to college out of state, let alone travel all the way to freaking Paris, so why keep kidding myself?"

Zeke scratched at the shingles again, getting the grit under his fingernails. "Dad would have wanted you to keep them up."

"Yeah, well . . . Dad wanted a lot of things."

Add it to the list.

Zeke stared sideways at his sister. He'd always thought she looked the most like their father, same bright blue eyes, same pointed chin and wheat-colored hair. But her expressions were all Mom. She'd obviously perfected their mother's frustrated frown.

He didn't really know what else to say, so he inched a little closer so that their knees nearly touched. He half expected her to scoot away, but she didn't.

"Sucks about the interview, though," she said at last, following it with one of her signature eye rolls. "This whole freaking competition. I don't care if he is the director of all that's good and right in the world, that Notts guy is a jerk. Was it really that bad?"

"It definitely didn't end well," Zeke admitted. "But no worse than the pickles, I guess."

"What happened to the pickles?"

Thankfully before Zeke could be forced to answer, they were interrupted by another squeaky voice from behind. "Hey, you guys ever coming back down?"

Zeke and Jackie both twisted to see Nate's spiky-haired head peeking up over the edge of the roof. He'd never climbed up the ladder by himself—Zeke had always been right behind him, making sure he didn't slip.

"Nate! What are you doing?" Jackie shouted. "You can't be up here. It's dangerous!"

"Cool your horses, sister. I've been up here before," Nate said dismissively, which earned Zeke a penetrating stare.

"Maybe once or twice," he confessed.

"Four times," Nate corrected, scrambling up onto the roof and crawling over to them. "This makes five."

"God, you're just like your brother, you know that?" Jackie said.

Nate grinned.

"It's not a compliment," she added.

"What are we doing up here anyway?" Nate wanted to know.

"Sulking mostly," Jackie said.

"And sweating," Zeke added.

Nate shrugged. "Okay." He plopped down on the other side of Jackie, who instantly grabbed hold of part of his shirt, anchoring him to her with a white-knuckled grip.

The three of them sat, only inches apart but ten years between them, looking out over the neighborhood and the handful of other kids with their feet firmly on the ground. You could just make out the edge of the park from here—the tip of the Rocket's tower glinting in the sunlight, ready for takeoff.

"Seriously, I'm not even sure why you guys even like it up here," Jackie said.

Zeke was about to say something about carbonated beverage bombs and bra parachutes, but Nate spoke up first.

"Things look better from far away."

"They do," Zeke confirmed.

Jackie nodded, agreeing with both of her brothers for once. "I can see that. We are *not* telling Mom about this, though."

That made two things they agreed on.

Which made one record set for the day.

They sat together for ten minutes more, which was as long as Jackie could take it before her nerves got the better of her and she insisted they all get down. She took Nate inside for a snack. Zeke went searching for Logan.

He found the cameraman in his usual break spot, except this time the camera was already packed away, along with the laptop. That was perfectly fine with Zeke. He wasn't interested in seeing Gordon Notts's face again anytime soon.

Logan had his book in his lap, finger pressed to the page. "Hey, kid. You all right? You kind of took off back there."

"Yeah. Sorry about that," Zeke said, shuffling closer. "Probably not how that was supposed to go." *Probably wasn't how any of this was supposed to go.*

"Don't apologize," Logan said. "Notts can be a little in-your-face sometimes. He means well, but he doesn't always see the trees for the forest, if you catch my drift."

"Not really," Zeke admitted.

"I think he sometimes forgets that humanity is made up of actual humans," Logan revised. "And don't worry about the interview: we agreed to just cut it off where you finish talking about your mom. It will be fine."

That was some relief, at least; Zeke doubted he would score many points for screaming at the director of charitable programming. "Thanks," he said.

"No sweat." Logan scratched at his beard with his free hand. "You know, my ma used to make all my Halloween costumes too. Except she wasn't very good at it. Some of the other kids would make fun of me for them, so when they weren't looking, I'd sneak up behind 'em and snatch their bags of candy."

"Seriously? You took their stash? Did they ever catch you?"

"Sometimes. But I still got a load of chocolate out of the deal." Logan smiled. "Not that I'm encouraging such behavior, of course."

"Of course," Zeke echoed. Don't dip your biscuits in another person's gravy. Everybody knew that.

"I mean, let's face it: we've all done things we're not proud of," Logan continued. "And some things that we are. Guess the big question is, which are people going to remember you for?"

Zeke looked at the office chair still sitting in the driveway, the broken jar, the pickles—eaten, uneaten, half-eaten. He'd have to get the hose out and clean up his mess before his mother got home. He couldn't expect anyone else to do it for him. Or he shouldn't, at least. He sat next to the cameraman and sighed a fifty-pound sigh.

"Tough week," Logan said. It wasn't a question. There was plenty of evidence to back it up, most of it on tape. "I bet you'll be glad when this whole thing's over, no matter how it turns out."

Zeke thought about everything he'd been through already in his quest for the title of World's Greatest Kid. Actual blood, sweat, tears, and vomit. No question, he would be relieved when tomorrow night rolled around and the final votes were cast. "Not sure it matters," he muttered. "I think I've made it pretty clear I'm not that great. Don't see any way I can win now."

"Not sure those are the same," Logan mused. "Besides, you've still got one more day."

"Right. You saw how *this* day went. What could I possibly do for tomorrow?"

Logan shrugged. "You're Ezekiel Stahls. Creative and curious and always pushing the boundaries. You'll think of something."

They sat in silence for a minute more. Then Logan riffled through the pages of his book. "Looks like I've only got one chapter left. Really curious to see how this whole thing ends."

Zeke had read that book three times, cover to cover, including once with his mom. But hard as he tried, he couldn't recall what happened in the last ten pages, which made him a little curious too. "I guess we could find out," he said, then added, "but just us. No cameras this time."

"Just us," Logan agreed.

He handed Zeke the book and showed him where to begin.

"And don't forget the voices," he said.

Promises to Keep

That night, Jackie made dinner.

Thankfully neither pickles nor applesauce were on the menu. Instead she boiled a pot of spaghetti, making sure to have it ready when their mother finally dragged herself through the door at almost eight o'clock, looking like she'd been blindfolded and beaten by a hundred mall teens armed with brooms. She barely had time to kick her heels off before she was tackle-hugged by Nate, who proceeded to tell her all about Zeke's earlier explosion in the driveway.

"I mean, there was puke *everywhere!*"

"Not *every*where," Zeke said, shrinking from Mom's look, which was equal parts suspicion and concern. "And I cleaned it off." The cracked jar was sitting in the garbage bin outside, so as not to stink up the place.

His mother's concern ultimately outweighed the suspicion and she placed a hand to Zeke's forehead. "Are you sick? Is everything okay?"

"Not sick," Zeke said. "Just spinning too fast is all." Not that this explained anything. Not that he *cared* to explain. She would find out before too long anyway.

Luckily, his mother was distracted by the smell of garlic bread, her eyes darting to the kitchen. "Well, this is a nice surprise," she said.

Jackie shrugged. "It's a two-dollar box of spaghetti and a jar of Prego. It's not chicken cacciatore."

"Who's Tory?" Nate wondered.

Their mother plucked a noddle from the strainer. "But *I* didn't have to make it. That makes it taste ten times better." You could tell she was grateful. And not just for the meal. All three of her children were in the same room, and none of them were pulling hair or pinning any of the others to the floor. Not yet anyway.

As she finished her appetizer noodle, Mom's phone buzzed: their nightly message from the Klein Agency letting them know that the four new videos had been posted and the voting had begun.

Zeke felt his stomach lurch. It had nothing to do with the prospect of his sister's overcooked spaghetti. It wasn't the failed challenges that worried him either; it wouldn't be the first time his mother had seen him attempting something ridiculous and/

or potentially hazardous to his health. She'd already watched him shoot down the Poop Chute on a skateboard after all.

No, it was the interview that had his insides tied in knots. What if Gordon Notts changed his mind and kept in the part about Zeke's dad? What if his mother heard what Zeke said about him? About what he was.

And what he wasn't.

But before Zeke could think of some excuse for them not to watch, his mother had set the laptop on the kitchen table next to her plate, Jackie on one side, Nate hoovering up noodles on the other. Zeke stood and looked over his mother's shoulder as she clicked her way to the Klein Agency's website. He stole a quick glance at the current tally, enough to remind him that Hailey Richter was in the lead, with Dom right on her tail and Aadya right on his.

And coming in a distant fourth . . .

Oh yeah? Just wait till they see your beautiful self-portrait, he told himself. *Wait till they see you face-plant in a bowl of applesauce. That'll convince them of your greatness. Especially if they get to watch you pitch a fit and storm out of your interview.*

"Whose should we watch first?" his mother asked. "Yours?"

Zeke shook his head and got to the laptop before she did, clicking on Hailey's picture instead, her overly cheerful face filling the screen.

"Sometimes, all it takes is a little music to brighten someone's day," she began in her sprightly voice. This was followed by a shot of her in a yellow sundress with stitched-on daisies, standing in a hospital room next to a kid with tubes snaking out of his nostrils.

This definitely wasn't clogging lessons.

Turns out Hailey Richter spent the first half of her morning volunteering at her local children's hospital, singing to sick kids with the aid of a pink ukulele. The camera followed her as she visited patients' bedsides, asking them if they wanted Billie Eilish or Ed Sheeran—the only two songs she knew, apparently. Even with that limited repertoire, all the kids smiled and tapped their fingers against their bed rails while she chirped and strummed. At one point in the video, a nurse joined in and she and Hailey did a duet. One kid hooked up to three or four different machines asked for a selfie with her.

"Now I know I have met an angel in person. And she looks perfect," Hailey crooned.

Her total ticked upward with each strummed chord. How could it not? Sick kids were as good as gold. Maybe even better than three-legged puppies.

The video then cut to her interview with Notts—hitting her with the same questions as Zeke. As expected, she promised to donate a portion of her winnings to that same hospital to buy books for the kids in long-term care, along with a promise to buy new ice skates for some of the girls at her rink, spending nothing on herself. And her heroes? Her gammy, who served in the air force, and Greta Thunberg. The video ended with the return of that selfie—Hailey Ukulele and that kid with cancer flashing peace signs and pretty smiles.

"Huh. *That's* gonna be tough to beat," Zeke's mother said.

Zeke moaned softly. Tough? Try impossible.

But Aadya Gupta certainly gave it her best.

The wiry, wry-smiled girl with the black belt showed up in her third day's video dressed in overalls and protective goggles instead of a gi, a hammer riding in a loop at her waist, talking as she walked purposefully past a pile of lumber. It reminded Zeke of a political ad, the kind that usually had old white guys with fake tans promising a better future for all.

"There's an affordable-housing crisis in this country," Aadya said, her voice sharp and determined. "But there doesn't have to be. This, at least, is one problem we can all fix if we try."

What followed were clips of Aadya helping other folks from Habitat for Humanity build a small house for a family who'd been evicted from their last one. There were shots of her driving home nails, measuring boards, even using power tools. *Couldn't be me*, Zeke thought; there was no way his mother would let him within twenty feet of a circular saw. But there was Aadya, dust on her goggles, slicing through two-by-fours with ease. Another tracking shot of her carrying bags of gravel on her shoulders like some serum-infused superhero.

And speaking of heroes, hers, apparently, were her auntie, who was a doctor, and RBG. Her video ended with the overalled overachiever hammering in time to that song by Phillip Phillips.

Just know you're not alone . . . 'cause Aadya G. will build your home.

Ugh.

"Okay. That was pretty good too," Mom whispered under her breath.

"She nailed it." Nate snorted at his own terrible joke.

"Come on. Anyone can hammer two pieces of wood together," Zeke said dismissively.

"Sure. Anyone *can*," Jackie said.

Their mother frowned and clicked on the second-to-last image and they were all looking at Dom sprawled on his carpet, surrounded by markers, doubled over a piece of poster board, though his head obscured what was written on it. Some sweeping strings and low horns could be heard in the background, clearly building to a climax. His disarming voice came in: "This week I was invited to take part in something special."

He didn't mean the competition.

The next thing Zeke knew, the kid was standing outside of a school building, looking out over a crowd of hundreds. His mother stood behind him holding the sign he'd been making while he, eleven-year-old Dom, *gave a freaking speech.* In front of all those people. With note cards and everything. It was a speech about equality and community and justice, quoting everyone from Mandela to Muhammad Ali. And it was *awesome.*

The people at KABAM didn't show the whole thing, obviously, only snippets—but they did make sure to show the huge ovation at the end.

The Stahlses didn't stand and clap; they sat and stared, dumb-founded and impressed. Zeke tried to think of the last speech *he* ever gave. Then he remembered: standing on top of his desk, ordering his classmates to drop their drawers.

But the real icing on the greatness cake came when Gordon Notts asked the kid who his hero was. Dom gave the man the answer he was looking for. *My hero is my dad.* The video faded out on Dom's poster, calling for liberty and justice for all. An infinitely nobler goal than seeing Micah moon Amanda Troxell.

"That kid is impressive," Jackie said.

Zeke's mom hovered the cursor above her son's picture.

"Maybe you shouldn't," he warned.

"What? Why not?" she asked. "I mean, I'm guessing you didn't build a house or give any big speeches or anything, but I'm sure you did something good today, and I want to see what it was."

Feats that inspire. Deeds that will go down in history. Pickles that will return in force. He was pretty sure she would never hear the national anthem the same way again, at least.

She clicked and there was Zeke in the living room with LEGO in his hair and a marker between his toes.

And there was Zeke stretched out in the kitchen with apple-sauce up his nose.

And there was Zeke spinning with the jar in his lap, around and around he goes.

There were no images of Zeke pounding on either podiums

or nails. No shots of him hugging sick kids and singing them cheesy pop songs. It was just Zeke being Zeke.

He watched carefully, not the screen but his family. His mother's face was a wrinkled tapestry of emotions. Amusement and confusion, revulsion and surprise. Jackie's was mostly just revulsion.

Thankfully Logan—or maybe Notts—decided to cut that last great act short, freezing for a moment on Zeke's green face right before he dropped the jar, a vague if slightly sarcastic subtitle at the bottom informing viewers that the attempt was "unsuccessful." He saw the totals of the other three contestants steadily rise, but somehow, shockingly, he was still getting votes as well. He wondered what that said about the world, that people would pick some kid snarfing applesauce over another kid fighting injustice.

It was kind of sad, really.

The next shot was of him sitting on his deck, bathed in sunlight, still looking a little queasy.

Hello out there, all you do-gooders.

Like all the other interviews, the screen was split, with Notts's double-wide grin on one side and Zeke looking sweaty and uncomfortable on the other.

He spied on his mother out of the corner of his eye, saw her smile when Notts got to the question of the grand prize and Zeke's faltering answer. "Really? You were going to fix the air conditioner?" she said. "I thought you wanted a moped."

314

Zeke didn't say anything. Because he knew what was coming next. He glanced at his sister, who frowned back at him.

Who is your hero?

"Ooh. Wait. Don't tell me," his mother said, snapping her fingers. "Looki? Lucky? The green one. With the horns.".

Zeke bit his tongue and continued to watch his mother's face, saw the sudden shift in her expression, a spontaneous smile when he gave his actual answer. *She's the one for sure.* Like Notts, she hadn't seen that one coming either.

And then the video ended, rather abruptly, cutting to the familiar message that read *To vote for Zeke Stahls, click on the button below.*

Zeke slumped back in his chair. Notts and Logan were true to their word, leaving the worst part on the cutting room floor.

But as the video faded, his mother's smile faded alongside it, replaced with a look Zeke couldn't quite place. She stood up wordlessly, gathering her half-eaten bowl of spaghetti, the clink of the fork hitting the sink as loud as a gunshot. With her back to all three of her children, she spoke in a quiet voice. "I need some air."

Zeke tracked her as she headed for the deck, shutting the door behind her, not looking back at her three children gathered around the table.

"What's wrong with Mom?" Nate wondered. "Is she mad about the pickles?"

Zeke could just make out his mother's outline through the

sliding door, standing in the shadows of the house that she and Dad had picked out together.

"One of us should go check on her," Jackie insisted. "Make sure she's okay."

One of us.

She stared hard at Zeke until it clicked.

The patio door stuck, because the patio door always stuck, but Zeke muscled it closed behind him. A little WD-40 was probably all it needed, but somehow even the simple fixes seemed like too much effort sometimes. He stepped out onto the deck next to his mother, who stood on its edge, rubbing her arms even though it was still plenty warm outside.

For a minute neither of them spoke, letting the cricket song fill that space. Finally she said, "It's not true."

"What's not true?"

"What you said in there. About me."

Zeke started to protest, but she wasn't finished.

"It was very sweet. Really. And I want it to be true. I do. But I just know it's not. It can't be." She let out a half laugh. "I mean, just look at me, Z." She brushed a hand over her wrinkled business suit. "What part of this says hero to you? I'm a walking disaster. I can barely drag myself out of bed each morning to get to work on time." She waved an arm over the backyard. "Look at this yard. Look at this house. Everything's broken, or if it's not broken, it's about to break. There're bills piled on the counter.

There's laundry getting mildewed in the washer. There's probably one fresh vegetable left in the fridge, if we're lucky. It's all a holy mess."

Zeke looked around. The yard *was* in dire need of mowing, approaching Amazon-rainforest levels of growth. And the only thing green in the fridge was a three-month-old burrito with an impressive crown of mold. And he had completely blanked on transferring the load of laundry he'd put in. She was right: things were messy. But that didn't change what he said or how he felt. He just wasn't sure how to convince *her* of that.

"Some hero," his mother repeated, making it sound more like a curse. "I'm hardly ever around. I can't even get home in time to make a pot of spaghetti; I have to have your sister do it . . . as if *she* doesn't have enough to deal with. I mean, honestly, Zeke, what kind of mother lets her kids climb up on the freaking *roof*?"

Zeke's eyes darted upward, past the sagging gutters, to the moon just peeking through the clouds. "How'd you know about that?"

"Mrs. Gwon texted me while I was at work. *Kids on the roof again* and a string of disapproving frown emojis."

Mrs. Gwon. Of course. Zeke made a note to TP her house the next time Halloween rolled around. "She's a nosy old lady with an ugly dog. What does she know?"

Mom sighed. "It's not just that. It's everything. It's like there's this giant black hole that I can't see, but I can feel it, tugging me, pulling me down, and I can't get away from it."

Zeke's mother bowed her head, her shoulders sagging under the weight. "You know right after your dad died, everyone said, this is it. This is the hardest part. The preacher. Our family. My friends. Just get through the next few weeks, they said, and it will get easier. Then when it didn't, they said, it's okay, this is the worst, just get through the next few months, and things will look up. The first year is the toughest, they said. Just hold on. But I've been holding on, and still it just gets *harder*, you know? Every day it's something else. The faucet drips. The brakes squeal. Your sister needs contacts. Your brother gets strep."

Your middle kid gets called down to the principal's office, Zeke thought. *For the third time in a month.* It was always something. He wondered how often that something was him.

His mother took a knuckle to the corner of her eye. He couldn't remember the last time he'd seen her cry. Not in front of him, anyway. They'd all gotten too good at doing such things behind closed doors.

"I miss him, Zeke. I miss his scruffy beard and his awful taste in movies, and his jokes, which somehow always made me laugh no matter how terrible they were. I miss how he hummed when he poured himself coffee. I miss how he used to put on his socks—scrunching them first and then slowly pulling them up, like it was some kind of magic trick, putting his damn socks on. I miss that look he'd get on his face whenever he'd come home after a long trip and see you running for him, your arms out like an airplane, jumping straight up, ready to fly."

Zeke nodded. He remembered. Of course he remembered.

"God, I'd pay anything to have one more day, you know? Just one more day with him. The way things used to be. It doesn't seem like that much to ask . . . for something that's impossible, at least."

Zeke reached out and took his mother's hand, his smaller fingers weaving with hers, squeezing tight.

"I still meant it, though," he whispered. "What I said. Even if you don't think so."

His mom managed a trace of a smile. "You're a good boy, Zeke," she said, squeezing back. "Don't let anyone tell you otherwise."

They stood like that for a while, hand in hand under the darkening sky, looking up at the stars.

Making silent wishes for each other.

Zeke didn't bother to check the totals that night before bed. He knew the hospital bards, house builders, and budding social activists would maintain their lead over the upside-down, upchucking push-uppers of the world. His video would speak to a particular audience: the TikTok challenge crowd. The *Impractical Jokers* fans. All of his friends at school (that was three votes right there). But it wouldn't be enough. Wouldn't even be *close*.

Which meant he'd have to do something spectacular tomorrow. Something completely off the charts.

Something impossible.

With the lights off and Nate out, Zeke grabbed the flashlight from the top of his nightstand and then bent over to dig beneath his bed, finding the cedar box and setting it near his pillow. He gently removed the lid, careful not to make too much noise, and spread the contents out beside him, their glossy surfaces cool and slick in his hand. He tugged his bedspread up and over as he had so many times before, enshrouding himself, creating a force field to block out the rest of the world, settling his flashlight's beam on the first card in the stack.

There were fifty-three in total. Fifty-three postcards from places Zeke had never been. Fifty-three images of sights that his dad had seen without them. They technically weren't Zeke's to take. Certainly not his to hoard, but he hoarded them anyway, like a dragon and its gold.

It didn't have to be the postcards. There were reminders of his father everywhere in the house. Framed photographs. The dusty golf clubs in the garage. The bottle of Calvin Klein cologne that his mother kept by the sink for three years, and sometimes, Zeke knew, spritzed as if it were air freshener—but only when she thought nobody was watching.

But these—these were the true treasure. He kept them hidden beneath his bed because he didn't want anyone to know that he had them, to know that he had snuck into his mother's room— *trespassed* was the word—standing on a suitcase that he'd never seen used, grabbing on to the hanger bar for balance, and swiping the box from her closet, Indiana Jones style, before slinking back to his room.

He'd taken them months ago. There had been nothing special about that day. Mom had whisked Nate off to get his hair cut. Jackie was out with her friends. Zeke was meant to be doing homework, but the loneliness got to him. The emptiness of the house. The quiet. So instead he took the box his mother had been preserving and he spent an hour flipping through his father's adventures—feeling the edges of the stamps with his finger, tracing the letters of his dad's handwriting. When he heard the van pull into the driveway, he hurriedly stuffed the postcards back into the plain cedar box she stored them in, but rather than rush to tuck them back onto her top shelf and risk being caught snooping through her closet, he decided to keep them close by. He felt ashamed for hiding them. For hoarding them. But he wasn't ready to let them go.

For the past three months, he'd slept above his father's words, taking them out whenever he felt himself sinking, just like his mother said.

Zeke spread the postcards out in an uneven rainbow, taking them in all at once. They spanned some fourteen years, the first ones addressed only to *my lovely wife and beautiful baby girl*, the salutations growing longer as he added one son, and then another. Their frequency increased as well, as Andrew Stahls grew more and more desperate to stay connected to his family, in whatever way possible. When he held one, Zeke imagined he could smell the places they were from. The one from Boulder, Colorado, held hints of pine. He could swear he smelled the salty tang of cold Atlantic waves crashing on the shores of Provincetown. He knew it was just his imagination, but he wanted to believe that these were more than just glossy paper and scribbled ink. He wanted to pretend that he was sitting in the cab, right by his dad's side, the windows down, the wind teasing his hair, the two of them taking in the mountains as they rolled by.

The postcards were from different cities and towns all over the United States—anywhere an eighteen-wheeler could go, most of them purchased at truck stops or greasy spoons. And they all came with a promise. From Sarasota to Sacramento and fifty-one stops in between, each one was a place Zeke's father always hoped to get back to. Like Jackie's posters, which Zeke supposed were still lying on her floor, each postcard was a *one day—one day* we will do this as a family. *One day* we will make our own memory here. Every postcard was a wish, gathered here in this box like so many pennies at the bottom of a well.

Zeke stared at the semicircle he'd made and reached for the first one, thinking he might read through them all again, but then thought better of it and grabbed the last one instead. It was from a place called Eden, New York. The postmark said it was mailed a little over three years ago. Zeke had no recollection of getting it, but then he didn't remember getting any of them, really. The postcards often arrived the same day as their sender. Sometimes they even came after, depending on how slow the mail was and how much road construction his dad had to contend with. But most of the time, a postcard meant their dad was on his way.

The picture on the front showed a narrow walkway disappearing into a sunlit woods. *Greetings from Eden*, it said. Zeke rubbed the postcard between his fingers and tried to conjure something rustic and woodsy. Something covered in wildflowers. His dad liked the smell of fresh flowers and would happily get his knees dirty pulling weeds and planting peonies side by side with Mom. At least that's what Zeke remembered. He traced his finger over the last words his father ever wrote.

Well, actually I'm in a rest stop in Buffalo, but I saw this card and thought it would be more fun. Apparently, Eden is this tiny little town in New York that almost no one has ever heard of. Guy I talked to said it used to be bigger, but everybody got kicked out. Get it? Still, how cool would it be to plant a garden here?

Seriously, though, this trip has been a long haul. Getting tired of being on the road. I feel like I should be at home right now, coaching Zeke's team or taking Jackie to her first rock concert or teaching Nate how to ride his bike. I'm thinking it's about time I switch gears, get out of this cab, and find some office job right down the block. Anything to spend a little more time with my four favorite people in the world. We'll see.

Miss you all. Be home soon.

Love, Dad

P.S. Why didn't Eve have a date with Adam? Because they had an apple instead.

Zeke smiled despite himself, which only brought back what his mother said: how Dad could always make her laugh. And how everything was breaking or broken now. And how she wished things could get back to the way they used to be. If only for one day.

One day.

Zeke only had one more day. One more day to become the world's greatest kid and win the grand prize, but he was thousands of votes behind. It was too much. It was just like Jackie said—it feels so far out of reach, so why keep kidding yourself?

He stared at the spread of memories arrayed on his pillow. Yellowstone and the Black Hills and New York Harbor. All the places they never went because his father decided to stop and help someone change a tire. "I could really use your help here," he whispered. "What can I do? What would *you* do?"

What would it really take to be the world's greatest kid, if only for one day?

Reaching for another postcard, his elbow bumped the flashlight, its beam shifting and falling on the bookshelf in the corner of the room. A handful of old favorites were stacked there, along

324

with Nate's book of world records. Mind-blowing feats. Stories to inspire. *We all know how* that *turns out.*

As he grabbed the flashlight, his eye fell on another book. One he'd read three and one-tenth times now. Including earlier today, sitting on his front porch with Logan's dog-eared copy in hand. The ending was fresh in his mind now: two friends walking off into the sunset together.

When you wake up in the morning, Pooh, what's the first thing you say to yourself?

And suddenly Zeke smiled through his tears. Because he knew the answer. How to be a great kid and get the votes he needed. The ones he needed most at least.

And it wasn't impossible. At least he didn't think so.

But he sure couldn't do it on his own.

The house was still. Mom's door was shut. Jackie's too. Rooms dark. TV off. Wineglass completely empty this time.

Zeke tiptoed to the kitchen, finding the business card stuck to the fridge where his mother left it along with the takeout menus they almost never used. *Gordon Notts, Director of Charitable Programming.*

He flipped it over to the back and the phone number scrawled there.

Breathless, Zeke grabbed the home phone and punched in the numbers. *Please be awake.* He sat through one ring. Three.

Five. Then, finally, a click.

"Hello?"

Zeke cupped his hand over the mouthpiece and whispered, "Hi. It's me. Zeke."

"Zeke? Man, do you know what time it is?"

The clock on the stove read 12:17. "Yeah. It's super late. And I'm really sorry to bother you. But remember when you said I'd think of something? Well, I did."

"Okay . . . and . . ."

"And . . . I have a *really* big favor to ask."

All Expenses Paid

He knew the smell would get her. It was always what got him.

Like the rats of Hamelin heeding the piper's call, Zeke's mother followed her nose down the hallway and into the kitchen the next morning, where she found her eldest son standing by the stove. "Is that coffee?" she grunted.

Zeke nodded. "*Fresh* coffee."

In school Zeke had learned that smell and memory were closely linked. It was true. That first note of bacon crisping in a pan reaching him through his closed door, drawing him out to the table where his father's feast was waiting. Zeke didn't have any bacon—not the real stuff, anyway—so the coffee would have to do.

"When did you learn how to make coffee?"

"Googled it," he said. It wasn't hard—once you realized you had to add the filter. Otherwise, way too chewy.

"And he's making pancakes!" sang a chipper voice from the table.

Zeke's mother blinked, sloughing off the haze of sleep to see the whole picture at last. The pile of dirty bowls in the sink. The skillet sitting hot on the stove. Her younger son already seated, rubbing his hands together, salivating over the plate of cakes still steaming on the table. Zeke dolloped out another cupful of batter that sizzled when it hit. He was wearing an apron, the one with the outlined picture of Yoda on it. *May the Forks Be with You.* A Father's Day gift from long ago. He'd found it tucked away in the garage at three in the morning as he was gathering the rest of his supplies. It came all the way down to his ankles.

"What kind of pancakes would you like? We've got sprinkley, chocolate chip, and cookies and cream . . . minus the cream." He also had three burned ones sitting at the bottom of the taped-together trash can, but he kept that part to himself.

"Oh, Zeke," his mother said. She stared at him with suddenly glassy eyes, but then her eyebrows caved. "Wait. I thought I banned you from using the stove until you turned eighteen?"

"That was the blender," Zeke reminded her. "You said I could use the stove as long as I was supervised by a responsible adult authority figure." He pointed to the doorway. There stood Logan with his video camera shouldered, already recording.

"Morning, Ms. Stahls."

Zeke's mother shook her head, her processors clearly at max capacity. Definitely time for some coffee. "Drink this. You'll feel better," Zeke said, handing her a cup.

She took a sip, then set her World's Greatest Mom mug on the counter. "Zeke. This is such a surprise, really. And those pancakes look . . . well . . . they look delicious, actually. But I need to go get ready. I've got to get to work."

"Not today, you don't. You officially have the day off," he informed her. "Also, if your boss asks, you have acanthocheilonemiasis."

His mother looked even more confused. "What?"

"Acanthocheilonemiasis. It's an infectious diseases caused by parasitic worms. When I called you in sick, I had to tell them something."

His mother shook her head. This was usually about the time the exasperation set in. "You called my boss and told her I have *worms*?"

"I didn't actually say the *word* worms," Zeke explained calmly. "I just said you were spending a great deal of time in the bathroom." His mother frowned even deeper. "They were very nice about it. Said they hoped you felt better soon. But honestly, you shouldn't have to work today anyway," he added quickly.

"Really? And why is that?"

Zeke smiled his usual smile. The one that worried her. The scheming one. "Because it's Sunday."

"Zeke, it's Thursday."

"Definitely Sunday," he insisted.

"Sunday, Sunday, Sunday," Nate chanted.

And then, all at once, it hit her. He saw it in her face. The pancakes. The apron. The coffee. Memories of a hundred lazy weekend mornings gathered around the table. She stared at Zeke with his spatula in one hand and a thing of rainbow sprinkles in the other. "It's Sunday," she echoed softly.

Zeke winked at her. "Go sit down. It's almost ready."

He went to flip the cakes bubbling in the skillet when a lion—or something like it—growled from the hallway. *Here we go.*

Jackie rumbled into the kitchen, her hair wild, eyes narrowed, jaw clenched. She was in her hippos-eating-tacos pj's. Hippos, Zeke knew, were some of the most violent creatures on earth. He took that as a warning.

"You little creepazoid! You did it again!"

Zeke glanced over at Logan still posted by the door, then looked back at Jackie. "Um . . . good morning?"

If his sister noticed or cared that she was being recorded, she didn't show it. Clearly she was over posing for the camera. "Don't good morning me, you little twerp. You were in my room again last night!" She turned to their mother but kept her finger pointed at Zeke. "He snuck into my room while I was asleep and put all of my posters back on my walls."

Zeke didn't bother denying it. It hadn't been that hard. Just like the night before, he'd managed to open the door and tiptoe in without his sister stirring. She didn't even budge when he accidentally dropped the tape right by her head.

Jackie glared back at Zeke. Zeke looked at Mom. Mom looked at Jackie. "Wait, what happened to your posters?" she asked.

"What? Nothing. I took 'em down, no big deal. That's not the point. The point is this sneaky little perv broke into my room again and—"

"What do you mean, no big deal," their mother interrupted. She didn't sound angry. Just concerned. "You've been collecting those posters for years now. I thought you wanted to see all of those places. Travel the world."

"I did," Jackie sputtered. "I mean I do. But . . ."

"But she's scared," Zeke finished for her.

This time his sister did steal a glance at Logan before settling back on Zeke. "What? I'm not *scared*." Her tone was all anger on the surface, but Zeke could hear the fault lines underneath. The questions and the doubts. Over the past few days, her shields had wavered. She'd let him in, just a little. And even when she didn't, he'd obviously snuck in on his own. Enough to see how she really felt, what she tried so hard to keep tucked away.

"You want to go, but you're afraid," he continued. "You're afraid of how much college is gonna cost. You're afraid of being too far away. You're afraid of leaving Mom all alone to take care of us by herself." Zeke pictured his sister where he was now, by the stove, making one of hundreds of lunches for him and his brother. Saw her standing in the grocery store parking lot next to him with clenched fists. Clutching the back of Nate's shirt on the roof. Sitting in her

331

bed, back against the wall, arms wrapped around the both of them as the storm raged around them. It was always there—you just had to be the world's greatest kid to see it. Or at least a better one.

"You feel like you have to always be around to fix things . . . but you don't. We've got this."

With a flick of the spatula, Zeke deposited a gorgeously golden, sprinkled pancake on the plate beside him and held it out to her. He hoped they were still her favorite.

Jackie stood there, speechless for once, staring at the offering, her blue eyes blinking instead of rolling. "You've got this?" she said, halfway between a question and confirmation.

"We've got this," he repeated. "There's whipped cream on the table."

"The spray kind!" Nate added.

Jackie hesitated, looking at her brother in the too-big apron, a streak of pancake batter on his cheek, then she nodded and took the plate, finding her usual seat across from Nate. She didn't ask about the mountains of food piled in front of her.

She, too, must have realized what day it was.

Zeke grabbed the bowl of blueberries and sat down in the empty chair next to his brother, who was already searching for the pancake with the most bits of crumbled cookie in it. He glanced back over his shoulder and pointed to the only empty chair. "Space for one more."

"You know me," Logan said. "Observe and record."

"If it were Thursday, maybe," Zeke countered.

"Come," Mom insisted. "Eat with us. It's the least we can do."

Logan set his camera on the counter and took his seat.

"Careful. It wobbles," she added.

"You get used to it," Nate said. He reached for the chocolate syrup, ready to drown his breakfast in the stuff, when Zeke cleared his throat.

"Um . . . if it's okay with everyone else, I'd like to say grace."

His mother looked skeptical, but she reached out and took Jackie's hand. Zeke took hold of Logan's and his brother's, the biggest and littlest. He closed his eyes and recalled the prayer his dad always used to say. The one that always used to make him giggle even though he knew it wasn't polite.

"Good food. Good friends. Good Lord. Dig in."

"Amen," his mother said.

"A-freaking-men," Nate echoed, changing his mind and reaching for the whipped cream so he could make a snowman on top of his pancake.

Because a great idea is a great idea.

It was total carnage.

Zeke had made his share of messes before, but the state of the table once breakfast was over could best be described as postapocalyptic. There were blueberries mashed into the wood and strawberries in Nate's hair. Everything felt sticky to the touch.

It was totally worth it.

They ate with relish—though thankfully not with actual

relish, which Zeke couldn't even *think* about without getting queasy. At one point Nate chased Jackie around the table with a piece of microwaved bologna—"hillbilly bacon" Zeke called it—snorting as he went, Jackie defending herself with a serving spoon. Their mom and Logan traded stories about their childhoods, which were both, surprisingly, full of mischief. Then Nate regaled the table with his knowledge of world records (most pancakes eaten: 113 in only eight minutes—it was his dream to one day beat it).

And when the topic of Daniel Timmerman's butt came up, as it was destined to, Jackie contented herself with pouring maple syrup into Zeke's orange juice in retaliation for teasing her, which he promptly proceeded to drink, just to show her.

His mother didn't scold them.

She laughed instead.

Not a grunt or a snicker or a snort. A genuine, full-out, carefree, unweighted laugh. And it was just like Zeke remembered.

Nobody said a word about Dad. They didn't need to. It was Sunday after all. They knew he was there.

Amazingly, nobody said anything about the contest either. Or the fact that this was the very last day of filming and Logan's camera was sitting on the counter while he shoveled in strawberries and told knock-knock jokes to Nate. *Who's there? Hotch. Hotch who? Bless you.*

Snort giggle snort.

When the massacre was over, his mom sighed and stood up,

grabbing her plate, but Zeke stopped her. "Nope. I'll get it," he said. "But not just yet. There's something else we have to do." He nodded to Logan, who stood up and headed down the hall to the front door, grabbing his camera on the way.

The smile on his mother's face faltered. "Should I be worried?"

"I actually don't think so this time," Zeke said. "Just give me three minutes and then meet me out front."

"I'm still worried," he heard her whisper to his sister.

"I'd go with that instinct," Jackie whispered back.

Zeke guessed he deserved that—but they would see soon enough. Breakfast was only the beginning. He licked the last of the syrup from his fingers and grabbed the bag he'd hidden in the hall closet.

Logan was waiting for him outside with the three helium balloons he'd stashed in the KABAM-mobile. Two said *Happy Birthday*. One was a narwhal riding a rainbow. "Sorry. Best I could do on such short notice," he said.

"They're perfect," Zeke told him, meaning they were plenty good enough. The front door creaked and Zeke turned to see his family emerge, huddled together on the porch, blinking up at the white sun already hard at work.

"What's all this?" Mom asked.

"Yeah, what's with the balloons?" Jackie wanted to know. "Did we miss somebody's birthday?"

In response, Zeke simply pointed to the sign he'd made and

stuck on Snoopy's hood, written on a scrap of cardboard because he forgot to make a request for poster board. The sign said: *Albuquerque Hot-Air Balloon Festival. One Day Only. Admission: Free.*

His mother took one look at the sign, and Zeke saw the recognition sweep over her. No surprise. The cedar box had sat in her closet for years. He had no way of knowing how many times she'd opened it without them. Maybe, like Zeke, she even had some of Dad's messages memorized. Maybe all of them. *Just float above it all*, Zeke thought. Out loud he said, "Congratulations! You won!"

"Really? We won?" Nate said. "Won what?"

"The trip of a lifetime. Hop aboard."

Of course his little brother was the first one off the porch, Zeke's sister and mother trailing cautiously. He handed them each a balloon, the narwhal going to Nate. "Hold on tight," Zeke told him. He nodded to Logan, who pressed a button on his phone and some jazzy piano rolled in, followed by Nat King Cole crooning in a smooth tenor. *If you ever plan to motor west, travel my way, take the highway that is best.* Zeke wasn't sure this song was all his father made it out to be, but he saw his mother swaying to its groove.

He beckoned his family to follow him as he circled around the driveway, each of them clutching their balloon. Logan followed behind, getting it all on film.

"Our first stop, Keystone, South Dakota. Population five hundred and forty. And if you look directly to your right, you will see the town's big claim to fame: the illustrious Mount Rushmore!"

Zeke dug into the bag hanging from his side and revealed his first creation: four dirty white socks stuffed with toilet paper sticking out of a shoebox and markered up in his best approximations of presidents Washington, Jefferson, Roosevelt, and Lincoln. Lincoln was blue because the black Sharpie dried out, and Roosevelt's mustache looked more like something an evil villain might twist maniacally, but it had been pushing three in the morning when Zeke drew their faces, and even though he'd used his hands instead of his feet, he'd still been running on fumes. The presidents should all be happy their eyeballs were in the right place.

Zeke half expected his mother to get on him for ruining two pairs of socks, but instead she took out her phone and snapped a picture as if she were actually standing in a national park in South Dakota gazing at the rocky facades of four dead white guys and not a northern Indiana suburb staring at socks.

"Oh look, the Lincoln sock even has a hole in it," Jackie pointed out. "How morbid."

Okay, *that* was unintentional. "Moving right along!" Zeke said, setting Mount Rushmore in the grass and urging his family to keep following him. "Next up, we have fabulous New York City. The Big Apple. The city that never sleeps." *Sort of like me last night*, he thought. "And is that . . . ? Oh yes. It must . . . the one . . . the only . . ."

Zeke snapped his fingers at Logan. Handing the camera to Zeke, he dug under one of the bushes lining the side of the house for the props that had been stashed there: the green sheet that he draped over his shoulders and the crown, which was really just a snowcap—much like the ones Hailey Richter knitted, except in place of a fluffy ball, it sported several sharpened colored pencils jutting out at awkward angles, carefully taped in place. Zeke's old math textbook served as a substitute for the tablet, cradled in Logan's left hand. The right hand held the lighter his mother thought she had cleverly hidden from Zeke in the laundry room. All decked out, the cameraman struck the proper pose.

He looked ridiculous.

"Behold, Lady Liberty in all of her majesty!"

Logan clicked the lighter, and a tiny tongue flame licked the air as he gazed stoically into the distance, sweaty beard glistening in the sun. Nate laughed. Even Jackie cracked a smile. "This is so stupid," she said, but Zeke could tell she meant it in the best possible way.

As if to prove Jackie's point, Lady Liberty took a moment to dab.

"Okay. Now I've seen everything," Mom said.

"*Not even close*," Zeke whispered to her.

His stint as a statue done, Logan quickly ditched his accessories and reclaimed his camera as Zeke led his family closer toward the back of the house and the big surprise that awaited them.

"And up here on the left, of course, we have Yellowstone National Park in the great state of Wyoming."

Yellowstone National Park, as it turned out, was nothing more than a TV tray taken from the garage with a two-liter bottle of diet lemon-lime soda sitting on top. The label on the bottle had been peeled off and replaced with a sheet of brown construction paper simply labeled *Old Faithful.*

"I really expected it to be bigger," Jackie snarked. Zeke smirked right back at her as he circled around to stand behind the little table, removing the preloaded paper tube of Mentos from his pocket. He thought back to last Friday, the day he found out he just might be the World's Greatest Kid. That was the same day he and Nate had taken the six-pack of Dr. Fizz up to the roof to play grenades. Quite a lot had changed since then, but certainly not everything.

He still liked to watch things explode.

"It looks like you all are just in time," Zeke said, pretending to check his watch. "Get your cameras ready."

Logan gave a thumbs-up and Zeke dropped his payload into the bottle, the breath mints cascading, *plip plip plip—FRSSSSSHT.* The reaction was instantaneous, the frothy suds shooting straight up, fountaining over Zeke's head.

"Oooh," said Nate. "Aaaah." The eruption lasted all of three seconds, maybe four, but the kid clapped enthusiastically.

"Ugh. Science fair flashbacks," Jackie groaned. Mom's phone

went *click, click, click.*

Zeke licked the soda suds that had splashed on his arm and glanced toward the backyard, suddenly doubting himself. *Expected it to be bigger.* Maybe Jackie was right. Maybe this wasn't enough. There were fifty-three postcards after all. Fifty-three memories that never got made, and this was the best he could come up with? A holey blue Lincoln, a dabbing Statue of Liberty, and a kindergarten chem experiment?

But then he saw the look his mother was giving him—a look that said *I see what you're doing here.* Zeke took a deep breath and peeked around the corner to make sure everything was still in place.

"And now, ladies and gentlemen, it appears we have reached our final destination. So if you would please disembark." Zeke took each of their balloons and extended one arm with a flourish, much the way he imagined Gordon Notts might do. This was it—the grand prize.

"Welcome," he said, "to paradise."

Perhaps paradise was stretching it. But it was the best that he could do given what he had to work with.

The leis alone had taken him the better part of an hour to make, fashioned out of tissue paper and fishing line borrowed from his father's old pole. Zeke draped one over everyone's shoulders, including Logan's, as he ushered them onto the deck, where a cardboard sign hung that read Aloha Stahls Family. The box fan that he and Jackie fought over days ago now provided the requisite "cool ocean breeze," courtesy of an extension cord and the Ocean Breeze–scented tree swiped from his sister's car. A plate of fresh-cut pineapple was already attracting honeybees on the patio table. Zeke cued up the luau playlist he'd found on You-Tube and Elvis immediately began singing about dreams coming true through the laptop speakers.

Zeke's mother put a hand to her mouth. His sister's eyes bulged.

"*Whoa*," Nate said.

There before them spread the tropical grandeur of Waikiki: a full six feet of pristine white beach line, courtesy of the three bags of play sand Logan had found at the closest Walmart, all spread upon two blankets to keep it from slipping through the cracks in the deck.

The "beach" butted right up against the "ocean"—another early-morning purchase. It had taken Zeke twenty minutes of huffing to inflate the extra-wide kiddie pool with the sunglass-wearing flamingoes strutting along the side, but it was worth it now just to see the look of wonder on Nate's face. "Is that a pool?"

"*That's* the Pacific Ocean," Zeke corrected.

"I thought that would be bigger too," Jackie teased, but Zeke could tell she was impressed by the effort if nothing else.

"When did you do all of this?" his mother wondered.

"Last night. All night." He'd snatched only fifteen minutes

of sleep, while waiting for the ocean to fill. "I got a lot of help."

The Stahlses all looked to Logan, who gave them a one-handed salute, his camera sweeping to take in the scene.

"Can I get in?" Nate begged, tugging on their mother's robe.

The kid was still in his pajamas, but Mom shrugged. "What the hell. It's Sunday. Go nuts," she said. "Just watch out for sharks." She looked at Zeke and smiled. Nate took a running leap into the kiddie pool, soaking his Avengers pajama bottoms. Jackie followed him. Logan captured them laughing and splashing. Elvis continued to croon.

Zeke felt his mother standing behind him, her hands on his shoulders. "You never cease to amaze me, you know that?"

He wasn't sure that was a good thing. He hoped today it was.

He turned to look at her. Logan was still by the pool, which was good: Zeke didn't want this next part on camera.

"I took the box," he confessed. "The one in your closet. But I'm guessing you already know that."

"Of course I know," she said with a nod. "I've known for a while. And it's okay. Those postcards have your name on them too. I probably shouldn't have kept them hidden away like that. It was just easier. At least, it *seemed* easier."

It only hurts when you touch it, Zeke thought.

"He would have loved this, though," Mom mused, gently running a finger along her makeshift lei. "The ocean. The beach. The music. All of it."

"You really think so?"

"It's everything he always wanted."

More than any man could ask for.

Zeke looked at the prints Nate had already left in the play sand, his feet close to the same size Zeke's would have been the day their father left for the last time. Fifty-three postcards. Fifty-three dreams. He should be here. It sucked that he wasn't. But it was okay, Zeke decided, to go on without him.

Jackie sat on the edge of the deck in the soft pile of sand with her pants pulled up, the cool ocean waters lapping at her shins as Nate pretended to swim. Logan stepped onto the island no longer holding his camera but instead armed with a couple of Seagram's tropical wine coolers, which were not on the list Zeke had given him. He twisted the cap and handed one to Mom. "Little early I know, but it's not every day you take a hot-air balloon all the way to Hawaii."

"Once-in-a-lifetime opportunity." She and Logan clinked bottles.

"To Sundays," Logan said.

"To the world's greatest kid," Mom added.

That's one vote, Zeke thought. He looked at Jackie and Nate getting into a splash war, their laughter from breakfast spilling over into the pool. *There's two more.*

Logan turned and gave him a wink.

And that's when Zeke realized the truth.

That no matter what happened, he simply couldn't lose.

* * *

Twenty uke-heavy ditties and a toe dip in the ocean later, Logan said he had everything he needed and it was time to pack up and head out. After a round of thank-yous and goodbyes, including a wet hug from Nate and an offer to pay for his air-conditioning services from Mom that was declined, Logan nodded to Zeke, who got the hint.

He met the cameraman around the front of the house, skirting past Wyoming and New York and South Dakota, leaving his siblings to play splashball without him, a newly invented game involving the kiddie pool, Nate's basketball, and a sadistic desire to get the other person as soaked as possible. Logan wasn't sitting in his usual spot on the porch this time. He was leaning up against the black KABAM van, his camera already stowed. That's how Zeke knew it was goodbye for real. It was the last day. The contest was over—or soon would be. They'd finished the book. All that was left was to settle the tab.

"I brought the money," Zeke said, pulling the wad of cash that he'd just taken from his musty soccer cleat. "How much do I owe you?"

"Let's see," Logan said, ticking off his fingers. "The wine coolers were on me, of course, but twenty bucks for the inflatable pool. Then, three bags of sand. Breath mints. Soda. Pancake mix. Strawberries. Blueberries. Spray whipped cream. Two pineapples. All totaled it comes to . . . sixty-five bucks."

Zeke winced. Hawaii was expensive. "I've only got forty-two." He handed his life savings to the cameraman. "I'll have to get you the rest later."

"Don't worry about it, kid," Logan said. "It's no big deal."

"But it *is* a big deal," Zeke insisted. "I woke you up and made you go to a freaking Walmart at one in the morning. That's insane. Not just anyone would stop what they're doing in the middle of the night to help somebody like that."

Logan looked thoughtful for a moment. "You're right. Not just anyone."

Touché, Zeke thought.

The cameraman took the wad of cash and stuffed it in one pocket of his jeans, then dipped into the other, pulling out a little red flash drive on a silver key chain. "Here you go. As requested."

Zeke cupped the drive in his hand. He knew he would never forget what happened today, but sometimes it helped to have something tangible to hold on to—a lucky rabbit's foot, a stuffed moose, a box of postcards. "I'm guessing Notts won't like this very much."

Logan shrugged. "He'll get over it. Besides, it could be worse. At least you weren't arrested."

"That's what I'm always telling Mom, but she says it's still no excuse."

The cameraman laughed. "Your mother's a fantastic human being. And Nate's a trip. And Jackie . . . well, let's just say I wouldn't want to be the jerk in the parking lot when she comes storming out."

"No. Me neither," Zeke said. He looked back over his shoulder at the one-story ranch with its rotted wood trim, this home that he shared with three pretty fantastic human beings, his eyes falling on the concrete step. Suddenly he knew how he could pay off the remainder of his debt. "Wait here a sec," he said.

Zeke bolted into the empty house—the rest of his family still basking in the sun on Waikiki—and ducked into his room, scanning the corner shelf until he found what he was looking for. Some things don't have to stop even when you think you've reached the end.

He came back through the front door with his prize proudly displayed, its cover sporting a few familiar faces: a bear and boy, pig and a rabbit. He handed it to Logan. "*Now* we're even."

The cameraman took it and flipped through the pages. "The sequel?"

Zeke nodded. "The one with the Poohsticks."

Logan still made a face. "And Tigger?"

"The best," Zeke confirmed.

Logan closed the book and nodded. "You're right. This makes us even." He extended a hand to shake on it.

Zeke stared at him for a moment. He'd only known Logan for five days, hardly any time at all, yet it felt like much longer. He'd seen Zeke at his highest and lowest—from the top of the Rocket to facedown in the mulch. Stood behind him in the parking lot. Helped him down from the tree. Even answered his midnight call.

A little more than just observe and record.

Zeke took a page out of his brother's playbook, bypassing

the hand and going for the hug instead, pressing his cheek into Logan's chest.

"I really did try, you know."

He felt the cameraman's big arms over his shoulders. "That's all any of us can do."

Zeke sniffed and nodded and finally let go.

Logan circled around and opened the door to the van. He had one foot inside, then stopped. "I think figured it out, by the way," he said.

"Figured what out?"

"The part about the Woozles. I think the first step—and maybe the hardest—is deciding what it is you're even looking for."

Zeke pictured the illustration—Pooh and Piglet tracking the footsteps through the snow, around and around and around the same tree, just going in circles. "And after that?"

The cameraman shrugged. "I'll let you know when I get there. As long as you promise to do the same."

Zeke said he promised.

Then he said goodbye.

And the Winner Is

That night the Stahlses had leftover pineapple and pancakes for dinner. There was talk of Ambrosia's again, but payday wasn't until Friday, and though it was Sunday, it was really Thursday, so second breakfast it was.

Not that anyone was complaining. Even reheated pancakes taste better when you eat them on the beach.

They'd spent the entire day just the way Zeke hoped they would: all together, soaking up sunbeams and kneading the sand, taking a break to clean up the kitchen as a team, the way a not entirely dysfunctional family might. It was decided that Hawaii could stay in the backyard through the weekend, at which point they would use the sand to refresh the neighborhood litter box. They would leave the kiddie pool out for the summer, though, just in case the air-conditioning decided to conk out again—or until the YMCA lifted the ban on their clan.

At some point in the lazy afternoon, Mom trounced all three of her children at Monopoly, rubbing her wad of fake hundred-dollar bills in their faces while Nate begged to play again using the "special rules." Afterward, Zeke and his brother invented their own live-action version of Bloons Tower Defense, tying the helium balloons to their shoelaces—Nate tying his himself—and chasing each other around the backyard, seeing who could pop the other one's first. But Nate's narwhal eventually got loose and drifted up above the trees, heading for the clouds. He pouted and kicked at the grass, but Zeke told him not to worry; that's just what happens to rainbow-riding narwhals sometimes. They fly away. And wasn't it pretty when seen from a distance?

It was while they were watching Nate's balloon soar free that their mother's phone buzzed. The final videos had been posted and the last round of voting had begun. "Should we go inside and watch?" she asked.

Zeke nodded hesitantly, knowing what was coming. He followed his family into the house, all squeezing together on the couch, each of them smelling of syrup and sunscreen, the laptop open on the coffee table in front of them. Zeke couldn't keep his foot from bouncing and noticed his mother's tapping too. The totals below the photos already showed the other three gaining votes. Zeke's tally hardly budged.

"We should probably do mine first," he said, clicking on his video. "Just get it over with." His family nodded.

There was no music this time, no dramatic intro or voice-over, just Zeke, back on the deck in front of the rosebushes and the broken wind chime, wearing the same clothes as this morning, which were the same as yesterday. The camera zoomed in, focusing on his smile—the sort of wistful one that was coming a little more naturally to him. Behind him the sun was still just starting to wake, painting the sky a muted orange, lighting one side of him better than the other. He spoke softly, the clip-on microphone picking up on the exhaustion in his voice. The exhaustion and the relief.

"Hello. My name is Ezekiel Stahls and this is my last video. I just want to say what a fantastic journey this has been and that I appreciate everyone who has watched me over the past few days. I want to take this chance to thank Gordon Notts and everyone at KABAM and especially Logan, the guy behind the camera, for this opportunity. I also want to thank my fellow contestants for inspiring me through their own videos, showing me just how awesome people can be if they try, no matter what age."

Zeke shifted uncomfortably on the couch. This was it. He took a deep breath. His video version did the same.

"It's for that reason I'm asking for anyone who might have voted for me in the past to cast their last vote for Aadya, Hailey, or Dom instead. There are a lot of problems in the world. Bigger problems than a busted air conditioner or a broken ceiling fan—and those three are actually out there trying to do something about them. I don't know if anybody can really be the world's *greatest* kid. In fact, if I'm being honest, I'm still not entirely sure what that word even means. But I do know that any one of them deserves the title a lot more than me and will use the prize to make the world a better place. So thanks again for watching, and don't forget to put those shopping carts back where they belong. Peace."

The camera lingered on Zeke's face a moment longer, then faded to black. It was over.

Nate shook his head, clearly confused. "Wait. What happened to the rest of it? The pancakes? The balloon trip? The beach?"

Zeke's mother studied him silently, no doubt wondering the same. He dug in his pocket for the red flash drive and held it out to her. The only copy of the footage from their nearly perfect day. "It was just for us," he said. "The whole day."

She nodded and smiled. "Just for us."

"But wait," Nate protested. "What about the contest? Does this mean we lost? What about the ten thousand bucks? The trip to Hawaii?"

Jackie bumped his shoulder with hers. "You just went to Hawaii, doofus." She caught Zeke's eye and offered her typical big-sister smirk, then she tilted her head toward their mother.

Mom was sniffling, blotting at her eyes.

"You okay, Ma?" Zeke asked.

She spread her arms and pulled all three of them even closer. One sweaty, sandy, sticky mess of Stahlses. "No, not quite. Not yet. But I will be," she said.

On-screen, the votes for three of the challengers continued to pour in, closing the gap between each other while widening their lead on Zeke. It was going to be a tight finish for sure.

"Should we click on the other videos?" Jackie asked. "Just to see?"

Zeke shrugged. He knew that whatever those three did for their last days, it would be amazing. Some people just aspired to greatness. Nate stared at his feet, bottom lip puffed into a pout, refusing to take the loss.

"Or we could go out for ice cream instead," Zeke said. "Be a good way to end a Sunday, don't you think?"

Jackie smiled. Nate sniffled but nodded.

Their mother reached over and closed the laptop, effectively casting her vote.

And then it was over. Officially.

At midnight the winner was decided. The World's Greatest Kid was named.

The phone call from Gordon Notts came the next morning.

It came before his mother left for work, in fact, having miraculously recovered from her bout with acanthocheilonemiasis—the cure, apparently, being six hours on the beach and a double scoop of rocky road in a sugar cone. Still, she wasn't sure she could handle Notts's showman's schtick so early in the morning, so she let it go to voice mail instead. Zeke knew what the message was going to say anyway.

"Hello, Stahls family. Sorry I didn't reach you. Just called to follow up on the contest and to thank you for your participation. I have to admit, I was a little surprised by Zeke's submission for the last day, but Logan told me he didn't want to be filmed anymore, and I have to respect that. It's got to be hard growing up nowadays, always out there, constantly judged, all the likes and follows and favorites. And there's a lot to be said for acknowledging the greatness in others. Still, it was a pleasure working with you all. Zeke certainly brought something . . . special to the competition. So thanks for taking part, and look for a survey in your email sometime in the next couple of days—I think there are some definite improvements we can make for next year and would like your feedback. Also, be sure to watch the livestream of the awards presentation tonight at eight. Cheers."

"Hear that?" Mom said, pocketing her phone. "You're special."

"So I've been told." Unfortunately being special didn't come with a ten-thousand-dollar check.

Zeke thought about the letter, the one that started this whole thing. *If for some reason this letter has reached you in error . . .* He still wasn't sure how he'd been chosen—if it really was a mistake, some glitch in the system, some fault in the formula. Maybe that was one of the definite improvements Notts had in mind, making sure nobody like Zeke slipped in accidentally. Then again, Kyo managed to make the top five too. Maybe it wasn't just a matter of how many hats you made or puppies you petted, how many

353

hobbies you had or what your overall grade point average was. Maybe there was no algorithm that could determine what a person was worth or what they were capable of.

Though if there was, Zeke hoped his numbers would have gone up at least a little over the last few days.

"So are we watching the awards tonight?" his mother asked, sipping from her new favorite mug.

"I guess. If you want to. Though I already know who won," Zeke confessed.

He'd snuck out of his room in the middle of the night to check. Purely out of curiosity. He was right. It had been close. A real nail-biter. Only a hundred votes separating first and second place.

"Yeah, me too," Mom admitted. "Not a huge surprise. Honestly, they would have been my second choice."

Funny, Zeke thought. *They were my first.* "I think maybe you're a little biased."

"Just a little." She ruffled his hair. He tried to squirm away. But not too hard. "Try not to antagonize your sister today. She's got that SAT retake coming up. And make sure your brother eats something with a vitamin in it. Where is your brother anyway?"

"Already at the beach," Zeke said. The benefits of oceanfront property.

"Of course. Silly me." She took her last swallow, set down her cup, and started scouring the counter for her keys. Zeke found them first and handed them to her. "Also, if you manage to get to the store, don't forget we still need milk. And eggs. And apple-sauce."

"Applesauce. Got it." Thank god she didn't say pickles.

She stopped at the door. "And, Zeke—"

"Yeah, I know," he interrupted. "Be good."

"I was actually going to say I was proud of you," Mom said. "But yes. That works too."

Zeke waited for her to shut the door, then rinsed out her coffee mug and dropped it in the dishwasher before heading back to his room. On the way he stopped by Jackie's door and listened to her practicing the violin. Later, maybe, he would ask if she wanted to do something, the three of them. Or maybe he'd let her stay in there so he and Nate could upgrade their zip line without her nagging them about not breaking their necks.

But first there was one more thing he had to take care of. Something he should have done a while ago.

He went to his room and crouched by his bed, reaching for the memories he'd been hiding underneath. His mother was right: it *seemed* easier, sometimes, keeping it tucked away, but you couldn't stay that way forever. Eventually you had to stop following your footprints in circles in the snow. You had to find a way to move on, to keep checking things off the list. It wasn't a matter of forgetting. It was the other one. The harder one.

Zeke carried the cedar box out to the family room and set it on the mantel, lid open.

Right next to the wedding photo that he liked so much.

Later that night, after a dinner of fish sticks and mixed vegetables, the Stahlses gathered back on the couch, Zeke and Jackie on opposite ends, Mom and Nate tucked in between. Nate was the designated popcorn-bowl holder. They could have picked other snacks, but sometimes popcorn was enough.

"What are we watching again?" Nate asked.

"We already told you four times," Jackie answered.

"Yeah, but I don't remember."

"*Zelnar Seven*. The one with the aliens with buckets on their heads," Zeke said, grabbing the remote and jacking up the volume so they could hear the dramatic intro music. There was always dramatic intro music. The framing of the opening shot was terrible. Logan would have done so much better. The spaceship looked to be made of tinfoil.

"It's not even in *color*? How old *is* this movie?" Nate protested.

"Just watch. You'll like it." *It was Dad's favorite.* Zeke reached across his mother's lap and grabbed a fistful of popcorn. They'd sprinkled a little sugar on it to go with the salt. All Nate's idea.

"Oh my god, I remember this one," Jackie said. "You're right. You can totally see the strings."

"He really did have terrible taste in movies," Mom said, sighing and grinning at the same time.

Somewhere, at this very moment, Gordon Notts was handing a giant check to a kid who would probably grow up to be on the cover of a magazine for cleaning up the oceans or fighting against poverty or curing some disease. Zeke figured he could always watch the recording later on the laptop if he wanted. Right now he was just where he wanted to be.

He reached for the bowl again, and his sister batted his hand away. "Don't be a pig," she said. Zeke stuck his tongue out at her. Nate snorted.

On the TV, the plastic spaceship shook and wobbled as it journeyed across the black sheet of outer space toward the dangling ball acting as a stand-in for some alien planet. His mother was right. It really was terrible.

But it was sort of awesome too.

March 28

Greetings from Myrtle Beach!

Okay. It's not Hawaii, but it's good enough for us. Just last week Jackie found out she got a scholarship to South Carolina, so we all came to visit over spring break. Turns out the college is only a three-hour drive to the coast, so we spent a few days jumping waves and burying each other in sand. The water's freezing, but I don't care. Some things are still worth it. And I have to admit, the sunsets here really are perfect.

How are things with you? Found that Woozle yet? If not, don't give up. It's out there. I'm sure of it.

Keep in touch. And remember, my porch is always open.

Zeke

P.S. What did the ocean say to the swimmer? Nothing. It just waved.

Acknowledgments

It's a lot of hard work becoming the Greatest Kid in the World. It takes a skateboard, a grapefruit, a hefty cat, a jar of pickles, and sprinkles in your pancakes just to try. It also takes a loving and supportive family.

Writing *The Greatest Kid in the World* was equally challenging. You can substitute can of Pringles for jar of pickles and ornery cat for hefty cat, but the loving and supportive family is a must. So here I offer all my gratitude to those who helped me achieve the grand prize of seeing this book in print. To Josh and the rest of the Adams Literary family, thank you for over a decade of undying support. To the fantastic managing editorial and design team at HarperCollins—Kathryn, Mark, Penny, Daniel, Vicky, Molly, and Amy—and to the tireless crew in marketing and publicity—Patty, Emma, Mimi, Christina, and the rest—your talent and hard work cannot be overstated (feel free to insert humblebrag here). Thanks to Rafael for another magnificent cover, and my deepest gratitude to Donna Bray and Deb Kovaks for continuing to make space on the shelf for my work. To Jordan, thanks as always for realizing that deep down—deep, *deep* down—there was a story here worth sharing. And for the candy, of course—those dark chocolate caramels were especially toothsome. Finally, to all the family, friends, and fans who continue to cast their votes for me even when I crash face-first into the mulch—you have my love and appreciation always.

Finally to my young readers, thanks for inspiring me on the daily. Squire Bill Widener once said—in a quotation immortalized by Teddy Roosevelt (the one with the mustache, third from the left)—"Do what you can, with what you've got, where you are." Like Zeke, I'm not entirely sure what it means to be great, but I'm guessing it starts there—with a desire to better oneself and make a positive difference in the world, no matter how small. So go out there and be great in your own way.

It's all any of us can do.